KT-232-686

B000 000 015 5056
ABERDEEN LIBRARIES

BEYOND THE HORIZON

BEYOND THE HORIZON

Ryan Ireland

ONEWORLD

A Oneworld Book

First published in North America, Great Britain and
Australia by Oneworld Publications 2015

A CIP record for this title is available from the British Library

Hardback ISBN 978-1-78074-597-8
Paperback (Export Edition) ISBN 978-1-78074-774-3
eBook ISBN 978-1-78074-598-5

Text design and typeset by Tetragon, London
Printed and bound by CPI Group (UK) Ltd, Croydon, CR0 4YY

Oneworld Publications
10 Bloomsbury Street
London WC1B 3SR
England

To my parents

for introducing me to the West

FIRST

ONE

I

At dusk he came limping from the ethered shadows. Perhaps the lamplight of the hovel attracted him as it did the insects—the grass flies, beetles, the moths. The man told his wife to stay inside once the stranger came into view. He went out and met the stranger. Collapsing into the grasses, the stranger panted. He asked for water, first saying water, then speaking in a different tongue altogether. The man called back to his wife for a canteen, made a drinking motion.

From the threshold of their abode the woman came, taper burning in a mason jar, canteen with the strap looped in the crook of her arm. She walked carefully, unbalanced, as she wore nothing on her feet and her belly bulged with child.

'Thank you,' the stranger said. He drank.

The man studied the stranger sprawled out before him in the grasses. The stranger wore a white shirt unbuttoned, but in good condition otherwise. His trousers were black, made with shiny fabric the man had never seen. He examined the stranger's shoes and noticed his foot had been crushed. The hide of the boot puckered into the puncture marks. Dried blood crusted off the edges.

'I saw your light,' the stranger said. 'Saw it from a dozen miles away. Seen it for some time now. Came this way hoping for some shelter.'

Shrugging the man said they didnt have much room.

'Anything would be good. I need to get my foot looked at.'

The man turned to his wife. He continued to stare at her though he spoke to the stranger. 'She can mend you—she does to me when I get in a bind.' Then he motioned to her, one hand circulating around the other, then pointed to the stranger's foot. She nodded.

The hovel barely accommodated three people. Planks of wood taken from the bed of a wagon covered the ground where the man and woman slept. One wall was constructed of stones piled haphazardly and reinforced with clay and swathes of sod. The adjacent wall was scrapped wood braced into place with a wagon yoke. Canvas oil cloth served as the ceiling, held in place by a stretch of rope. A ragged blanket hung as the door.

'Gonna have to cut the boot off your foot,' the man said.

Stranger nodded, said he figured so.

The man nodded to his wife and she used a straight razor to saw through the upper of the boot. Twice she nicked the stranger's leg, but he did not flinch. He studied her movements as a child might.

'How'd you do it?' the man asked.

'Do what?'

'Get your foot like you did.'

The woman began pulling away the strips of leather. Scraps of flesh clung to the piecemeal of the boot. The stranger turned his head to look directly at the man when he spoke. 'Had a horse go bad on me.'

'Lost the horse, did you?'

'I did.'

The woman cleaned the blade of the razor with the fray of her skirt, sterilizing the metal in the flame of the candle. Without a moment's hesitation she cut into the darkened meat of his wound. She sliced out the infected flesh. Still the stranger talked. 'Beauty of a horse, white like snow. Light in her step too. I could ride up on someone. Theyd never hear me coming.'

The woman wrung hot water from the rags she boiled and began wrapping his foot. Steam rose from where the blood soaked into the still wet cloth.

'What'd you say you did?' the man asked.

'Horse kicked me off. I told you.'

'No,' the man said. 'Your work.'

'My work?'

'How do you go bout makin a livin?'

'I dont. How do you go about doing such a thing?'

The woman finished wrapping the foot. Already the fabric hued pink with the stranger's blood.

'We scavenge,' the man said. 'Live off the land.'

'Scavenge.'

'I got a piece of land, got some wheat, some beans.'

'Tobacco?'

'No, no tobacco.'

'Thats too bad.'

'Caint say I'm much one for smoking.'

The woman nodded. The foot was dressed.

'Does she speak?' the stranger asked.

'She does—just not in our tongue.'

The stranger smiled at the woman and thanked her.

When he awoke, the man thought the stranger to be an apparition, a dream of some type. Where the stranger slept an hour before now lay vacant. It was dark, still before morning. He went to the flap door of the hovel and looked out. The stranger hobbled through the grass. The man called out and the stranger looked back over his shoulder. A gnarly piece of driftwood fashioned a crutch for the stranger.

The man walked out to the stranger. 'Just woke,' he said. 'Mustve stirred me when you left. Woke up an thought you was a dream.'

The stranger closed his eyes as if meditating on the man's words, inhaled through his nose. 'Wasnt sure myself.' He opened his eyes. 'Then I woke.'

The man scooted his hat back on his head so it canted at an unnatural angle. He placed his hands on his hips. The stranger laughed. Then the man laughed too. Murky rays of the rising sun broke over the horizon, announcing the coming of the day.

'Wanted to see the piece of land you told me about,' the stranger explained. 'The patch of wheat and beans.'

The man nodded, pointed, said it was down yonder way.

'Yonder way,' the stranger repeated.

'Thats right.'

A few seconds passed with only the two men studying each other, their forms coming into full shape with the gradients of daytime breaking apart the night.

The stranger's gaze shifted over the man's shoulder. 'Your wife is up,' he said.

And she emerged, swinging open the flap door of the hovel. She wore the rags of a bustier, her full stomach protruding and bare. Both men watched her yawn, stretching her arms over her head. Dark blotches of hair nested in her armpits, their shade matching the tangles that hung down between her breasts.

'Should I avert my eyes?' the stranger asked.

The man looked downward, toward the stranger's unshoed feet. 'She aint my wife.' The man looked up to gauge the stranger's reaction.

'Shes not yours?'

'Her nor the youngin.'

The woman looked out over the grasses at the men and she obscured herself, for now she stood naked.

They ate beans and chaff meal ground together and thickened with water from the south-running creek. They drank from canteens.

'Had some coffee here a piece back,' the man said. 'Traded it with a passer-through.'

'Did you?'

'Did. Rationed it a while, but it ran out.'

'As things do.'

The woman took the men's plates once nothing remained of their meal and put them in a kettle.

'Fine place you have,' the stranger said.

'It's a scavenging way of life.'

'You told me,' the stranger said. 'How'd you get here?'

'Had a wagon break down. Whole axle gave out, snapped. Still got the mule. Keep him out by the creek.'

'Saw him,' the stranger said. 'Why didnt you try to ride him out of this place?'

'Figured I'd make it out here on my own.'

The stranger nodded like he understood. The man sucked meal from his teeth.

'And your woman?'

'You askin where she come from?'

The stranger's tongue probed over his teeth, pulling at chaffs of meal lodged there. 'Yes. Does she have a story?'

'She was passin through like anyone else.'

'And she stayed.'

'They left her behind.'

'They?'

'Her people. Got darker skin, dirty skin, they call it. Skin like hers.'

The stranger pinched another glob of meal from the bowl. He ate it.

'They left her cause she was with child?'

The man gulped from the canteen, swallowed, said yes, thats what happened.

'This is hard country.'

The man did not know what to make of this statement.

The stranger elaborated. 'These people all going west, they say they want to start a new life.' He laughed to himself. The man did likewise, but only to emulate his guest. 'You could mark their progress with bloodstains. Track where theyre going by listening to them talk in their sleep. Dont know what theyre really heading into.'

The man nodded like he understood. They ate in silence. The woman came and went.

'Baby'll come soon enough,' the stranger said.

'Reckon so?'

'It's a hard country.'

II

On his third day at the hovel, the stranger trapped and caught a rabbit using a snare he rigged up outside what he supposed to be a nesting den. He skinned the animal using a bolt honed into a shank, cloth wrapped around the end in a handle. The woman dried the meat with what little salt they had and boiled the bones with some turnips from the creek.

The three sat together in the hovel. Outside the heavens clouded over. Wind rustled through the grasses like a thousand voices crying out across time.

They ate in silence.

The woman ladled the broth into cups wrought from stoneware.

Days since the stranger arrived were fruitful enough. The bucket of meal overflowed with seed and chaff. Vegetables dug and scavenged from the land numbered in the dozens. Though the stranger did not disclose the location of the rabbit den, he said he hoped to snare a few more in the days to come.

'How long you plan on bein?' the man asked.

The stranger stopped, his cup hovered near his lip. He asked what the man meant before drinking.

The man and woman exchanged glances.

'We like you well enough.'

'Yes.'

'Yessir. But we—my woman and I—like it out here ourselves.'

'Yourselves.'

'Thats right.'

'But this isnt yours.'

'What isnt?'

'This.'

Again, the man looked at his woman. She cast her gaze downward at the barren spot on the dirt floor.

'Well, theres plenty of space for everone. You can get a piece down aways.'

The stranger shook his head. 'There isnt plenty of space. You live right where a thousand years of people have lived.'

The man set his cup on the ground. 'Dont rightly see what youre gettin at here.'

'Getting at?' the stranger asked. 'I'm saying the same words people have been saying since this place was a stew of water and sludge and blood.'

'That right there,' the man said. 'Dont rightly know what you mean by all that talk.'

The stranger looked at the woman. 'Los errantes están condenados. Los quienes se quedan están muertos. Todos—todos se sucumben al fuego y se ahogan del polvo.'

The woman's hands wrapped over her womb. Her eyes glassed over.

The stranger addressed her smiling and talking softly, kindly.

'Now what the devil tongue you speakin in?'

The stranger looked at the man. 'I am a man of medicine. She should be grateful.'

'You told us you didnt have no profession.'

The stranger seemed to weigh the man's incredulousness before replying. 'I was a doctor in the army. I'll resume my practice next time the men of this country start killing one another. It's never long.'

A week passed before the man broached the stranger's departure again. Theyd walked out to the creek to feed the mule, water him and check the tethers that kept him bound to the deadened sapling.

'Wife an I think your foots healed up about right,' the man said.

The stranger stroked the coarse tuft of the mule's mane. He used his tongue to make clucking noises at it.

'You probably already knowed that, being a doctor an all,' the man said.

'All the more reason for me to stay.'

The man made certain he looked the stranger in the eyes when he said his wife didnt want him around. The stranger nodded. He looked out across the plains, first west, then east.

'Hysteria,' he said.

The man's brow furrowed. 'Whats that again?'

'Hysteria,' the stranger repeated 'Hystericus, from *hysterikos*—from the womb. Condition having to do with your wife's pregnancy. Carrying a baby can make a woman insane.'

'Shes losin her mind?'

'For a time,' the stranger said. 'Thats why she needs me. Thats why shes scared. She doesnt know what shes thinking.'

The man shook his head. 'Dont seem like her minds gone.'

'Takes a doctor to recognize it.'

The man pretended to busy himself with the feedsack and filling the water bucket for the mule. He dropped a few larger stones into the bucket to weight it down, keep the animal from knocking it over.

'I'd help you make a place of your own,' the man offered. 'Still got some parts of the wagon left. Good slope to dig into about a mile north of here.'

The stranger smiled. The suddenness of his elation startled the man, the same as any other beast baring its teeth might. 'We could share this land,' he said.

'Guess we might.'

The stranger made a definitive nod. 'Be a fine idea. I could be around to help.'

The man tried to match the radiance of the stranger's smile with his own, but found it too difficult to maintain. 'Be a good thing I reckon, have a doctor around to birth the baby.'

'Be hard for her to do it on her own.'

The man reissued his straightforward look. 'Hows that?'

'Well, you'll have to register the baby and her out at the territory seat.'

The man nodded as if he knew what he had just been told.

III

As it was told to him, the stranger found the hillside one mile north of the hovel. It would take a fair amount of excavating to cut into the leeward side of the slope enough to create a livable space. He stood at the base of the elevation, grass knee deep, and envisioned his future home: two rooms, he postulated—an outer and an inner room. Be good to keep out the winter. The outer room would serve as a porched area. Some of the beams from the wagon could fashion the uprights. He could build up the walls with some of the dirt from the hillside.

The inner room would hug up against the cut bank of the hill. He'd fell a few of the saplings from the creekside to reinforce the dirt, be nice to have something to aid the lithe trees with the reinforcement. He figured this to be the space where he would sleep. Be a good place for it—dark and quiet, secure against the earth.

If he dug down far enough he could get below the frost line, have a place to store meat in the summer months, place to store liquids in the winter. He would make it a secret though. The opening for the cellar would be hidden in the inner room, perhaps where he slept. A large flat rock from the creek might make a sufficient cover for an aperture.

He climbed to the top of the hill and surveyed the lay of the land, saw it go out a hundred miles in each direction. So long as he dug in the proper direction, at the correct angles, he would progress faster than the man. Doing the geometry of the situation proved easy. But he knew too that men's actions are wily and there would yet be an equation to solve the dilemma of what so many would term the human condition. Once he came out on the other side of the tunnel, there'd be no returning; time would only telescope toward cataclysm.

'Could be crazy,' the man said to the woman. She listened rapturously as if she understood the words being spoken.

'El hombre es peligroso. Es un hombre malo,' she said. As she spoke, she grabbed the man by the forearm.

'I know it,' the man said, though he had little idea of what the woman actually pled of him. 'Sent him to scout out the hill a mile away from here. Figured we shouldnt send him away all together. Not like hes actually dangerous. Little unhinged, maybe.'

He rested his hand on her belly, the belly button sticking out like a nose. 'Says he can help birth the baby.'

The woman's eyes widened and she leaned in close to the man, gripping his arm ever tighter. 'No quiero que esté cerca del bebé.'

The man used his free hand to loosen her grip. He rubbed her womb. 'You neednt get worked up,' he said. 'You'll catch a hysteria.'

Some nights the stranger still ate with the man and the woman. Other nights, most nights now, he dined by himself, eating solitary in places unknown. When he did arrive for mealtime, he brought small game with him—some bird, a rabbit, stray rodents he dried into sinewy strips.

The woman cared not for the conversation when the stranger visited. She ate quickly, refusing his contributions to the meal. Then, with an uttered pardon, she excused herself. The men repeated the word hysteria lowly and they silently and secretly studied her. Once she exited the hovel, they spoke freely.

'How she seem to you?' the stranger asked.

'Fine most of the time,' the man said. 'She gets real strange when you come round.'

'Hysteria can make people suspicious of outsiders; it heightens the part of the mind where superstition is formed. Women can see things that arent there.'

The man shook his head. 'Hard to think of her like that—like shes goin crazy.'

'That baby inside of her,' the stranger said. 'Hes got a mind too. Having two minds in one body creates chaos. If shes hearing voices, could well be the baby's voice.'

'Dont really make sense,' the man said.

'If it made sense, we wouldnt call it crazy.' The stranger smiled as if he had just told a joke. The man mulled on a string of meat, his eyes focusing on something distant. After a minute he asked if the stranger's home was coming along all right.

'Best I can get it,' the stranger said. 'Be better if I could get some of this oilcloth you got yourself here.' He stretched out his arm and ran his fingertips down the tented wall. 'Real tough material, it is. Be good for bracing the dirt wall.'

'If you want some, I got some extra,' the man said.

The stranger didnt seem particularly surprised by the offer, even in this spartan place. He sat cross-legged, arms resting on his knees. He craned his head all around, examining the way the cloth draped and wrapped over the ragged frame of the hovel. 'I'd take some cloth, if you could spare it.'

The man crawled over to a chest that served as a table and cleared the top of it. He opened it up and shuffled some of the contents about and pulled out a folded square of cloth.

As he held it, the stranger noted the seams along the edges, how thick the fabric felt, how it textured closer to canvas.

'It's a sail,' the man said. 'An old boat sail.'

This sparked some amusement on the stranger's face. 'Strange place for a boat sail to end up.'

The man nodded, said it was his father's doing and went outside in search of his woman.

IV

The stranger's abode progressed surprisingly quickly. In a matter of weeks he dug out what he said would be the porch and most of the inner room. He began reinforcing the walls with branches and saplings when the man came to visit.

'Comin along real well,' he said.

The stranger draped the oilcloth over the exposed dirt and braced it with the poles. 'Should be a real fine piece once I'm done here.'

The man nodded in agreement. He dismounted the mule and pretended to show a detailed interest in what the stranger was building.

'Had a question about that registerin business,' he said.

The stranger unfurled a length of cord and laced it between the poles to hold the cloth flat. His lithe fingers worked quickly, tying knots. 'What about it?'

The man looked out beyond the homestead, out beyond where the sky and earth met. He squinted. 'You said I'd have to go to the territory seat, to register her an the baby.'

In his throat the stranger made a grunting noise. He asked what about it again.

'Caint say I ever heard that bein done,' the man said.

'It's a census year.' The stranger said it real flat like the answer should be explanation enough. Then, as the man opened his mouth to ask for clarification, the stranger continued. 'You said your woman was a wayward—her people left her here. Something tells me that shes not part of this country. And something tells me that baby—the one you have nothing to do with creating—hes gonna be dirty skinned too.'

'Dont see what thats rightly got to do with anything.'

'There'll be a census marshal coming around. They find out youre housing a couple non-citizens and they'll take them away.'

The man appeared to be physically knocked off-balance and he staggered about for a second. 'They caint do that,' he protested.

Stranger nodded in agreement. 'They cant if you register them out at the territory office.'

'Whereabouts that?'

For a moment the stranger closed his eyes and appeared to be visualizing a place of myth, constructing it in his mind. Then he opened his eyes. 'A ways from here, place I never been before.'

'How far?'

'You know,' the stranger said, 'you could not register your family. You could hide them whenever a passer-through came near.'

'Office is far away then.'

'It is, yes.'

'Whereabouts?'

'Farther west, out Colorado way, place called Fort James.'

'You be able to get me direction of some kind?'

'Yes,' the stranger said. 'But you should be warned: this might be hard country here, but out that way, thats no country at all.'

★ ★ ★

The next night provided more of the same—the man insisting on legitimizing his woman and the baby, the stranger reluctant to provide details.

'I can find Fort James just fine,' the man said.

The stranger grunted as he used a piece of driftwood to brace the porch roof. 'It's a ways from here,' he said.

'Need a headin, a direction—thats all.'

'You sound confident. Did you used to be a scout in the army?'

The man squinted, folded his arms. He did a rare thing and considered his words before he spoke them. 'Got some maps,' he said. 'Know how to guide myself usin the stars.'

The stranger quit working and devoted his attention to the conversation at hand. 'You know celestial navigation?'

'No,' the man said. 'Just know how to follow the stars to get where I needs to go.'

The stranger snorted. He threw his head back to look into the sky above. Evening swirled the tongues of red cirrus clouds into the mellowed lighter shades of aged day. A ghost moon, nearly full, waned into existence. There were no stars yet. It wouldnt be long. The stranger looked at the man. 'You'll have to travel in the night then,' he said.

'I know it.'

'Some people say the country is more dangerous at night.'

'They say that. I figure it's about the same, just darker.'

The stranger chuckled to himself. He went back to constructing his porch space. After a moment he quit again.

'Wheres a man like your kind learn to travel by the stars?' he asked.

The man seemed to anticipate the question and his delay in answering seemed to be a predetermined measure for effect. 'Father was a sailor,' he said.

The stranger nodded. 'Thats where you got the sails from, the oilcloth.'

'Took them when I left.'

'Took the maps too.'

'Thats right. Took whatever I could fit into a wagon, said I was gonna sail the ocean on the other side of the country.'

This truth pleased the stranger and he smiled. 'Instead you end up in this place—place like the Sargasso.'

The man's eyes sharpened. His lips drew tight and constricted until they were white.

'Say something wrong, friend?' the stranger asked.

The man shook his head slowly, not taking his eyes from the stranger, who smiled at him like a fool. 'Just never heard another man talk bout the Sargasso, no one this far inland anyhow.'

'I'm well traveled,' the stranger said. 'Now we'll need to plan for your leaving. It wont be easy on your woman.'

V

The man did as the stranger told him to do. He prepared his woman a drink of boiled leaves and squeezings of wild chives. It would help calm her hysteria, the stranger had said. It would also cause in her a deep sleep.

Only after she fell into slumber did the man leave, kissing her once on the cheek and again on her swollen stomach. He took the saddlebag he filled with meal and maps, the shiv he'd fashioned from a bolt.

'You must leave in the night,' the stranger had instructed him. 'The worry—the anticipation of your leaving—could cause the hysteria to grow.'

'An what'll you do then?' the man had asked.

They had sat in the nearly completed interior room of the stranger's abode to discuss the matter as the woman only appeared more and more uneased in the presence of the stranger.

'I'll bring her here,' the stranger said. 'This is a discreet place, a safe place for her to give birth.'

'An youve birthed some babies in your time?'

'I have.'

The man looked about the shelter. Secretly he was impressed with the stranger, how fast the place took shape. He'd asked how someone goes about making a home so fast once and the stranger simply said such things were a matter of time.

'You marked out how to go to Fort James?'

The man nodded. 'Gonna wear my mule down tryin to get there an back so quick though.'

The stranger smiled the same awkward smile he rarely let happen. 'You'll be back before you know it. You'll have your woman right with the government. Son'll be legal too.'

'You think it'll be a boy?'

'I have a sense about these things,' the stranger said.

The man kissed his woman's stomach once more and stole off out the door. He nearly ran into the stranger as he slung the flap door open. In the moonlight both men appeared with shallow features and muted shades.

'Thought you'd be around tomorrow,' the man said.

'Best if I'm here to explain everything in the morn,' the stranger said. He patted the man's shoulder. His hand felt warm, soft. 'Better if you go now.'

And with that the man left on his mule. He looked over his shoulder once he made some distance, but saw nothing behind him. He looked up into the cosmos, saw Virgo sprawled out, Spica glowing the brightest.

The woman started awake at the touch of foreign hands around her womb. When she saw who the hands belonged to she scuttled back on her bedding.

'Eres satanás.'

The stranger smiled. 'Me confundes con otra persona. He venido aquí para salvarle.'

'No,' the woman said and she pulled her skirt down in an attempt to keep the stranger away from her unborn. He approached still. Outside some birds shrieked. Sun came glowing through the canvas roof of the structure. She cried out for her man.

'Él tiene un objetivo para los tontos.'

The woman shook her head and cried silently. She wrapped her arms around her stomach. Inside the baby kicked.

'No hay razón de resistir,' the stranger said. He smiled kindly and extended his hand to the woman. 'Este es el diseño general del universe. No hay nada más para usted.'

The woman sniffled, realized whatever the stranger meant, he would ultimately be correct. 'Por favor,' she said. 'Hágalo rápidamente.'

Her request was simple and he would oblige. Then he told her it would all happen in due course.

The plains went on for some time. The man rode the mule through the nighttime hours as he said he would do. During the day he draped his shirt over his face for shade and slept. He awoke in the evening when the silken purpled rays of the sun provided just enough light to study his maps. He ate a handful of meal and drank from his canteen and waited for the stars to emerge from the darkness.

First the North Star flickered into existence where the dusk met the land. Low on the opposite horizon the Hydra snaked across the sky. Mighty Ursa Major rotated in the heavens. The man rode without regard for any certain destination, his gaze set far out into the great nothingness beyond.

The stranger did as she had asked and killed her quickly. He performed the deed using a metal band pulled from the edge of a wagon wheel. He'd taken a rock and hammered the edge into a jagged blade, teeth of metal forming wherever the impact landed. While the woman waited, she wet herself. The metal band proved a clumsy tool, never intended for this use. In the end the stranger made three blows—two to the woman's head and one to her torso, taking care not to strike the womb—and then she was dead.

The stranger performed the task without ceremony, carrying out the act as silently as the woman received it. He collected the stray parts of her body—the hand she'd futilely raised to deflect the first blow, the fragment of skull bone with the scalp still attached. He bundled the vestiges together in her dress and tied the skirt at the top and bottom. Since she was small he could easily carry the makeshift sack into his now finished abode. The flat rock he'd slaughtered her on lay covered with blood and feces. He studied the skies and figured it would rain soon enough and clean the spot. Time now became important. The fetus would only live on for a few more minutes.

He went to the inner chamber and lifted a wooden door to the tunnel he'd bored down into the earth. Roping the sack to his waist, he began to crawl—this tunnel plumbed deep at a steep angle and then fell nearly straight down. Siftings of dirt fell as he crawled, dragging the body behind him. He went deeper, until the loose dirt packed harder and morphed into clay. Water seeped from all sides of the tunnel. Gravity and the angle of the tunnel caused the sack containing the body to fall against the stranger. At once he became soaked with blood, water and urine. He scraped his hands against the rocks, the fissures of the labyrinth winding their way through complete darkness. He came to the end of the tunnel.

The way into the tunnel seemed to no longer exist. He crouched low in what he suspected was a pool of spring water. He placed a hand on his bundle and still felt the baby stirring, kicking. Perhaps the way down here had collapsed. Or maybe his route had become so circuitous no light could meander its way to these depths.

'Este es un lugar bueno para ser sepultado,' he said. Finally, the baby moved no more. Then he tried to stand, but did not have enough clearance. He began laughing and let the echoes resound throughout the chambers within the earth, channeling and mapping out the landscape beneath the land above. He laughed louder at the sound of his own mania and the noise amplified to deafening levels. The rocks began to shake and wisps of dirt crumbled from between the cracks of stone. A rumbling louder than any laughter resonated from deeper than any charted cavern of the earth's bowels.

TWO

I

Several days out the man saw a troupe of men. Distant things. It was daytime now and he readied himself for sleep. The men on the horizon corkscrewed their way through the grasses and up the slight gradient to where the man pitched camp. Though they remained otiose things, he could see one of them waved his hand. The man set down his meal of dried grains and mush and searched in the saddlebags for his shiv.

'You there,' the distant figure called. Again he waved his arm.

Uncertain of how to return the call, the man simply waved his arm.

There were three men in the troupe—each dressed in a uniform that might have once looked regal.

'Had injuns attack our division,' the man with ropes around his shoulder said. He was an officer. 'Lost most of my men. Apaches—thats the kind of injun we're talkin about.'

The man shook his head. 'Caint say I ever heard of em.'

The two other officers exchanged a look. 'You aint never heard of the Apache?'

'No.'

'You live out here an you aint never heard of the Apache?'

'Caint say I have.'

All three men laughed heartily.

'Dont see whats funny,' the man said.

'You must be bout twenty years old,' the officer said. 'Now I'd hand over my entire army paycheck to have your kind of stupidity.'

The two other soldiers bellowed laughter in agreement. When the man did not join in their laughter, they redoubled their glee at the man's ignorance.

The man took out his shiv and brandished it at the officer. 'Go on now,' he said. 'You just settin here takin up my time and funnin me. Get out of here.'

But the display the man made only caused further wails of laughter. The officer pulled a saber from his waistband and waved it in the air. 'I'm a goddamned grizzled uncle-dad,' he hollered. 'I smell bad enough even the redskin niggers leave me lone.'

The other two men hooted and took out a hatchet and a bayonet respectively.

'Put that shank away, boy,' the officer said, turning suddenly savage. 'Hate to chop you up like I did to the niggers we took prisoner.'

Without hesitation, the man slid the shiv into the side of his boot. 'Would appreciate it if you fellas got a move along. I'm restin up so I's can travel through the night.'

'That so?'

'It is,' the man said. 'Figure you fellas are probably lookin to head back to your fort.'

The officer snorted. 'Why'd we do a fool thing like that?'

The other two soldiers nodded in agreement. One took a swig from his canteen. 'Got a whole different set of skills,' one said. 'Might as well be dead for all the army knows.'

'You gonna just do what—steal an kill?'

'Whatever makes a livin.'

'You gonna kill me?'

All three of the men exchanged glances casually. The one's gaze fixated on the mule. The man's hand began sliding back down his leg, toward the shiv in his boot.

'Afraid you got nothin even worth killin you for,' the officer said.

'Maybe you'll learn what an Apache looks like,' the other one said.

'Be the last thing you learn,' the third said.

With that the three men stood up and mounted their horses. 'Thanks for the conversation, stranger,' the officer said. He tipped his hat and they rode on.

The man watched the soldiers go until they became lost in the shifting grasses of the plains. Unnerved by the visit, the man decided he could not sleep and he packed up his gear and began riding again.

Riding during the day required a different type of navigation than at night. Instead of familiarizing himself with the stars, he had to know the path of the sun, the time of day. Navigation by the sun consisted of knowing time and space. To travel westward as he was, he needed to travel away from the sun in the morning. At noon he would be wise to stop for rest as it was the hottest time of day and the sun cast shadows without direction. Once the sun canted past the noontime peak, he would progress toward it.

These few lessons were what he learned from his father.

'Maps can be wrong,' his father said. 'Men draw em up, make money on em.'

He remembered he asked his father why any man would want to make a map poorly. But this angered his father, being interrupted. Often he spoke just to hear himself talk. 'Why do you think?' he asked. Now the boy stayed silent. 'How they gonna sell the next one, if this map is the best?' He shook his head. Normally when he became this upset, he said he should have left the boy with his mother, that loose bitch with crotch rot.

His father leaned on the rail of the boarding house balcony, suddenly calm again. He watched the waves roll in and out, smelled the air. 'Lotta sailors now trust the maps,' his father said. 'They dont know how to gauge the sun. They dont know bout seabirds an what they mean. Lotta capns wont take me on cause I dont read maps—or anything really. Worse thing we ever done was come to shore.'

And it was true. Life at sea made for easier living than this place where they ended up. At least when they moved on the sea. The Sargasso told another story all together. 'Cmon boy,' his father said. 'Time to get some shut eye.'

The boy's hands gripped the railing. Far off in the village streets he heard laughter and strange music.

II

For nearly a whole day the man rode with occasional breaks to water his mule at streams. He rode into the night. Though sore in buttocks from the journey, he pressed on, his head drooping every now and again with slumber. He jerked his head back up. Moonlight, brilliant and glittering, lit a path before him. He thought to look around, study the far stretches of darkness pulled out in every direction. But manmade light, there was none.

His thoughts wandered. He imagined his woman back at the hovel, wondered if she'd given birth yet. He thought about his son. In his mind he became certain now that the stranger must have been correct, it would be a son. He pictured her cradling the baby in the crook of her arm, singing those listless songs in her foreign tongue. Thoughts of the stranger, how he tended to her, infiltrated the periphery of his fantasy. First he imagined the stranger holding the baby, smiling at his wife, speaking to her as he had that one time. He would say things to her like his father used to say to the women at the wharfside houses.

Then he imagined the stranger and his woman in bed together, her still loosed from birth, but wanton just the same. Somewhere in the hovel the baby cried while they fornicated.

The man shook his head, as if the thoughts could be flung right out into the darkness around him. In doing so, a memory took their place. He remembered his father's breath, hot with wharf house grog, telling him to watch.

His father stood naked over the bed. His body hewed lean, tanned all. Stray hairs and scars marred his skin.

'You want him here?' the woman asked. She lay in the bed next to the boy. She was naked too.

'Needs to watch,' his father said. 'Needs to see a man give it to a woman.'

The hired woman craned her head around to look at the boy. He'd drawn himself up against the wall, pulling his legs to his chest.

'Aint a thing to be scared about,' she said. And as she said this, his father pulled her leg to the side and inserted himself. The woman's brow flinched and she groaned.

The boy looked out the window by the bed, which began to rock rhythmically.

'Hey,' his father said. He snapped his fingers to draw the boy's attention. 'Keep watchin. This is how men do it.'

When the man awoke, the daytime returned. His mule had stopped to graze on some reed grass by a spring. The man gauged the sun, guessed it to be late morning. If he had been dreaming, the thoughts were a fog now. He dismounted the mule and squatted by the spring, refilled his canteens. The chaff meal ran low, maybe another two days' worth.

He made a half-hearted attempt to forage something, but found nothing here. He looked out behind him, half expecting to see back as far as the hovel. But there was nothing. He turned his back to the sun and looked ahead. Faint and jagged, farther out than the rest of the land before him, lay the mountains.

The stranger ate dinner with the troupe of soldiers. He looked over the insignia on the officer's uniform, looked at the faded patch of fabric where a name used to be embroidered. The two other soldiers sat on a length of driftwood, eating from their mess kits.

'Want to thank you for the dinner, the kindness,' the stranger said.

'Cant let a man go hungry out here on the plains,' the officer said. He didnt make eye contact when he said this. He looked at the boots the stranger wore, looked at the roped clumps of black hair on the stranger's head.

'Good for you theres not a whole lot of men in these parts then,' the stranger said.

The officer poured both him and the stranger cups of coffee. The two soldiers declined theirs. 'Hot if you want it,' the officer said setting the kettle on the ground by the fire.

'Run into many men?' the stranger asked.

'Few, yeah. Mostly the desperate type.'

'That so?'

'Some men with no business bein out here like they is.'

The stranger raised his eyebrows. 'And what business is it that should keep a man at home?'

The soldiers on the driftwood tended to their weapons, conversed between themselves.

'Ran into a fella,' the officer said. 'Never heard of an Apache.'

'Is that right?'

'God's honest truth, right boys?'

The two soldiers paused their conversation long enough to grunt in agreement.

'And what business do you have out here, in these parts?' the stranger asked.

This question caused all three men to give the stranger a hard stare.

'We're soldiers, infantry,' the officer said.

'But youre not going back,' the stranger said. 'To your fort, I mean.'

'No,' the officer said. 'Cant rightly say we are.'

The stranger looked at the two companions, each sharpening his weapon. He studied the smaller of the two men. A skittish sort, the man used a flat stone to rub the face of a hatchet.

'Youre scalping,' the stranger said.

The officer snorted, slurped at his cup of coffee. 'Doin whatever pays, whatever keeps us goin.'

The stranger wrapped his hands around the tin cup, letting the warmth flood through them. He looked once at each of the men before addressing the smallest. He smirked. 'Ik zal je vermoorden duren,' he said.

The officer nearly spat out his coffee. 'What in the hell'd you say?'

The stranger stayed calm. Men usually became worked up when he spoke a native tongue to them. But this younger soldier, the one with the hatchet, he understood.

'Youre a fur trapper,' he said to the soldier. 'Een bonten handelaar. Started out in the sylvania country other side of the Mississippi. Never fought in any war though. Thats why your uniform is so ill-fitting.' The stranger closed his eyes. 'You took the clothes off a dead man so you could reap all the army benefits.'

'Hold on here,' the other soldier said. The stranger silenced him by raising his hand. He addressed the interrupting party directly. 'Youve had these thoughts yourself, sometimes when your comrade in arms mispronounces a word, when he stays silent while you and your officer here are laughing at a turn of phrase.'

The officer slurped at his coffee, studied the soldier in question over the edge of his cup. Still, the stranger kept speaking, this time rotating his oration between all three men in his audience. 'You'll say I'm making this all up. And I am. The story never existed until I put it into your head. Doesnt make it any less true.'

He sipped at his coffee. The soldiers exchanged glances. The officer spoke. 'You of any value?' he asked the stranger.

'You saw me walking,' the stranger said. 'No horse to speak of, no possessions.' He looked at the soldier with the hatchet again. 'Ah, maar de bonten handelaar. How fitting.'

The soldier stopped sharpening his blade, letting the rock fall into the grasses. He gripped the stock of the hatchet. The other soldier thumbed the edge of his knife.

'Whats that mean—*how fitting*?' the officer asked.

The stranger laughed, gulped down the last of the coffee. 'You all are going to cut the scalp right off my head, claim it as an Apache's. Youve been eyeing my hair since I sat down. My value to you is as a corpse.'

The officer gave the soldiers a nod and the one with the hatchet lunged at the stranger. But the stranger pulled out a shank of his own, a scrap of metal. It cut the man across his bicep. Flesh flapped limp and the arm fell deadened to the man's side. He howled in agony. The stranger seized up the hatchet and in one broad stroke split the other soldier's skull from one orbital cavity to the next. He whirled around, missing a jab from the officer's sword. Two more hacks and the officer lay broken in the grass.

The stranger squatted by the officer's corpse and undressed him, pulling the uniform jacket and trousers from the body. He stuffed the trouser legs into the sleeves of the jacket and tied the clothes around his waist. Then he stood up.

The fur trapper tried crawling away, his arm with the cloth and muscle and bone all unfolding. He panted. The stranger sauntered over.

'How far ahead is the man who hasnt seen an Apache?'

'Lieve God.'

The stranger clucked his tongue, kicked the man in the arm. A scream rang out. 'Waar is hij?'

'U zult mij doden?'

The stranger smiled. How quickly men wanted opposite things. One moment it's life, the next theyre hoping for death. 'Yes,' he said. 'How far out was he—how many days?'

'Drie.'

The stranger nodded, saying he had one more task. He scooped the man up like he might a babe and carried him across the plains. 'You cant die just yet,' he cooed. 'We've got to find a decent resting place first.'

In his arms the fur trapper sobbed.

In the evening hours, after the blue of the sky succumbed and bled into the redder hues of the passing of the day, the stranger and his bounty came to a low-built sodhouse. The plankwood door creaked back and forth in the breeze. Neither lantern light nor smoke from the tin pipe chimney gave indication to life inside. The stranger smelled the air, noted a rankness he associated with rotting meat. Then he spied the dismembered corpse of a woman. The Apache had been here. He must be close on their heels.

'Slecht land,' the fur trapper murmured, dizzy with delirium from losing too much blood.

The stranger shushed his captive and heaved the man to the ground. He scanned the land about him. He shut his eyes and smelled the decay of the place full in his nostrils. He sauntered away from the crumpled form of the fur trapper toward the homestead. He creaked open the door.

'Dia duit.'

All inside—the father and two sons—lay dead. The stranger allowed his eyes to adjust to the darkness. He picked up a biscuit from the supper table, still set. It tasted fresh enough.

He swiped his finger through the blood on the stovetop. It hardly smudged and had a tack to it.

A clay pitcher sat on a stool by a bed. The stranger picked up the pitcher and smelled the water. He closed his eyes and inhaled again. He poured the water from the pitcher, the stream splashing off the table and trickling across the dirt floor to the doorway. Once the pitcher drained completely, he untied the uniform from around his waist and crammed it into the stoneware vessel. He walked back outside. The fur trapper still lay where he had been left. The stranger turned his attention to the pitcher. He knelt, putting his hand to the ground like an Indian scout might. Then he nodded and used his bare hands to scoop out a hole in the earth.

Once the pitcher lay buried, he hefted the fur trapper back onto his shoulders. The man stank of feces, of blood and sweat. Still he breathed, a shaky inhalation and a wheezing exhalation. Pause. Then another rattling.

'Last thing most men do on this planet is shit themselves,' the stranger said. 'Natural thing—the bowels open up, shit just rolls out.'

He walked a hundred paces and looked at the Y-shaped post hanging crooked over the well, a rope looped in the elbow. 'It's because we run out of energy, cant keep it tight,' the stranger laughed. The fur trapper, in his delusional state, chuckled. 'Killed a baby a piece ago,' the stranger said. 'Most babies are born right into shit with the mother pushing so hard. It is as if I summed up all of life by pre-empting it.'

The stranger looped the rope from the well around the

both of them, binding the trapper's arm and legs to his torso in a clove hitch. Then he jumped into the well, waiting for the rope to pull tight.

III

Mountains loomed closer with each passing hour. Yet they stood as artificial things, jags of glass set out on the horizon only to tease the man. He consulted his maps. If the cartographer who drew this scape years ago were not a liar, then Fort James lay on the other side of the mountains. A thin dotted line noted where one might pass without much weather, without too much struggle.

When the mountains came closer still and took on dimension, the man stopped to study them. He had traveled through most of the day again. He had forsaken his appetite, his desire to slumber. But he knew here in the evening hours, with shadows masking entire slopes of the mountains, the tips of white shimmering like capstones of an ancient Aztec temple, he knew it to be wise only to travel into the folds of the mountains in the daylight. A rounded rock could turn his mule's hoof. An elevated trail might take an unexpected turn. He'd heard stories. Stories told by lantern light from the mouths of sailor men. He was young then and his mind made the tales bigger, he knew.

The mast rigger told the other men how he learned his trade in a jungle land. Said he swung from vines and shimmied up trees to escape from the injuns there. 'Weird ones they was,' he said. 'Twigs in their faces, tattoos all o'er their bodies. All of em skinny though. Probably from all the runnin.'

The boy's father, a navigator and quartermaster on the schooner, said the mast rigger was lucky, theyd be fatter if theyd caught him. Everyone laughed, even the Portuguese deckhand.

But the Norseman had the best stories. He told of his days in the mountains of his country—only there the mountains were called alps.

'No travel in the night,' he said, his accent only growing thicker with imbibing grog. 'Men like beasts eat night travelers. Best to make fire.'

The other sailors laughed loudly at the anecdote. But the boy remained captivated. The biggest threat in every story involved being eaten. 'You were a mountain man?' he asked.

The Norseman agreed with a sailor's aye.

'How'd you end up on a boat?'

'It what Norsemen do,' he said. He quaffed back the last of his grog and swayed with the lilt of the ship. 'There none mountains i oceanen.'

Later, the boy's father said it wasnt true, what the men in the galley had mentioned. 'They were drunk,' he said. 'They invent stories to out-talk each other. Dont want you gettin the wrong ideas bout the world.'

The boy asked if he would ever see the mountains. For as far back as he could remember he had lived on a boat, enlisted with his father as a deckhand. On his eighth birthday he learned to keep the galley, how to trap and kill rats. Once he could brave the open deck he swabbed and fetched and rigged.

'Not if I can help it,' his father said. 'Aint nothin inland that you need to see. Bunch of nonsense there.'

The mountains were grander in scale than he originally supposed. It took him another day to reach the foothills and he camped where the land began a steep grade into a canyon. He mixed the last of his chaff meal with water and swished it about his mouth. If he was lucky, pieces of the meal would stick in his teeth and in the morning he could suck them out for sustenance. He tethered his mule to the tree and looked up at the thick band of stars sprawled out, composing the Milky Way. Deep in the southern sky Corvus and Centarus danced together.

It had been this way on the ship. Some nights his father seemed a softer man. He stood at the bow rail, pointing out the constellations to the boy, telling him how to chart a course by following the stars. 'Had a Spaniard teach me bout the stars while back,' he said. 'Before you came along.' The boy ignored the sudden angst that embittered his father's speech. In a moment's time, he continued talking. 'Spaniard said the stars are like million suns throughout the galaxy—whatever that is. I think it's the same as heaven. He tried to tell me what we see in the sky is a history of what happened. Said it was like getting a letter: we can read what happened and what we're readin seems like it's happenin now.' He shook his head as if he'd lost his way in talking. 'But it already happened, we just see the past for a moment.'

The boy said he didnt understand.

His father chose his words cautiously. 'This man—the Spaniard—tells me we could very well be lookin at some stars that already done burned themselves out. He told me, sober as a mission priest, the stars with their energy, can navigate the distances between places. But they can also guide us through time.' He chuckled. 'This is why I dont want you to take what these men say as bein true.'

'You dont believe him?' the boy asked.

Again, the man considered his answer before replying. 'Aint that you cant trust em. It aint that. But these stories they tell, theyre like a half truth—partly something they made up. Hell, they might even believe it any more. Spoke it right into life.'

The boy nodded. He smelled the air, looked at the stars. Other men could have the world, he'd take the sea for himself.

When he woke, he scarcely recognized his surroundings. Light bathed the slope and there was no escaping it. He sat up, put his hand to his gut. He had terrible hunger pain. He sucked the meal from his teeth, but that did little to assuage his appetite. He picked the crust from the corners of his eyes and ate of it too. Leaving his mule hitched to a patch of scrub, he wandered the hillside, flipping rocks over in search of insects, looking for a place where ground varmint might store their winter food. He came to a flat spot on the hill—bald, the dirt bleached white by the sun. An odd place, the man figured, with no hope of food. Yet the strangeness drew him in.

Atop the slope there a scrag tree stood, branches sprawled out in petrified order. Wood scorched down to grey, looked to be blistered by lightning. A vulture perched on the topmost limb. A flitting shadow caught the man's attention and he looked to the sky. Above him a half dozen more buzzards circled in slow arcs.

Beneath the tree an oblong hole gaped, a few round stones scattered about it. The man slowed his gait and studied the scene. Only his mule hitched a quarter mile yonder moved. The buzzards too. A corpse lay next to the open grave. It was a man's body nearly decayed beyond recognition. Rags of clothes—a pair of trousers and a flimsy shirt—covered the rough-hewn leather of his skin. He lay face down and for that the man was grateful. First thing the vultures take is the eyes.

He came close enough to peer into the grave. And what he saw there began to puzzle him. He crouched down by the body and scanned his surroundings in all directions. No human as far as he could see was afoot. He looked back into the grave, into the pinewood box. All seemed reasonable: the grave was shallow certainly; but the ground was hard. There was a coffin and that too seemed reasonable given the vista. At one point in time maybe the scrag had bloomed with flowers. It would be a pleasant place to rest for an eternity. Even the displaced corpse could be a product of coyotes or scavengers, graverobbers. Men did do such things. He'd heard stories.

The second body, the one in the coffin, bothered him. His skin stretched tight, still intact; he looked to be asleep, though judging by the angle of his neck, he was not. Even so, the man said sir a couple times before inching forward. His death must have been recent—he still had his eyes in his head.

The man tried to concoct a plot wherein this man could have been robbing this shallow grave and fallen in, breaking his neck. He shook his head. Then he searched the fresher corpse's body for valuables. The corpse wore a serape and the man had to unfasten it to search through the dead man's pockets. But there was nothing, save a canvas bag of jerky. The man immediately ate a strip of the meat, swallowing it with barely a chew. Bigger pieces meant the meat would stay in his gut longer.

The corpse still had boots on his feet. The man wadded a long, translucent strip of jerky into his cheek. Squelching the juice from the meat through his teeth, the man thought of the abnormality of such a crime. He looked around again, this time taking longer and more squinted glances into each horizon. Nothing moved. Now even his mule stood stock still in the sun.

'It aint graverobbin,' he said out loud. His voice carried harder in the wide open than he thought it would. It startled him. Even the mule, a quarter mile away, redirected his gaze at the man. He justified the action in his mind as he tugged a boot of rich red leather with stamped designs in the upper off a stiffened foot. Fine things like these left to dry rot, left to feed some roving band of coyotes. As the second boot slid off the corpse's foot, a couple dollars held together with a silver clip and a pouch of tobacco fell out. The pouch was made from the scrotum of a quarter horse, a tendon woven around the opening as a drawstring.

Without another hesitation he pulled on the boots, stuffing the money into the upper, the tobacco into his pocket. He walked briskly back to the mule and rode into the mountains.

IV

Deep in the mountains proved a strange place. Trees with no business being alive still thrived, rooted in rock and sheltered on each side of the box canyons. Contrasted against the evergreen cover, the soil red and raw and rocked appeared as an open wound, a scab on the earth. Ancients had lived here, people who ground their sown oats into meal, who drank from clay pots like urns. Anasazi people would build their shelters in cliff overhangs and cubbies, who constructed labyrinths of apartments in the sides of mountains. Petroglyphs—their rudimentary form of snaked and swirled written language—adorned the walls in chalked white paint. Whether the original inhabitants had anything worth saying, the stranger knew not.

He wandered through the stooped doorframes of the structures these people made. Crumbling bricks composed of nothing more than straw and mud had weathered a thousand years. The stranger ran his fingers over them. He closed his eyes and his mind went into a dark place. Someday other people would find these ruins—first some stray cowhands, then locals rife with curiosity. Not long after the locals discovered this place, then the rest of the world would come to know of it. Flocking here in droves, on paved roadways, bringing their families with them and no intent to settle, they would trod trails, led by an hourly paid outdoorsman in a wide-brimmed hat and pristine uniform. A ranger—root word range. Little placards would describe what they saw, telling them what men who spent more time in school than the rest of the world gave as truth.

He opened his eyes. Where his fingers had pressed against the brick, flakes of adobe broke off.

The man took the low pass through the mountains. He stopped an hour into the foothills once his path merged with a trickle of a stream. Both he and the mule drank readily. Using his bare hands, he clawed at the soil and uncovered some small white tubers. He washed them in the stream, smelled them and ate them. It might hurt in his gut if they were bad fruit, but he did not eat enough to cause sickness. That much he knew.

On the ship they had thrown their bad food overboard. As part of his quartermasterly duties, the responsibility of disposing of the rotten goods fell on the boy's father. In good times, it was only a few fruits, a crate of flour squirming with mites. The captain would come to the father's room—a cubby beneath the deck stairs with a sheet hung up for privacy.

'Got a couple more need taken care of,' the captain said.

The boy lay on the top, shorter bunk. Without a word his father nodded. Theyd wait a piece and his father would take a taper from the footlocker and together theyd go to the cargo hold.

The captain marked the crates with Xs. Tonight there were five in total—big crates too.

'All the foods nearly gone,' the boy said.

His father hefted a crate, said to grab the other smaller one with plantains in it. The boy did like he was told. Tiny flies flocked out of the slats of the box. The plantains themselves smelled overly sweet. It made him hungry.

'Doin this'll save someone from dyin from the shits,' his father said. They carried the goods up the stairs to the deck. Men were still up; the boy could hear them muttering to each other, to themselves perhaps.

'Cmon,' his father snapped. They lugged the cargo to the rail of the ship. 'On three.' He counted one and two and they shoved the boxes overboard. First a protracted silence, then a splash. With the boat in the doldrums, every sound could be heard.

'You there!' The nightwatchman scampered out of the shadows. 'What'd you throw?'

'Bad food,' the boy's father said. 'Rotted all the way through.'

'Better than no food.'

Another man came up from below deck. It was the first mate. 'Whats this?' he asked. He looked the father over, then the boy. He licked his lips in thirst.

'These two throwin food overboard again,' the nightwatchman said.

'Capn's orders?'

The father nodded, said in fact it was; there were still a few more boxes under deck.

A few more men gathered around to watch the confrontation. 'You an capn seem awful friendly like,' the first mate said. 'He givin it to you or you puttin it in him?'

'Theyd be the only ones getting their pricks wet,' one of the deckhands said.

'Rotten food,' another simply said.

From the stern of the boat, the captain's voice rang out. 'Should stop drinkin the salt water,' he said. All turned to look at him. In his hand he held a taper, the wax smelling of flowers. 'Salt water makes the mind go crazy.'

'But we aint got any fresh water,' the nightwatchman hissed. 'No rain since we got here.'

By now all who dwelled on the ship had come above deck. The Portuguese man clung to the rail, ignoring the exchange. The rigger sided with the nightwatchman, stating that salt water quenched better than no water at all.

'We're all sailors here,' the boy's father said. 'In right times you know you cant stuff yourself with rot food and salt water.'

'These aint right times.'

'That food probably aint even turned.'

'You and capn are tryin to kill us.'

'How in hell we end up in this place?'

'Sargasso,' the Portuguese man said under his breath. The boy heard when he said it, for there was no wind, no weather, no movement to speak of.

The stranger toured the rectangular towers of the Anasazi village, ducking through doorways, padding up the crumbling steps carved into the sloped rock, making use of a rickety ladder left in place for a thousand years. He climbed through the tunnels. Most of the tunnels were little larger than the breadth of his shoulders. Inside he heard only his own breathing, the shuffling of his hands and knees on the stone, could see nothing more than the light at the end burning white hot. He emerged and there were more ruins. He muttered to himself. These structures had brick at their core—he could see it where the adobe mud fell off in slabs. The ancient homes rose from the landscape like alien things, gaping doorways, postholes where the wooden beams once rested. He crawled into the porthole doorway of one. Shards of a clay pot littered the floor. Scent of rotting flesh ruminated in the small space. In his desperation, he went to crawl through a hole connecting this apartment to the one behind it. He heard the squeak of a mouse as he crawled and before he could avoid it, his knee crushed the rodent.

When he came out the world was again a different place. He looked around the earth, little more than rubble from a tower fallen and scorched land. Touched by nothing except the sun. He cursed under his breath, to himself. Then he began running in circles, his head shaking back and forth, trying to survey the ground.

He cursed again and ran back to where he began. But there was nothing there. The tower—he said it out loud. He ran to the fallen tower and with a renewed fervor, began slinging bricks aside. A small opening showed black and amorphous underneath. What light penetrated through the abyss glimmered at the bottom of the well. He moved some more bricks. Once the aperture augured wide enough, he raised his hands over his head, ready to dive headlong into the darkness.

There he stood, rigid and arms upraised, holding his breath, eyes closed. He released his breath and opened his eyes. This wouldnt be enough. The ancient formula of progress—men plunging headlong into darkness—needed casualties. The ties of the New York subway were the ribs of migrants. The chambers of the Hoover Dam a mausoleum for a score of men. The locks of the Erie Canal little more than a deathbed. Death is progress.

First the stranger just stood by the opening, looking around for anything moving, anything milling about. But there was nothing. Far off, barely even visible, he could see birds, buzzards with their long necks circling. The stranger smiled at the irony: these were beasts in search of the dead. He lay down in the dust, next to the opening, shutting his eyes, pretending to be dead himself.

A time passed, neither long, nor short, when he heard the flapping and rustling of feathers. He held his breath and kept his eyes shut. The buzzard reared its wings open again, danced its sideways waltz to the stranger.

Then the stranger inhaled slowly through his nose. In his mind he visualized the vulture perched on a small stone, its clawed feet wrapped gnarly around it. He rolled and grabbed in one motion. The bird cried out. And they both fell headlong into the aperture.

The stranger climbed through the darkness—darkness so thick he had to scoop it out of the way one handful at a time. His mouth filled with the darkness and he had no choice but to ingest it. Mealy, muddy and rank, he gulped it down, wormed his body through the space. Swallowing the space, it pushed through his throat, plopped foul and full in his gut and continued on slogging its way through his bowels and eventually was expelled behind him.

Then—light. A faint glow of light and he reached toward it, found it to be bleeding through the slatted cracks of the wooden trap door of his dugout home. With a single shove, he pulled himself out of the hole and looked around the interior room. This place was nearly complete, a handsome shelter. He stood and walked out the door to the plains.

He continued on, past the flat rock where he would eventually slaughter the woman and drag her body into the depths of the caves. He walked on, his path intersecting the man's eventual trifle to a fool's errand. In spite of himself, he whistled, long and low, an unnatural action for him to take, but a spirit of some type moved him.

'Fancy seein your likes out this way,' a voice said.

Before he turned around, the stranger smiled.

The stranger looked back at himself. 'Cant be more than one of us, you know,' he said.

'You know better.'

'So do you.'

And they knew each other completely; it was true. The one knew what would unfold, the other keeping the knowledge of his thoughts on seeing himself inside his head. But they shared the humor of violating the laws of existence.

'Only so much material in the universe.'

'We'll solve it all soon enough,' he said. 'Feel the earth spin a little slower once I showed up?'

'Saw everything get a little dimmer, knew someone must be sucking the energy right out of creation. Didnt know it'd be me.'

'You will realize it, only too late.'

Without needing any further cues, the strangers sat, studied each other.

Finally the stranger from the time before asked if he had to be killed.

'Has to happen that way,' the stranger said.

'Cant be rewritten.'

'Afraid not,' he said. He leaned back on his hands, looked at the sky, the clouds passing by. Distant things. 'You'll understand soon enough.'

Together the stranger and his reflection walked a new path out toward the stream. They walked quietly and the stranger told him how he'd kill the woman and her baby and make short work of the troupe. He described the ruins in the mountains and gulched foothills with the open grave. 'Goddamn,' he sighed. 'It's a beautiful place, this world.'

THREE

I

Food became more plentiful in the mountain pass. Pine nuts were easily plucked from the low-hanging boughs of the trees while he rode on the mule. Come time to stop in the midmorning, the man might set up a snare for some ground squirrel using a length of twine and a sharpened stick. If he chose to ride through until the afternoon—which he did more often now—he would make a game out of baiting the squirrels with his gathered pine nuts. Then he sat on a boulder, crouched, stone in hand. He chose the stones carefully, preferring the rounded ones as big around as his thumb.

When a squirrel came close enough to the pile of nuts, he slung the rock, sidearmed at the creature. More often than not, he killed the animal on the first throw. Eating squirrel wore on his gut, especially when he sliced the flesh too thick and it didnt dry by morning. But he had to eat what he had.

Thats what the first mate had said to his father.

'Got to eat what we got,' he said. The captain tried to speak, but the men interjected with nonsense vulgarity.

'Ever night you an quartermaster come up here, dump food overboard, tell us it's no good.'

Just as the men had nights before, they congregated on the deck. Staring up at the slivered moon, Scorpio and Draco chasing each other in endless fight. They chanted like byzantines, demanding rain. But none came. Only a gentle lapping of the mossed sea rocked the boat in the doldrums.

The captain held the candle up to the first mate and examined his face. 'You drank from the sea.'

The first mate drew back into shadow, said he did; it was the only thing to do.

'Não há nada mais aqui. Isto é o Sargaço,' the Portuguese said. He limped to the first mate's side. The other hands grumbled, some asking what the old coot who lived in the hold just said.

'Sargasso,' he said again. Then he reached his fingers out and pinched the flame of the candle between his thumb and forefinger. A hiss sliced through the quieted darkness and a small festoon of smoke snaked in the air. No one moved, all bewitched by the old Portuguese. The boy watched as the Portuguese took from the captain's hand the candle. He watched as the man ate the candle and said in another tongue that all was satisfied.

The stranger watched the husband leave his woman at the hovel, watched his double converse with him in the moonlight, wishing him godspeed. For a time, he stood there watching this form—fully him in the flesh and blood, yet something completely outside of his own existence—just stand in the grass. The silhouetted figure began walking away in pursuit of the man.

The stranger waited until morning to come for the woman. Fear washed across her face when she woke. She reached for the man's body, but he was not there. Saying no several times, she crab-walked backward into the tarpaulin-and-board side of the hovel. But the stranger had not moved. She pulled her skirt tight down between her legs.

'Usted consume la luz,' she said. 'Vaya ahora.'

'Hemos hecho esto antes, mi amor,' the stranger replied. He smiled, complacent and toothy. 'Usted no puede cambiar lo que ya ha pasado.'

Then she began to cry. 'Usted es loco.'

Still the stranger knew the path of the man. He followed the man through the night, walking in the tracks the man left behind. What traces the man left behind from his camps—a scrap of cloth, a matchstick or some flecks of grain meal—the stranger gathered and ate.

And though the man stopped for the night, the stranger had no such luxury, for he had no mule, no horse, no train or bus or car. He walked. Sometimes he closed his eyes and imagined what the man saw, what the world looked like at that place at that moment. How simple it must be.

He thought of the man's story, how much the man must have forgotten and how much of it was now a thing of fiction. He laughed out loud while he walked. He thought it comical how certain people are when they create their stories. Foolish things. You cannot know what has already been written until you read it. And at that moment, it's supposed to be new.

As the man recalled it, the captain was killed that night on the boat. He called the Portuguese by a name not familiar to any of the men. And the old man walked away without incident.

Later that same night the first mate crushed the captain's skull with an eight-pound mortar. When he told the crew of this, he said the captain was chanting in his sleep. They carved the flesh from the captain's bones and drank his blood after it had been boiled.

The father and son stayed in their quarters. 'Stranded at sea can cause men to go crazy,' his father said.

The boy nodded. Above them men whooped and sang, stomped across the deck. Below them the sea slapped the boat rhythmically. 'If we stay out of sight, stay quiet, they'll leave us be.'

And for a time, the crew did leave them alone. The men stayed on deck, cursing at the sky, drinking from the sea. When the rigger died, they ate him too. Blood seeped through the deckboards and dripped on the boy's bunk. He touched the spot of blood. It was cool and wet. His father didnt notice when he licked it off his fingertip.

At that moment the stranger understood the man. He had to see him as a boy, know what happened, what could never be undone. He had to see the memories of the man and how they were different from what the story was really about. If he bothered to ask the man what happened, it was this. But the stranger knew better—he knew what shaped the man was kept in the darkest wells of his mind, a place where terrifying dreams wake us into being.

II

At first he tried to take the woman by the hand as a gentleman from another time might. She spat on the stranger, cursed him. He knew then how it had to be. With one hand he seized both of her wrists. With the other hand he grabbed her hair. She screamed. He pulled her from the hovel and out into the grasses. She jerked her head to the side and left him holding a tuft of hair. Stumbling only a few more feet, before the stranger grabbed her by the ankle, she resigned into sobs. Without the crying she might have been a pretty thing. But now her face contorted, tears dragging dark streaks of dirt to her chin. Her breasts swollen with pregnancy heaved with each inhalation.

The stranger sat next to her, his mind far away. Finally, when her tears subsided and she sniffled, she asked if it could be quick.

'Usted pudiera aprovecharse de mí y irse,' she said.

He shook his head. 'No puedo perdonar la vida,' he said. 'Tengo que acabarlo. Su tiempo aquí se ha acabado.'

The news did not surprise her, she figured this to be the case. Again she asked for it to be quick. 'Sí,' the stranger said. He stood and extended his hand. This time, the woman took it and they walked out to a flat rock, to where a wagon broke down years before, splintering its wheel on the stone.

The woman sat on the stone and watched while the stranger pulled the steel band off the outer edge of the wheel. The band held to the wood with tack nails; one of them sliced his fingertip open. He put the finger to his mouth before going back to work. The strip of metal wavered awkwardly as he held it up, gauging its usefulness.

The woman turned her attention elsewhere; she looked out across the plains. The skies were clear, not a chicken hawk or buzzard in sight. The thwap of the rock against the metal pulled her attention back to the stranger. He raised a stone above his head and brought it down against the band again. Where the stone impacted, the metal edge of the band became spiny and dented, forming a jagged blade.

'¿Será rápido?' she asked.

And it was.

Pitiful how she whimpered before he swung the blade, how she raised her hand as if this would deflect the blow, how her other hand cradled around her womb as if she could save the unborn from this fate.

The man crossed the plains as he would in the lifetime before, encountering the solitary trees left from antediluvian times and spared being scorched into salt. He saw the occasional being, the troupe of scalpers and a man riding distant on a beast. At night he watched the stars, tried to reach out and touch them while he lay on his back.

The stranger followed. He followed where highways and

billboards would eventually slice the land and blot the sky. The horizon remained unbroken, not a guy wire to a radio tower or the vapor trail of a jumbo jet marring the expanse. He walked over a sop of grass still quelling with dew from the night before. In time this place would be quarried, chunks of stone pulled and pulverized and ground down into pea gravel, used to set sidewalks and level commercial housing. While men in hard hats and diesel construction vehicles toted the stone away, bones from dinosaurs would be discovered, discarded and tossed into the tumbler with the gravel.

At night, while the man placed his trust in the long-burned-out stars of a universe bent on crushing itself, the stranger guided himself by the street lamps, casino lights and reflective stripes of the freeway. The stranger would lay down to sleep at dawn, his head resting on a scrap of driftwood or a stone. The sun glowered up from the crags of mountains and baked all that splayed out on the altar of midland America.

Each man had visions—one of the world as it had been, the other inventing the story of destiny as he came upon it. Both of them envisioned the time in the Sargasso. A month, maybe more, had passed since there was any breeze to speak of. Several of the crew committed suicide by weighting themselves down with chains and throwing themselves overboard.

'Keeps them from being eaten,' the boy's father said.

The crew of the ship roamed the deck like sleepwalkers. They burned their clothes and trolled for food naked and despairing, letting the sun take its toll on their bodies. The men's skin boiled and dripped, ran with blisters and puss. In the night they sodomized each other, taking the boy and his father up to the deck and holding them down.

Up in the crow's nest the Portuguese sat as a silent sentinel to the events unfolding below. The men called up to him as they beat one another and groped at the unwilling participants, but he ignored them, staring off into the ocean as if there was a place beyond here.

III

Taking the body of the woman into the hatch proved more difficult for the stranger than he imagined. He stopped from time to time as he tunneled farther downward to scrabble for his baggage. He located the abdomen of the woman and placed his hand across the expanse of her belly. The baby inside stirred; less so than a few moments ago when he last checked, but still alive nonetheless.

He went deeper into the total absence of light to where the soil hardened into stone and the caverns ran slick with moisture. Drips from stalactites echoed. There was still deeper to go. He crawled frantically, following a path from a memory he had yet to form. The palm of his hand slid on the rock and he tumbled forward, the sack and body falling with him. He landed in a shallow pool of water, the bell of the skirt undone and the body in pieces around him.

The water rippled, but instead of coming to a calm around him, the liquid continued to swirl and torrent. The walls of the cavern shook and stones crumbled in on either side. The stranger closed his eyes and did his best to imagine the world he had told himself about.

The man woke in the midafternoon. Some vision—a dream—had been circulating in his head. Something called from the outside world and filtered through his memories and formed into a new experience all together. He sat up. Nearby the mule grazed, lazily swooped his tail at some flies. The man had sweated in his sleep, sweated right through his shirt. No more than a few hours passed since he let slumber overtake him.

He took a canteen from the saddlebag, drank from it. He swore, shook his head. Out on the horizon whence he came there was nothing. Even as he rode away, he cast a glance over his shoulder. A feeling of being watched welled in his gut and propelled him forward.

At the end of the tunnel the sky showed as a spot of blue. The stranger scrambled through, toward the source of light. He heaved stones aside and freed himself from underneath the rubble. He looked around the landscape at the fallen adobe brick tower, at the vultures circling above. If there was a way out of here, he had already taken it. Now was where he needed to stay.

Ruins from the Indians folded limply in the rumpled hills. Little stood as it had decades, centuries before. The bricks, once dried and blocked with sharp edges, had eroded into egg-shaped curiosities, things unable to be stacked. Walls spilled over, the mortar turned to grit and cake. Occasional storms as they blew in this part of the country had taken their toll on the place.

The stranger rested his hands on his hips and gauged the sun. He figured it to be midafternoon, figured it to be a time when America was still a geographical location. Somewhere hundreds of miles, several time zones away, Johnny Appleseed was littering the Midwest with fruit trees, a stove pan on his head. In the south Pecos Bill wrangled tornados, shot holes in the sky. Hiawatha trolled the rivers of Iroquois territories, trying to bring his people together.

'Well, then,' the stranger said aloud. 'I suppose I have some work to do.'

FOUR

I

What possessed the man to keep on traveling as he did baffled the stranger. Rarely did the man pause for sleep. He rode on through both day and night, stopping only when the mule tired. Traces of the man became more scant. The stranger picked up his pace until he came to nearly a trot. He seemed to be racing against the day, trying to duck under the sun as it collided with the horizon. If the man slept any length of time, the stranger figured it must be in the saddle. Nightmares woke the man often. And of all nightmares—those realities born from our wakeful lives and perpetuated in our minds—the man thought of his rescue from the ship.

At first both he and his father took it for a hallucination. Dusk and the hours following it on the deck of the ship proved good for this. Every couple nights another man committed suicide because of these visions. Some men murdered men because they were told to do so by long-since-eaten crew members.

'Do you see it?' his father asked.

The boy nodded meekly, too afraid to say anything, afraid the other crew might hear, afraid the vision would dissipate. Around them the crew slumbered away, snoring. In the captain's quarters, the first mate was having his way with a younger deck hand. For the last five nights he came for the boy afterward. Twice his father successfully defended him. Three times now his father had to watch.

The canoe glided stealthily through the water, two shadowed figures inside dipped their paddles and stroked in unison. Behind them, equally as clandestine, came a fleet of canoes. What moonlight there was cast the mystery men's shadows long into the placid waters.

The father instructed his son to follow him. They clambered down below deck and into their quarters. Above them they could hear the rhythmic thrusting of the first mate sodomizing another boy. Hearing this gave the father pause and he looked at his son. Then he took a kerosene lantern—the only lantern whose fuel hadnt been imbibed. He lit it, held it in one hand.

'Take the other end of the footlocker,' he said. The boy did as he was told. 'If these visitors is what I think they is, tonight ends it.'

The man had not slept for two days. He rode the mule until it staggered off the trail and cantered in a circle in the brush. The man shushed the mule, dismounted and rubbed its muzzle.

'Been ridin you too hard,' he said. 'Suppose we oughta set up here for a day, maybe two.'

Even as he spoke he glanced around, looked down the path, up at the slopes on either side. Alone as he ever was, he knew there were eyes upon him, though he could not see them. As he set up camp, he kept the shiv in hand. Darkness came on quickly here in the depths of the valleys. Soon the black behemoth mountains hulked darker than the sky, which unfurled like singed parchment, blotched indigo and purple, stippled with stars.

He sat upright against a lean tree listening for the sounds of visitors. He squinted into the blackest of the shadows to adjust his vision to the night. Then he shielded his eyes from the glow of the sky and scanned the passage he'd taken between the mountains. It could have very well been a trick of the mind, but the man saw something dart from one shadowed space into another. He clutched the shiv in his hand and squatted by the tree. He stopped breathing and listened. But again there was nothing. The mule snuffled, and in his mind the man cursed the beast for being so noisy. Then, very distinctly, a twig snapped.

Without much further thought the man looked to the mountain. He knew it to be bouldered and littered with scrag. He ran to the incline and grappled at whatever he could. He came to a perch—a flat rock jutting from the slope. He climbed atop the stone table and lay flat on his stomach to peer over the edge. Below, his mule brayed lowly. He watched for some time, squinting against the night, trying to see who prowled about his camp. Eventually he relaxed and rolled onto his back. He would sleep here tonight.

When the boy and his father came back up to the deck with the footlocker, the planked wood beneath their feet ran with blood. The natives from the canoes stood silently over the dismembered bodies of the crew. A hand cut longways—just the ring finger and little finger, most of the wrist—clung to a railing, tendons hanging loose at the end. The Portuguese man hanged from the rigging, his entrails dangling, his feet amputated. The boy stayed close to his father.

'Got a footlocker a supplies,' his father said. The natives circled them. Their blades—a scythe, a saber and a sickle—gleamed in the moonlight. 'My boy and me, we havent eaten nobody, havent killed no one.'

He held the lantern up to illuminate the faces of the natives. They had no eyebrows. Beneath the smears of blood they were tattooed, their nostrils stippled with studs, intricate scarring adorned their foreheads and chests. They were naked.

From the captain's quarters another native appeared. He ducked as he came through the threshold. Where his nipples should have been, two swathes of scar tissue shined in the lantern light. In his hands he held the head of the first mate. It may have been a thing of fiction in the boy's recount of the incident, but he believed the first mate's mouth still moved, his eyes fixated on the last surviving members of the crew. When the native turned his head to speak to his men the boy noticed his ears were cropped flat across the top. He exchanged a few short syllables with the men and they went below deck.

He looked back at the father and son, grunted and squatted. He held the first mate's head by the scalp in one hand and used a dirk in his free hand to stab out the eyes. When he was finished he set the head on the deck and rested his elbows on his knees.

'Heard a story once,' the father said. 'Heard some fellas bought an island big as a country from some injuns for some stain glass and beads.'

The native stared at them blankly. The boy imagined the natives who disappeared into the shadows just moments ago would spring forth any moment and kill them just as they had everyone else. Still his father spoke. 'We're just askin for you to not kill us. I got stuff to trade.'

He motioned to the footlocker and the native nodded. His father unlatched each side and flapped open the top. The natives stepped over the head and inspected the contents of the footlocker. A bird of bright feather flew from the night and perched atop the opened lid. He cooed and the boy and his father exchanged looks. A bird meant the promise of land. First the native shuffled through the miscellany of items, then he tried a few out: holding the telescope up to his eye, examining the maps, unfolding and refolding the jackknife. He did not touch the clothes folded in the bottom of the box.

It satisfied the natives well enough. The native stood and whooped, his jaw moving in unnatural form, his tattooed tongue coming to rest between his teeth. From the shadows the rest of the native men appeared, weapons in hand. The native spoke in whoops and yips, his eyes alighting and his tongue flapping like a rabid animal. The father put his arm around the boy.

They each felt a hand on their backs and they walked to the edge of the deck where the canoes were moored beneath.

⋆ ⋆ ⋆

The stranger lost the trail of the man. He had not anticipated a pace so vigorous or a man so scant in his markings. For many stretches the stranger ran. He ran through the flats where someday farms with circular fields dictated by irrigation systems would dot the landscape, etching rows of corn that would make them look like LP records to the crop duster pilots. He ran in paths where power lines would one day swoop and dip from one skeletal structure to the next and eventually come to a relay station that rose like the frame of a great cathedral, buzzing with the electricity of a ghost choir.

He cut through a housing plat where balloon construction homes would crop up overnight and dice up the land with sidewalks, fences and driveways. He followed in the track of a coast-to-coast rail line with oil tankers toting one behind the other like a caravan of fallen silos, boxcars and freighters chugging by like assembly line coffins. He felt the energy of this world pulsate in him; radiation and microwaves, cellular phone signals and fallout—bits of data and memory floated about him as if they had become part of space. And the stranger knew, in the deepest wells of his mind, these broadcasts only appeared to fade or become lost to time. If he could chase a radio transmission far enough—out into the outermost reaches of our solar system, the galaxy and greater universe even—the voices would be just as they were, young as the day the signal was born, old as the day it turned to static on a transistor radio.

And there would be highways with overpasses, roundabouts and single blinking yellow lights, roads lined with streaks of brine and salted for the winter truckers and nine-to-fivers. Routes would be augured through the crests of mountains—thousands of years' worth of mud and sediments compacting and metamorphing—scooped out by steam-powered crawlers with teethed shovels. The things that thwarted Lewis and Clark and Sacagawea meant nothing to the future. The borders of civilization were leveled by the telegraph wire, plowed under by fiber optic networks, and forgotten by the satellites that glided silently above the earth at ten thousand miles per hour. Rivers and oceans—the Sargasso Sea—became cemeteries for foolish men whose vision of the future extended no farther than the water's edge.

'No comprende ingles,' the Mexicano said. He looked up at the out-of-breath stranger, sag eyed and sweaty.

The stranger smiled wide and goofy, plopped himself on the ground. It was a nice enough spot for rest. They both looked at the sun; it seared high in the sky and seemed to quiver there, unmoving.

'¿Alimento?' The stranger's pronunciation was off, a little weak.

The Mexicano looked at him sideways—an incredulous squint. 'Sí.'

He moved his serape to the side and pulled out a canvas bag. He took out two strips of jerky and gave one to the stranger. The stranger bit his and chewed. The Mexicano did likewise.

'Buena vista,' the stranger said.

Again the Mexicano nodded, said, 'Sí.'

The stranger looked over his shoulder at the deadened tree, the bald spot on the hillside. The limbs of the tree spread out against the sky like fractures caused from thunder blasts.

'Este lugar tiene la enfermedad del muerte,' the stranger said.

The Mexicano looked mildly surprised at the stranger's sudden facility with language.

'¿Por qué diría usted eso?' he asked. He took a pouch of tobacco from his boot and some rolling paper from his pocket. '¿Cigar?'

The stranger smiled and declined the cigar. He pointed to the tree, to the patch of soil beneath it where the dirt was fresh packed and a few round stones lined the grave.

'¿Un amigo suyo?'

The Mexicano placed the tobacco in the paper and licked the edge. He rolled it and held it between his lips. After he lit the cigar and puffed on it a few times, he asked how long the stranger had been following him.

This made the stranger laugh. 'Desde el principio de tiempo,' he said.

The Mexicano replaced the tobacco pouch into his boot. 'Tengo el dinero,' he said. He knew the offer was in vain.

The stranger stood and dusted off the seat of his pants. 'Pase. Camine conmigo.'

The Mexicano did as he was told and followed the stranger over to the fresh grave under the tree. A shovel crafted from a tin can lay beside the tree. Using the toe of his boot, the stranger burrowed a hole in the dirt. 'Usted pulla.'

It took less than a half hour for the Mexicano to excavate the grave. The sun still suspended over the site, baking everything beneath it into wrought forms. The coffin was a pine wood box buried less than a foot beneath the soil.

'Ábralo,' the stranger said.

There was a moment of hesitation before the Mexicano complied and used his hands to claw at the slat board cover. The nails popped from the wood and the lid came loose. Inside the corpse lay face up, the skin gnarly and the clothes ragged. The body had wintered somewhere, been dead a season or two.

'Sáquelo,' the stranger said. The Mexicano protested in hurried pleadings and the stranger let him talk. Soon the Mexicano exhausted all pleadings. He stood and straddled the grave, grabbed the corpse by the shirt and hefted him up in one motion. He staggered, holding his breath until he set the corpse on the ground. For a moment, maybe more, the stranger and the Mexicano stood over the body, examining it like it might spring back to life. The Mexicano mumbled to himself and his eyes glistened with either sweat or tears or both.

'¿Por qué estás haciendo esto?' he asked.

The stranger studied the Mexicano, his rakish serape and burlap trousers. He thought for a moment to respond, then thought better of it. He seized the Mexicano as the corpse had been handled. They fell to the ground. The Mexicano cried out and the stranger hugged his body close. Together they rolled across the ground until they fell into the empty coffin. The lid fell shut. There was a moment of darkness and the men cuddled. The stranger positioned one hand under the

Mexicano's chin. '¡Dios mío!' he called. Then the stranger snapped his neck.

II

The man woke with the sun baking the flat rock on the side of the mountain. Whatever mystics the night had cast on his mind were clarified now in the daylight. He looked down the slope at his mule and few supplies. All remained untouched.

He tottered down the mountainside and packed the satchel for the mule. He went to untie the hitch that bound his animal to a tree and saw a figure out of the corner of his eye. Slowly he turned to face the man. And the man did not try to hide. Most of his head was shaved, his chest and face painted. He wore a necklace of teeth.

'You an Apache?' the man asked.

But the Indian did not reply. There was a rustling behind the man and two more Indians emerged from the brush. One held a hand ax and wore a stovepipe hat; the other held no weapon and simply wore a loincloth made from a human scalp. In his pocket, the man felt the weight of the shiv. No one moved.

Farther down the trail another Indian rode on a white horse. The purity of the animal struck the man as odd; he'd never seen something so clean. As the horse and rider drew closer, the man could see the Indian more clearly. He wore a suit of armor constructed out of bones. Around his torso was a ribcage and vertebrae. The crown of a skull capped his head and dark hair ran out from under it. His hands were also outfitted with bones from human hands—everything bound together with leather strings.

The man stood still, his arms hovering at his sides. He tried to swallow some of his spit so he might speak, but his mouth was too dry. The mule tossed its head and brayed.

The Apache chief trotted around the man and his mule and exchanged glances with the other Indians. Then he came close to the man and looked down on him with a hardened gaze. The Indian smelled like chalk, like stoneground flour, like dust and nothing.

'I aint even worth killin,' the man said.

The Indian chief leaned forward as if he hadnt heard what the man said. The bones of his armor clacked together as he moved. The other Indians inched forward; the one raised his ax.

'Your people are good,' the man said. 'Your kind gave my father and me passage once. We're friends, your kind and I—we're amigos.'

The chief considered the words for some time as if he understood what the man said. He nodded and sat upright again. He motioned to the other Indians and they cut the mule loose from the tree. The man did not protest as they departed and took his mule with them.

His father had called the natives friends. They had taken them to an island and fed both the boy and his father smoked fish. They drank fresh water flavored with fruits and pollen and flower petals. Still, none of the natives spoke or looked at them. It was as if for a short time they were treated as demigods. Each morning a woman naked from the waist up with teeth pierced through her nostrils left food by the shelter. She set the food on the ground on a bed of palm leaves. Tentatively she opened her mouth as if she was about to speak, but she never did. Instead she backed away with her head bowed.

The boy saw her come and go, but the father slept through the visitations. A week passed in this fashion: father and son would walk about the island in silence, the natives always present, but never obvious. They would eat and drink their fill and nap in the afternoon. In the evenings they built a small fire from dried driftwood and fell to sleep by it. By then father and son were ready to converse as if they had spent the entirety of their day speculating what the other would say and then finding the correct answer to steer the conversation in his own direction.

'Where are we?' the boy asked his father. They sat opposite from one another by the fireside. Waves rolled in from the ocean. It seemed impossible now that those waters were in the same ocean as where they left the ship burning, the rankness of flesh cremating.

The father said he figured them to be in the Caribbean, in the gulf somewhere. 'Hundreds of islands round here,' he said. 'Dangerous routes for ships too what with the reefs and all.'

'So you know where we are?' the boy asked.

'Close enough,' his father said. 'Stars like I never seen before down this way, stars I only seen drawn out—didnt believe they existed.'

'Are we gonna leave this island?' the boy asked.

'Not certain we can,' his father said. 'We'd need a boat.'

'Do you want to?' the boy asked. He clarified. 'Leave?'

His father stared out at the ocean, the endless horizon, the clouds and birds. 'If we do, I think we should head inland, toward the coast. American mainland.'

'Whats there?' the boy asked.

'Nothing,' his father said. He dragged a stick through the sand. A minute later he asked if the boy would be all right.

The boy didnt know what his father meant and he said he was fine.

'Best to forget what you saw—forget about that place altogether,' his father said.

'Sargasso?'

'Dont even say it.'

'What am I supposed to say?'

'Make something up.' The father snapped the twig once, then twice and a third time. He tossed it into the fire. 'Just make up a story and that will be what happened. What happened out there'—he pointed to the darkened horizon, out into a slate of black wind—'that was unnatural.'

'You said that was the way desperate men act.'

Again, his father shook his head. 'No men act that way. People dont eat—they dont stick their pricks—' It was the only time the boy saw his father cry. 'If we make it back to a place with laws and proper folks I'll show you how a man acts.'

* * *

It was night in the cliff dwelling. The stranger looked up from the bottom of the ceremonial pit, the kiva used only by the men of the Anasazi male order. First he noticed the sky, stars sprawled out. Closer to him, close enough for the heat to warm his skin, was a fire. The fire had been built in the hole in the center of the kiva; the same hole where ritual fires were set ablaze a thousand years ago. The man sat hunched by the wall, half in a stupor of sleep. The stranger stood on the other side of the flames. Yes, this was where he desired to be, to walk in step with the man. But this was too soon. The man seemed to stir from his slumber and his eyes fluttered into wakefulness.

'You,' he said. He hunched over and squinted past the light of the fire into the shadows on the other side of the pit.

The stranger stayed quiet, knowing he appeared to the man as little more than a shadowed vision. A scarab scuttled by on the stone floor. How insignificant most of the life in this universe is. And how unwitting this insect is. Years from now philosophers would attribute the origins of the universe to a complex system of events and would credit the flap of a butterfly's wing as the catalyst for such things.

He stooped and plucked the bug from the ground.

When he looked at the man again, the Indian chief—clad in his bone armor—stood at the edge of the pit looking down on the unwitting subject.

'You,' the man called again. He passed from cobwebs of dreams into full reality. The stranger crushed the bug between his thumb and forefinger as he stepped into the fire pit.

III

The man took to traveling at night again, this time by foot. Since his encounter with the Apache, an uneasiness settled over his every move. He felt watched, the most intimate moments of his life interrupted by others' voyeurism. He gauged the stars circulating above, noted a streak of white that blipped in and out of existence. The course he took kept him in a low and vulnerable spot. He looked to the rock ledges on either side of him, the pine trees nothing but wire silhouettes in the moonlight.

Once the sun crested over the ridged peaks of the mountains, the man gave his surroundings a quick survey, then darted off the trail and into the groves of pines. He crouched by the trunk of a tree and listened. In his hand he gripped the shiv. He held his breath. Somewhere farther off—down on the trail, maybe from the yonder ledge—there was a noise. The sun kept rising, cutting through the gauzy haze of early morning. He listened for another noise but fell into sleep instead.

He woke again when the cool damp of night stirred him from his dreams. Upon realizing he was awake, he held his breath and listened again. If there was a noise, he did not hear it. Still, he imagined the eyes of the skeleton man on the horse fixated on him from one of the ledges, his gaze able to pierce through the night. The Indians, he thought, trolled the trail behind him, picking up artifacts from his travels and destroying the prints he left in the soil. He couldnt go back onto the trail; it was too open, too visible. He resolved to keep to the forests.

Shiv in hand, he meandered through the trees and thought little as to how the stars above him aligned with his predestined path. He came to a clearing and had the sudden urge to urinate. He put his back to a tree and placed the shiv on the toe of his boot so he could easily find it in the dark. As the urine pittered on the pine-needled ground he thought he heard something a second time. His stream weakened and he glanced around the forest. Again he felt the eyes on him.

His father had watched him defecate on the island. The boy kicked sand over the feces as a sanitary measure.

'Whats that?' his father asked. He pointed to the clumps of turd now dusted over with sand.

'Took a shit,' the boy said. 'Do every morning... Thought you werent up.'

His father kept staring at the spot in the sand. His lips curled up in disgust. 'What bout the blood?' he asked.

The boy shook his head, picked at his fingernails.

'What about the blood in your shit?' his father asked again.

'Been like that since the first mate shoved his piece up there,' the boy said. He stammered and felt hot when he admitted it. But he did not cry.

His father's throat lurched like he might vomit. If he did vomit, he swallowed it back down.

'It's better than it was,' the boy offered.

His father refocused his gaze on the boy. 'Whats that?'

'Aint as much blood—gets less every day.'

His father grabbed the boy by the shoulder and forced him to the ground, pulled him by the hair to the pile of sand and feces. The father used his own hand to scoop the turds out of the sand and hold them up to the boy's face. 'This aint natural,' he said. 'You dont bleed when you shit!' He wiped the feces on the boy's face and it left streaks of brown and red, flecks of earth. 'It's not human!'

The boy rolled over once his father loosed his grip. He cried now, writhing in the sand. His father staggered away then emptied the contents of his stomach by a palm tree. From the tree line the native chief and the half naked woman watched as silent witnesses.

The stranger turned along the creekside trail, the path eventually parting ways from the water and lifting around the skirt of the mountain. As he walked the trail flattened, growing wider. He smelled the smoke of sulfur, manganese, bauxite. Again the trail inclined, becoming steeper. Pine tree roots irrigated and dammed the soil, creating a natural staircase up the slope. Where the pine boughs parted and looked out across the valley, the stranger stopped. A slight haze of grey hung like gauze in the air beyond the next mountain.

The stranger focused his sights in closer on the foreground, at the adjacent mountain slope. A tailing of loosely packed till spilled out from the mountainside as an unnatural ruination of the landscape. He strained his eyes looking through the yonder pines, trying to see what he knew lay in the depths.

In the future, steel pylons would support a span of concrete and asphalt over this gulf of space. In the valley below cigarette butts and foil wrappers would blow around like confetti. The adjacent mountain, not yet tapped for minerals, would be discovered to house a fortune in copper. Men would die by the dozens extracting the stuff of electrical transmissions and striking effigies of Honest Abe. Within a hundred and twenty years nothing would be left of the mountain. In fact a void, a pit, would be left in its place. The pit would eventually be filled with garbage added in layers and bulldozed over with dirt until a mound like those of the Miami Indian burial grounds took its place.

It was the evolution of the world—mountains and pits and garbage. The stranger thought how odd it was that someday after the great fallout, the next generation of species would unearth the landfill thinking it to be a place of significance. They would dig through each layer finding the things not yet decomposed to be worth something—something at least of numismatic value, if not historical significance. History is only made by burrowing into the earth, by digging out what will become the annal crypts of our past. Just as the early archeologists extrapolated the skeletons of entire dinosaurs from a single tooth, the stranger saw that these future dwellers would use these clues to reconstruct the myth of a place and a time called America.

How wrong they would be—America was never done being constructed. It was a ghost of a place since it was stumbled upon by Columbus or Vespucci, Saint Brendan or Leif Erikson—whichever brand of lore parents spun their children at bedtime. And after the stories were told—in our dreams—that is where America exists.

★ ★ ★

'Wake up!' his father said.

The boy opened his eyes. His father looked down on him with eyes like a man possessed by isolation. His body moved rhythmically back and forth in a rocking motion. It took a moment before the boy realized his father straddled a body under him.

He sat upright and pulled his legs to his chest. The body was that of the half naked woman lying face down in the sand. The food she brought them lay sprawled out across the sand floor of their lean-to. She murmured incoherently and lifted her head. His father grabbed her around the waist and hefted her pelvis back into his. Her head fell, catching a mouthful of sand. She coughed and called out.

The boy witnessed his father insert his penis into the orifices of the woman over and over again with strange fascination. At first the woman's hands flailed about, but her arms were too short to reach the father. Once or twice the woman almost appeared to squirm away before the father seized his grip on her again and forced his way back inside her.

She screamed out and looked at the boy. Her eyes were wide and bloodshot. She said words that could only be pleadings for help, for mercy. But the boy sat inert.

'A woman,' his father grunted. 'Men and women.'

The woman screamed out and his father grabbed the woman's hair and forced her face down into the sand. He continued thrusting at her while her cries were muted in the dust. Her hands scraped at the sand around her face.

'Papa,' the boy said quietly. It felt as if he had sand in his throat.

'Shut it,' his father said. All the sudden there was respite and his father craned his head back as if examining the sky—but his eyes were closed. The woman sprawled out limp in the powdered earth.

IV

Slopes of the mountain passes became steeper as the man traveled on. The soil bleached out from brown into red and again into a dust like crumbled adobe. Pine trees took over the landscape, their roots webbing across the hard-packed soil. The man's path eventually took on a certain predestination as he entered a canyoned place. Walls of stone reached up far on either side. Some trees took root in the rock and seemed to spire just to meet the sun.

The man, with his intrepid pace, slept not but a few hours at a time and upon awakening he would gauge either the sun or the stars or the ghostly moon that marked the transitions from day to night and night to day. Then he began to walk.

In the daytime he noted some markings on a reddened rock. The illustrations appeared to be that of a child. He took pause long enough to study the chalked lithographs. He noticed how hungry he was as he stood still. In a crook in the rock face he spied a bird's nest. For a long time he stood still, waiting for the bird to return, but it did not. He walked to the nest and looked inside. Two eggs no bigger than his thumb lay in the tangle of sticks and mud. He picked one up, smelled it, then ate it. The viscera leaked out from the crackling shell sweet and frothy. The second egg was not the same. When the man crunched down on the shell, something distinctly meaty squished under his teeth. He kept chewing, the taste of blood flooding his mouth. He swallowed hard, the fleck of eggshell and bits of bone like hair, scraping the length of his esophagus. Then he continued on.

When the native chief and several of his warriors came to the lean-to, the boy and his father did not resist them. The woman still lay face down, her legs spread apart in an unnatural angle, the father's jizzum leaking out. One of the warriors lifted the woman up over his shoulder. The natives guided the father and son through the forest, through a grove of palms and thicket. The father did not protest; he simply let the natives take him and the son. The boy trembled. He looked to his father, but his father only looked straight ahead.

They walked for some time before coming to a cove. It was a deserted spot on the island, the beach sodden with sandmites and strewn with vine. The chief looked as if he might continue walking, walking right out onto the ocean. He turned and looked at the father and the son. He pointed to a canoe farther on down the beach.

'You want us to leave?' the boy asked.

But the chief did not answer, nor did he cast his gaze upon the boy.

'You aint gonna kill us, is ya?' the father asked. He sighed and nodded, looked out into the sea.

The warrior went to the canoe and slumped the woman into the boat. Another set their footlocker on the sand. The chief broke his gaze and the native band retreated into the forest, leaving the father and son on the beach. Together and exiled, they inspected their sailing vessel. The canoe was made from the dried trunk of a tree. It had been hulled out through a series of scrapings and burnings. Eventually the trunk formed an oblong bowl, the inside black with carbon from being set aflame.

A knife made from a stone like glass lay next to the woman. The warrior, whether by accident or as a type of courtesy, must have dropped it there. The boy's father hefted the footlocker into the boat.

'More supplies than I expected,' the father said. He grabbed the bow of the boat and began to shove it down the beach toward the surf.

'But the woman,' the boy said.

'Bodys ours now,' the father said. 'Think the chief wouldnt take it so kindly if we left her.' Then the father told his son to get in the boat. The boy did as he was told. Blood dribbled across the bottom of the vessel. 'Think the point is we're supposed to take everything with us—leave the place like we was never here,' he said and launched them into the ocean.

In the twilight hours the stranger arrived at the mine. The trail led him there naturally, taking a course that dipped back across the boundary creek, the thread that sliced the mountains into mirror images of each other over a million years. He stood atop the tailing. Besides an overturned crate, a broken shovel and a few stray bottles, there was little evidence anyone had ever inhabited this place.

A dried pine, naked, its limbs wizened and gnarled, stood by the mouth of the shaft. He postulated that latent amounts of uranium poisoned the tree. He sniffed, walked past the tree and into the shaft.

Wooden uprights and ceiling boards supported the tunnel as it cut straight back into the mountain at a low grade. Keeping his head down, the stranger proceeded into the manmade cave. Instantly the air grew colder, moister. The chiseled path on the floor was made slick with trickles of runoff. The slabbed walls sweated condensation.

He proceeded slowly into the shaft, letting his eyes adjust to the darkness as he went deeper. He stopped and bent down, picked up an object lying stray by the cave wall. It was cylindrical and it sweated too. It smelled bitter, acrid. He carried the dynamite as a man might carry a taper as he descended into total darkness. Along the way he gathered more sticks of the explosive. Down deeper still he found bundles of dynamite held together with twine. He gathered those too, slinging them over his shoulder by their fuse lines.

He stopped, partially because the headroom clearance had dropped considerably, and partially because his load had become cumbersome. He sat on the granite floor. The seat of his trousers soaked through. Whether it was night outside or not no longer mattered; it was night in here.

FIVE

I

The man came to a place where the pines thinned out and grew even taller. They hugged the cliffsides. The air smelled sweet, like boiled tree sap. It was strange land like he had not seen before. Mountains were cut flat across the top with mats of green blanketing the plateau surface.

From time to time he still felt the presence of the Indians. Feeling their eyes upon him caused the man to move more quickly until he plodded through the pylons of tree trunks. He came to a cliffside and craned his head back. Through the openings in the branches, he could see caverns bored deep into the yellowed stone. Farther up, past the reach of any man, he could see the scribblings of men who had been here decades before. He approached the foot of the cliff and saw a series of footholds. Somewhere distant in the forest he heard a pinecone crumple under foot of something clandestine. He figured it to be an Indian—the one with the hand ax, maybe the one with the suit of bones. Could be the one with the scars over his nipples and the stipples in his nose. He shook his head. No, that place was gone now. He began to climb.

Each foothold and cubby for his hand was well measured and he easily scaled the cliffside right to the cavern opening. He pulled himself inside. For a moment he sat catching his breath and took in his surroundings. A mortar and pestle sat on the floor amongst shards of a broken clay pot. A ragged animal skin lay on the floor. The man lifted the pestle from the mortar. Meal crushed a thousand years ago still piled deep in the bottom. The man ate it. Grit from the crushing stone sifted through his teeth. When he was mostly done he finally looked out across the vista. The sight made him swear out loud. Up here in his cliffside perch the world spread out vast and small.

The ocean appeared much the same way to the boy. He and his father had been adrift a week in the canoe. The meat his father had cut from the woman's legs and dried on the broad side of the knife ran out a day ago. They had both tried to eat the leg meat as if it was jerky. Each of them nibbled on the flesh, then vomited. Her body had since spoiled and bloated. His father stripped the corpse of what little she still wore. Because the canoe was so narrow and unevenly weighted the boy and his father could not simply dump the woman's body overboard as they would have on the ship. Such an action could cause them to capsize. For six nights they wallowed in her blood, smelled her rot. Maggots began to hatch in her sore spots.

'Damn island injuns,' his father said. 'Put this whore in here with us just so we'd have to deal with the flies.'

The boy looked out over the plaintive waters, trying to ignore what was happening right there inside the canoe. His father took the stone knife and wedged it under the woman's arm.

'Help if you hold her wrist down,' the father said. But the boy made no move to touch the woman. 'It'd help me get the blade tween the bones there.'

The boy did not move. His father readjusted his posture until he had a foot on the woman's hand. He cleaved the blade back and forth until the bone splintered and flecks of blood splattered on the boy. The father took the arm and tossed it into the water. 'Wouldnt of gotten you soiled like that had you helped me,' he said.

In the evening, as the stars began speckling the sky, the father heaved the torso from the vessel. The canoe rocked back and forth violently. The boy's father sorted through the footlocker. He began to speak to the boy, but thought better of it and muttered to himself as he rummaged through the maps and sails. The boy had already settled into the bottom of the boat where he slumbered.

When he awoke his father was still awake. If he had slept, the boy did not know. He did not ask. Instead he asked his father what he was doing.

'Making a sail,' his father said. Indeed he busied himself by taking one of the smaller sails from the footlocker and cut it down with the knife. 'Cuttin the cloth like this.' His father set down the knife and formed his fingers to make a triangle.

'Gonna make a rope of sorts out of our clothes and tie it to the top there, run the rope back here and I'll hold it. You'll sit up in the bow there and hold down the other two corners.'

'I'm not strong enough,' the boy said.

'Wont have to be,' the father said. 'Take your trousers there and tie a leg to each corner. You'll just have to set on the trousers and not get blown away.' Then he laughed. He laughed hard enough for the canoe to bounce in the water.

'You drink the ocean water?' the boy asked.

His father stopped working. He looked wide-eyed at his boy. 'Did you?'

'No.'

'Why you ask?'

The boy's brow wrinkled. 'You laughed,' he said. 'Aint never heard you laugh.'

II

As the stranger lay amongst his dynamite and the nitroglycerine soaked into his skin, he thought of the future. He thought how he would lie here in state for a decade or more, the climate of the shafts preserving most everything except his flesh. How the earthquake would bury him. How the dynamite would continue to age like gourmet cheese and grow sharper, more volatile. Most people spend their energies trying to go from one place to another. It was a trifle, this life. Time moves everything if you wait long enough. Our lives are usually just too short to wait out the universe.

But in here, unlike men, the stranger had time. Universes would intersect here, he knew. In the meantime, he would tell himself bedtime stories, replaying the defining moments of this world as he knew them.

He fell into a type of coma thinking of the boy and his father. He thought about how they stripped naked, shredding their clothes and tying them into rope. Then the boy's father said they needed to shit. In unison they sat on opposite edges of the boat facing each other, shitting into the ocean. The boy bled some and the father watched.

Then, without a word to one another, the father wrapped his portion of the rope under his arms, his son sat on the trousers to hold down the bottom of the sail. Though the cloth hardly functioned as a proper sail, it provided them some propulsion, an almost vertical lift.

'We must be caught in a current a some type,' his father said. The boy had been awake, but kept his eyes shut. 'Wont be long.'

And the father had been right. The stranger thought of when they spotted land, saw a boat sitting moored in a harbor. A boat flying a pennant flag. He thought of the promise they both saw in a bird, a sprig clamped in its beak, long before the land and ships came into view. Both the father and his boy hooted, called out in nonsense verse, waved their arms. The canoe nearly capsized.

When they arrived a group of men—longshoremen—gathered at the end of the dock. They tossed a rope out to the canoe. Most of the longshoremen turned away, for the father and son were both naked and stained with blood and feces, dried charcoal from the interior of the boat.

'Good Christ,' one man said. He touched his forehead, his gut, then each shoulder.

'D'où êtes-vous?' another asked.

'Where are we?' the father asked.

'Port of Tobacco,' one man said.

'Wheres that?'

A protracted silence followed the father's inquiry. Then one man answered, said this was America.

The man took to exploring the cavern dwellings of the cliffside. Most everything was connected in one fashion or another. Handholds and footholds led from one apartment dwelling to the next. The caves looked to be bored into the cliff through natural means. Sometimes a crawlway made passage between two apartments and the man recognized these as chiseled by human hands.

Nonsense script adorned the walls, smoke stains plaqued the ceilings. Every once in a while the man came across a rock worn down by usage into a tool of some type. It was quiet in here—he could hear no one following him, tracking his progress to Fort James.

At night he continued worming his way through the apartments, emerging now and again to scale the cliffside laterally by means of hand and footholds. He found a hole toward the rear of an apartment. The opening was lined with mud bricks and the man knew this path was one constructed by whoever dwelled here ages before he came here. He crawled in.

The darkness was instantaneous: no moonlight could navigate the angles needed to illuminate his way. He slurked forward, stomach grating on the grit and stone floor, reaching one hand out in front of him, groping at nothing. On his face he felt a rush of cool air. He pulled himself forward, prying at the cracks in the stone with his toes. Suddenly there was nothing beneath him and he tumbled downward.

To the stranger, the events of the man's life unfolded as if they happened right before his eyes. As he lay in wait he saw what happened as if this were his own life. He slept with the man, ate with the man. He saw the bits of the man's life that lapsed with memory—moments the man distorted and blocked. He was with the man when he and his father were jailed in Port of Tobacco, taken by the longshoremen into town.

'Not that we dont trust ya,' one said. 'Just that you look crazy as a loon.'

'And that injun boat of yers,' another said.

The Frenchman agreed, saying, 'Oui.'

The boy and his father, surrounded by the dock workers, walked the dirt road into the town. A well-established place, Port of Tobacco had several buildings cobbled together with stones and mortar.

A man with an apron stood in the door of a squat structure. 'The hell is this?' he barked.

'Castaways.'

'Came in on a nigger's boat.'

'Dont look like injuns.'

'Caint never be too certain.'

They laughed and pushed the father and son forward.

They were kept in a root cellar below a medicine shop—a space with no greater height than the deepest hull of a ship. The father and son were given clothes, though only a set each. Two buckets were provided for them: one for their refuse, the other with fresh water. Twice daily a man flopped open the hatch to the cellar and swapped out the buckets.

'What you gonna do to us?' the father asked.

But their visitor wouldnt look him in the eyes. On the planked floor above, the boy could see the boots of several other men standing, watching, listening.

'Could use some more bread,' the father said. 'My son and me—we been out at sea for a piece, nearly starved.'

The man climbed back up the stairs and the hatch shut. The boy could hear the wooden bolt sliding in place. Light came in only through the fissures and knotholes in the floor.

'Aint as sunny as that island,' the father said.

But the boy did not answer. He listened to the muted voices of the men above conversing with one another.

'Least theys white men, people like us,' the father said.

Then the boy told him that nobody was like them. 'Thats why we're here,' he said. 'They aint never seen people like us.'

The father knew this was true. At sea theyd met lots of men of different types. They traded with those to whom they could relate—if they had a man aboard speaking in the native tongue, if the customs one displayed were that of decipherable measure. But those who were nothing but foreign to them—they killed them without hesitation. This boy and his father, they shared no commonality with these people.

The man woke inside a brick structure. The hole he had pulled himself through punctured the rock wall and the sun shined through a square window. The top of the structure did not have a roof. Instead a stone ceiling seemed to suspend over the whole of the building without any support.

He sat up. A gash ran the length of his forearm and oozed with purpled blood. He made a fist and pain raced up his arm and burned like venom. His body ached. He limped from the structure to investigate his surroundings.

There are times in the human mind when things are so unfamiliar that the brain simply does not let the eyes see. Little bits of the information are edited down into fractured granules of information—single frame photos, a single exchange of words. We construct the rest around what we think to remember.

So it was with the man. He walked around the village of ancient roofless bricked buildings. A great expanse of stone stretched over the entire village. The alcove in the mesa opened up into a flat-bottomed canyon filled with scrub and brush. Other mesas cropped up somewhere between here and the distant jagged mountainscape. Whoever inhabited this place recognized the natural opening as a place for shelter—a place to house an entire village. The man walked the narrow alleys between the buildings, his eyes darting from one window to the next. But nothing moved. He was the only one about. Artifacts from those who lived here littered the ground, sat dusty in some forgotten corner of a squared adobe brick building. The cave dwellings on the adjacent side of the mesa must be growths from this place, the man determined. Toward the back of the alcove, where the ground met the roof of the cave, the rock slicked with water. He put his mouth to the stone, his lips scraping against the lichen. The water tasted of the earth. He stayed in place—an awkward position like a penitent man genuflecting before his judge—licking at the rock. When he had his fill, he sauntered back through the abandoned village. Once he arrived at the mouth of the cave, he sat with his legs dangling over the cliffside. The sun now slanted at such an angle that he could sit in the light. Come evening the alcove, the village, would be bathed in the fiery splendor of a dying sun. For now the sun stayed high in the sky, weltering down on the alien place without pity for those who did not have the shelter of the cliff dwellings.

Last he'd seen the stars Virgo graced the sky. Boötes began to peek over the horizon. He wondered about his woman, if she suspected that he wouldnt return. Such promises are broken on a regular basis—worse still are the ones kept. Christopher Columbus kept his promise and returned to the New World once it became just another world. Perhaps if he'd only come once, those tribes that greeted him would have considered it salvation; it is the returning in which we are damned.

As the man stood to go back into the mammoth cave, he noticed a movement, a discreet fleeting down in the canyon. He did as he learned as a boy and cupped his hands around his eyes, making holes to narrow and magnify his vision. A bush of scrub shook and something flitted behind it to a boulder. It was the Apache with the stovepipe hat. The man uncovered his eyes and stood to flee into the cave. When he did so, he saw the skeleton chief on the white horse. He rode without guise or protection, the man's mule in tow. The man retreated into the village, searching for a place to hide.

Two weeks passed before the boy and his father had a different visitor. The cellar hatch opened and a man descended the ladder. He had a kerosene lamp in hand. He paid no mind to the captives in the room as he trimmed the wick. The light illuminated his face. He had burly white sideburns and wore a suit and hat. Someone above handed down a round stool. 'Thank you kindly,' he said and set the stool on the floor. Once seated on the stool with the lamp by his side he addressed the captives. 'Come here and let me have a look at you.'

The father and son emerged from the shadowed space where they had stood observing their new visitor. The father placed a hand on his son's shoulder.

'Lots of rumors circulating about you two,' the man said. 'People saying all types of wicked things, terrible things, things that no human could ever possibly imagine.' He stopped and frowned. 'But yet here they are, these settlers, spewing off falsities as if they were true. The mind is a dark place.'

'Who are you?' the father interrupted.

'You buy people?' the boy asked.

The question seemed to surprise their visitor, although his inquiry, in reality, had no such effect. 'Now why would you ask such a thing?'

The father squeezed his son's shoulder. No one spoke until the visitor decided to continue speaking. 'It's because you saw humans bought and sold, yes?'

'What sort of man are you?' the father asked again.

The visitor sighed, smiled wearily. 'Thats a more difficult question. To a seafarer like yourselves I might be called a witch doctor—'

'A witch doctor.'

'Yes. I know, I lack the usual appearance—the adornment of bones, the nose piercings… I dont live in a hut.' He chuckled. 'Indians might call me a medicine man.'

'You dont look like a savage.'

'You do. Thats why I am here. I'm here to judge you.'

'Hows that?'

'Guess you might rightly call me a judge.'

'Dont look like a judge,' the father said.

The doctor said, 'And what are you supposed to look like, sir?'

The boy's father stood dumbfounded.

The doctor continued. 'These people will make up stories about you and arrive at the inevitable conclusion that you should die—a creative conclusion, certainly. But I decided to intervene. I will change the end of your story if I see fit. They believe my stories over their own eyes... Can I examine your son?'

The father let his hand slip from his son's shoulder. The boy took a step forward and knelt down before the witch doctor. The doctor grabbed either side of his head and stared into the boy's eyes. He did not lock gaze with the boy, rather he looked past whatever anguishes were housed there. He pried the boy's mouth open and examined his teeth. Then he groped at the boy's body as if inspecting him for concealment of a weapon. He held the boy close and asked if the boy ever saw someone bought and sold. The boy replied that yes, he had.

'Thought so,' the doctor said. 'But you all werent slave traders. No.' He cocked his head to the side. 'You were scavengers of a different type. Wheres the rest of your crew?'

'Dead,' the father said.

'All of them?'

The father nodded.

'Perhaps,' the doctor said, 'it would be best for you to tell me the entire story of how you came to be here.'

The man formulated plans in his head of how to confront the Apache as he searched the village for weapons. But there were no weapons to be found. He took the shiv from his pocket and squatted by the doorway of a rectangular tower. He figured he could kill the Indian who came through the door first, yoke the body up in such a way as to deflect the blows from the

Indian who came in next. He imagined he could commandeer a weapon, fight his way free.

He squatted by the threshold for some time, until his legs burned. He stood and knew it was futile. He placed the shiv into his pocket and stepped out into the alley. As he walked the narrow path between the bricked buildings he picked up stray pieces of driftwood, the occasional bundle of brush.

The man found a large stone pit, a place excavated into the ground and paved with cut stone. In the center of the round pit there was a hole in the floor. The man built his fire there. He struck a rock against the shiv and the sparks set the brush aflame. He knew the skeleton man on the white horse would see it. That the Indians would come here, to this place, and cut him into pieces. He did not know of prayer, but this wish that he be killed quickly came as close to prayer as he had ever been. It quieted his mind.

He had not been asleep long when he stirred from slumber, feeling another's eyes upon him. He started awake and squinted against the flames of the still raging fire. A tall figure stood opposite the fire looking at the man. He was familiar. Haze from sleep still clouded the man's vision. The figure moved and picked something off the floor. The man hunched forward and suddenly recognized the figure to be the stranger he had entrusted his wife to.

'You,' he said aloud. His voice resonated in the stone cavern of the kiva.

The stranger stepped forward, holding whatever it was between his fingers like an alm offered up to some deity. His boot came down on the log, sending embers flurrying up into the air. He looked up over the head of the man. The man looked to the same spot.

The Indian chief stood there. The white horse stood by his side. The man jumped up and treaded backward. He looked for the stranger. The stranger was gone—no more than part of a dream. Frantically he searched his pockets. He pulled out the shiv and shook it in front of him.

'Come down here ya nigger and I'll run this through yer eye.'

The Indian chief appeared slightly bemused by the man. He watched as the man pantomimed stabbing him through the eye. As the man danced around the fire pit, the logs collapsed into coals and a few licks of flames now and again.

'Send yer other nigger with the hat down then,' the man said. The resolve had left his voice and when he issued the challenge it was tinged with resignation. He stopped moving around the pit. A dull clank cried out in the night when he dropped the shiv. Then he sat on his haunches. Though his words were no more than murmurs, than sobs, the acoustics made his ramblings audible to the chief.

'Just go on an kill me if thats what you aim to do,' he said. 'Do it quick if you can. Wont be the worse that ever been done to me.' He cried for a while, head down and eyes scrunched shut, anticipating a blow to the back of the head at any moment. When he opened his eyes and looked back up, the chief still watched.

'I's just trying to get to Fort James,' he said.

The chief's eyes went alight.

'You know it,' the man said. 'You know Fort James?'

The chief raised his index finger, the hand of bone flexing with his own, fleshed hand, pointing seemingly at the stars. The man began to stand up, but a hand on his shoulder spun him around. He came face to face with the painted Apache. The Indian raised a hatchet into the air and brought the blunt butt side down on the man's eye. Blackness engulfed him.

The boy and his father were released from the cellar immediately. Though a dulled cloudy grey, the light outside caused in both of them a temporary blindness. They were afforded a room at the inn down by the docks and given clothes. The innkeeper did not look the father in the eye when he said the room was already paid for. Whatever fortunes had been bestowed on them, their benefactor remained unknown.

The boy had his suspicions though. It was when they were telling the witch doctor about the Sargasso. The boy had been struggling to find a proper lie when his father interrupted.

'It was the Sargasso,' he said.

'Yes, the Sargasso,' the doctor said. 'Heard of it. Doldrumed place.'

'Aye.'

The boy decided he needed to say the rest. 'Men there acted like animals.'

'Your men? Your shipmates?'

The boy nodded. 'Did things like eat each other, stick their pricks in each other—' The father coughed abruptly. 'The Portuguese ate a candle.'

The doctor's eyes went alight. 'A candle, as in a taper?'

'Yes,' the boy nodded eagerly.

The doctor shifted his weight on the stool, straightened his back. He stroked his sideburns. 'I am a well-traveled man,' he said. 'Been to many strange lands—been to a place where two men were born of one backbone; their faces looking in opposite directions. Ive sat at the head of a table—if you could call it that—and eaten a dog. Birthed a baby in a barren place.' The father began to interrupt, but the doctor continued. 'I know more than most men will ever know. If you collected all the seafarers, magicians, priests and teachers in the world, they have only heard of a fraction of what I know, what Ive witnessed. The world is a goddamned beautiful place, friends. And what I say now, I say with certainty: you are meant to wander, boy.'

'What about me?' the father asked. 'Am I meant to do anything?'

'What does wander mean?' the boy asked.

'It's what you will spend the rest of your life doing,' the doctor said. He shifted his focus to the father. 'If you had purpose, it's done now.'

He stood and shifted his hat on his head. 'No ones going to lynch you. I cant say what happens will be any worse.'

With that he left. Together in the dankness of the cellar, the shadowed space, the father and son contemplated what the witch doctor said.

'They just gonna turn us loose,' the father said. 'We'll be on our own again.'

'But he said that was worse than dyin.'

'Hes right. What we gone through is already worse than whatever the next life holds.'

The hatch in the floor opened, a pair of boots visible. 'Come on up outta there, you dirty redskinned niggers,' a man called. 'That witch doctor says hes done with you.'

Again the man came to in the Indian village. One eye was swollen shut. A splintering pain gnawed at the side of his face. He tried to lift himself off the ground, but his vision began to blacken and he let himself collapse back to the ground. It was daylight now. The logs from last night had long burned down to coals. The coals, now cooled, were little more than ash and char.

The man lay on the smooth stone. The cold rock felt good on his skin. He tried to shut his good eye, but that made him dizzy. Each time he inhaled, his head mushroomed with pain. His body felt like it was pulsating. If he died here, years from now some good Samaritan would come along and insist this miscreant had perished without a proper burial. They would dig a shallow grave somewhere and, assuming these bones were those of an Indian, wrap them in cloth and leave the resting place unmarked. But these were not his thoughts.

Instead, he thought of his woman. He tried to imagine what she might be doing at this very moment. It's a common thought of those who are separated. And like most of the departed, he did not actually imagine what she would be doing. He simply recapitulated the things he had seen her do.

He sat up more slowly this time. He leaned against the wall of the kiva. From above, at the kiva's edge, there was a noise. His mule stood, tethered to a rock. A gourd with a lanyard sat by the rock. Unbemused as ever, the mule swished his tail. The man used his legs to push his back against the wall of the pit. With considerable difficulty he pulled himself from the kiva. He lay on his stomach for a moment, anticipating an ambush. He would not have fought. After a minute or more of silence, he rolled over, reached for the gourd.

A trail at the mouth of the alcove climbed the plateau. The Indian had pointed up, as if that was the trail he should take. He cared not if this was a path into perdition. Life, he imagined, would either continue or cease; there isnt anything between the two. The trail was steep as no other man had taken his mule on it. He knew it was a practical thing to guide the mule by the reins, guide him up the slope. Doing otherwise meant risking both their lives. He resolved to ride the animal anyway.

Twice on the slope the mule faltered, its hooves chuffing off a stone smoothed over by wind and sand. The man slumped over the head of the mule. With his arms wrapped around the animal's neck, he could feel each breath it took. The climb was taxing. He turned his one good eye to the crest of the slope, where the land broke flat and even. The sun baked down at the topside of the mesa. The man determined it must be noon.

They rounded the top of the trail and the man yawed back on the reins. The mule stopped. It was an open place. Ghost mountains on every side of them. The man used his hand to cover the damaged eye and studied the distant sights in more detail. Far out, sagged up against the nearest mountains, the land looked to be nothing but powder. The man figured it to be a sand desert, a place meant for certain death. But here atop the plateau there were at least some small indications of life. Sticks of grass cropping out of the coarse soil. Birds, not of the predator kind, fluttered about. Out farther on the mesa, barely dotting the horizon, was shadow.

'Gee-ah,' the man managed to say into the mule's ear. He slapped the beast's shoulder and they sauntered forward. Waves of heat rising off the ground distorted the distant visions of this place. At moments it looked as if nothing was there, but then the place would reappear with more detail than before. They passed the threshold of illusion and the man could see this was a civilized place indeed. A band of men trolled through the grasses a quarter mile out from the settlement. As the man passed by them, he asked what this place was called.

Most of them ignored his query. One looked up; he had eyes of solid white and seemed to look directly at the man. 'Wie heisst dieser Ort?'

'This place,' the man said. 'Tell me this is Fort James.'

'Ja,' the blind man said. 'Das ist Fort James.'

SECOND

ONE

I

Making bricks was new to the stranger. He had participated in many things in his time, but brickmaking was not one of them. After stating that he had work to do, the stranger set out in search of anything that might be used as a tool—a length of metal, a board of hardwood, a flat-sided stone. Some miles from the Indian village he happened across a broke-down crate. He dusted the powdered earth off the wood. The sun and aridity of this place nearly petrified the wood. He brought it back to the Indian village.

By fixing the pieces together with some cord and bracing it with rock, the stranger formed a rectangular mold. He knelt by one of the walls of the fallen tower, which had buckled under its own weight. At its base some of the Indian bricks still fitted together, giving shape to what was once a sturdy structure. The stranger scraped his index finger between two of the bricks, pulling out mulled bits of mortar. He tasted it. Each one of these bricks was formed from a mold and left to bake. This place was like a kiln. All that lived in this place was formed from dirt. From the beginning, there was nothing else other than rock and dirt. But then some men, if they were even that, came along and spat in the dirt and made mud. They wiped it on their foreheads and found it to be a way to keep the mosquitoes away. It cooled their blisters.

Within a thousand years these cavemen, while wallowing in their own filth, would come to plop gobs of mud one on top of the other. They formed rudimentary walls. Then slept in shallow pits, huddled next to whatever mate theyd found. Give these men another thousand years and they achieved what the stranger had already made—a brick mold.

He sat cross-legged, looking at his invention—the empty wooden box. In here he would shape not just the future of this place, he would recreate a past that never was.

The boy and his father were shown to the town's boarding house. They were given a room on the second floor. The woman who took them there did not speak to them; she simply unlocked the door and ushered them inside. Clothes lay on the bed—some for the boy, some for his father. At the far end of the room there was a door that led out onto a balcony. The window by the bed provided the same view. The walls were washed grey, the plaster chipping away from the lath.

The boy took a step toward the bed, toward the door and window. The floorboards creaked. Outside, the vista opened up across the ocean. Any lands beyond here were non-existent, swallowed in the tides.

'This gonna be our home?' the boy asked.

His father walked past him and sat down on the bed, pulled off his boots. The rank odor of sweat and mildew soured the air. 'Reckon it's as good a place as any,' he said.

Reaching his destination gave the man extra strength. He entered the town proper under his own power. When he dismounted the mule, he led it by the bridle. Short flattened structures made of adobe bricks, walls buttressed with scraps of driftwood, lined the long barren patches of soil demarcating the streets. A shack made of tin metal wafted flames inside, a wiry man swinging a mallet against a giant metal slab. His foot pumped a bellows and the inside of the shop glowed like the annals of our molten world before it cooled into rock.

'¡Tenemos bolsas de comida!' a woman with a dead eye called out. 'Usted está cansado. Coma. ¡Coma!'

Street urchins called out from under their blanket awnings. 'Puedo decirle su fortuna,' one called out. The man shook his head.

A plank wood building with an oil sheet over the window holes appeared to be the most established place. The man set his course for it.

'You there,' a man called from atop one of the buildings. He stood a full body height above the man. 'You sellin that mule?'

The man shook his head.

'I thinks you are.'

'I caint,' the man said weakly.

Some dark-skinned boys ran through the streets between the clusters of vendors and mendicants, the urchins and vagabonds. One stopped and stroked the mule's mane.

'Give you ten pounds coffee, five pounds lard for that mule,' the roofman said. He put his hands on his hips.

Again the man said he couldnt sell the animal. He began to explain how he needed the mule, how he would only be here for a day or two, but he was interrupted by the boy cursing. '¡Su caballo sucio mordió la mano!' The boy doubled over, holding his hand to the core of his body. A cloaked woman ran to the boy. He cursed again.

'He nip ya?' the man asked.

Some of the boy's friends, in noticing their playmate's absence, circled back around to the scene. The woman swaddled the boy in her cloak, whispered to him.

'If you dont trade me that donkey,' the roofman said. The man turned his back on the roofman, but the roofman kept talking. 'If you dont want to deal, I can foller you to wherever youre asleepin and I'll steal im from ya.'

Before the man could turn around to respond, the old woman shoved him. The roofman laughed.

'Cortaré el pene si mi hijo se muere de la septicemia,' she said.

'Su hijo es una molestia en nuestro pueblo fascinante bruja vieja,' the roofman called to the woman.

The woman's eyes sharpened. 'Y usted no nos sirve para nada. Háganos un favor y deje que este señor se le mate,' she hissed. Then she spat on the ground and pointed up at the man. Without another word, she whisked the boy away.

The roofman turned his attention back to the man. 'I'll kill you too.'

The man blinked. 'You'll kill me?'

'Cut your throat open.'

The man stood long in the bustle of the road, smoke and children swarming around him. He collected his thoughts. Somewhere farther on, people were singing. He tried to locate the source of the noise.

'Need my mule,' he finally said. He looked up to where the roofman had been standing. Now he was gone.

He waited a moment for the man to resurface. From across the street, the old woman and the boy with the bitten hand glared at him. He tugged at the mule's bridle and they continued gravitating to the slatwood building.

'Hey-a mister,' a woman with olive skin and pocked cheeks called from a doorway. She pulled at the crotch of her dress. 'Queira ter um fogo entre as suas pernas?' She licked her lips and pulled an armstrap of her dress down to expose her breast. 'Faça-o muito. Faça-o vir duas vezes.'

The man looked away, to the other side of the street. The woman called at him again, but her words were lost in the din of the street. A man with little hair on his face and a flattened top hat stood on a wooden block. He had a black boy on the block with him. 'Miracles and wonders!' he called. The man stopped to see whom the auctioneer addressed. But the streets kept moving, no one paying him any mind. 'This boy, blind from birth, will see today.' He leaned forward, the boy motionless at his side. 'How, you ask? My secret formula—the base a mud dredged from the Rio Mancos and the ancient healing ways of the wild Indian, strong enough to sap a snakebite, potent enough to scar over a bullet wound. Now people always ask me the same thing: does it work? And the answer is yes; it most definitely does.

'Yes, friends, I have done my time in the cavalry, been to old Mexico, shot a few Indians and cured a few men. In fact this medicine recipe was given to me by an Indian shaman on his deathbed…'

The man pressed on, uncertain where he could stop for respite, where he might be safe. The slatwood building seemed less promising the closer the man came to it. A gap between two buildings provided a dark alleyway and passage to a quieter section of town, a part obscured by these structures. Halfway through the slotted path the man noticed a Mexican slumped against the wall, apparently asleep. He nudged the Mexican with his boot. He did not stir. The man knelt down and shook the Mexican by the shoulder. Only then did the man notice the stab wounds in the Mexican's torso.

'You,' a voice called down. The man craned his head straight back, mouth a-yawp, to look directly above him. He recognized the voice instantly. It was the roofman.

'You kill that dirty sumbitch?'

'No,' the man said. 'I jus found him.'

'Like hell,' the roofman called down. 'You probably got his blood all over ya. I could call for the law and theyd flog ya right to death tomorra morn. They'll do that if you cut the heart out of a man.'

The man looked at the Mexican's body, realizing for the first time just how concave the chest cavity appeared. Blood, still warm, continued to soak through the garments.

'You do this?' the man asked.

The roofman laughed. 'What—How'd I do that? I'm up here. One of youse down there did that. Probably some other Mexicano hiding just down the alleyway a piece. Waitin to gut you, dry your guts out and sell em to an injun.'

The man looked down the alleyway. Pockets of darkness shrouded either side. Only a dusky haze marked where it opened up on the other side.

'Leave the mule,' the roofman said. 'Leave him and I wont call out for the law. Just go back out the way you come in. I'll see to it that you dont get cut up.'

The man continued staring off into the shadows. He looked back in the direction whence he came. It was also blinding, but in a different way. He could hear the mishmash of voices. He let the mule's reins fall from his hand and he crawled on all fours under the animal. As he stood to run he could hear the roofman's laughter echoing through the channel behind him.

II

Simple deduction led the stranger to the well. If a civilization had been in this place before, then there was surely a source of water. He closed his eyes and smelled the air. In his mind, he thought of another time, when he decided to kill the buzzard and dive down into the rubble of the tower. There had been water in there, near the bottom. How the Indians of ancient times came to know there was an aquifer here was beyond him. He drank deeply from the waters. Then he stripped off his clothes and bathed. This far down and sheltered as he was, there was little light. This place was cold and he shivered. He dunked his clothes, wrung them out, then waterlogged them again.

He slogged his sopping clothes back to the surface. First he rolled in the dust, letting the dirt stick to his wet skin. He appeared as another color. Then he took his clothes and wrung them out into the soil. He squatted so the tip of his penis grazed the ground. He used a stick to mix the water and dirt together and slopped the concoction into the wooden box.

The sun beat down on the hot flat pan of the rubbled village. The mud on the stranger's skin dried and cracked, peeled up. Meanwhile the brick also baked. But unlike the stranger's flesh, which boiled and blistered, softening with sweat, the mud hardened.

At dusk, when the sun was finished with this place, the stranger used the mixing stick to pull the rectangle of mud from the wooden case. He held it up for inspection. In the evening sun, the whitened block of mud glowed red, like this brick was pulled from the forges of an infernal world.

In time he had piles of bricks. He wandered the horizons to the north and south, to the east and inevitably to the west. There he gathered more boards, some lengths of burlap, a handful of metal rivets. He found the bones of a dead steer, picked clean by vultures, bleached by the sun. He took only the cow skull, figuring the brain cavity to be a good mortar, the horns a possible tool.

From his findings the stranger was able to make another set of casks to dry bricks. Now he could set six bricks at a time. On hotter days he could fire two sets of bricks in a day. While the mud dried he took the horns and scraped down the old Indian adobe bricks and fashioned them into more rectangular objects. The stranger trapped mice and snakes, buzzards, and cooked them in the sun alongside the bricks. He ate them and tossed their bones and innards into the well. Still he drank those same waters.

III

The quieter side of town was no less rambunctious than the market side of town. Several wagons lined the street. A large brickwalled structure with a wooden gate appeared to be the hub of activity. The gate opened and closed often, men in uniforms carrying out pallets of dry goods, crates with different color dots of paint on them.

'You there,' a soldier called. He pointed at the man. 'Give us a hand.'

The man did as he was told and grabbed the edge of the pallet they were hoisting up onto the back of a wagon.

'Man just stole my mule,' he said.

'Lift on three,' the soldier said.

He counted out loud and they hefted the pallet up the rest of the way and onto the wagon. 'Get it outta here,' the soldier called to the wagon driver. 'Commandante says he wants it there in three days' time. Best not to disappoint him.'

'Think the fella that stole my mule also killed a man.'

'A soldier?'

'A Mexican.'

The soldier shrugged and turned back to the outgoing cargo.

'Need my mule to get back to my wife.'

This gave the soldier pause. 'Get back?'

'I'm just here to register my family for the century.'

'You dont got a job?'

'What do you mean?'

'You dont work here, work in Fort James?'

'Caint say I do. I'm just here to register my family.'

The soldier laughed. 'Ever mans got a job, got something he does.'

'I do,' the man insisted. 'I'm here to register my family.'

'Need a job, friend. Commandante will see to that.' He pointed over the man's shoulder. 'That your mule?'

The beast wandered in the street and the man ran to it, looking at the rooftops around him.

Not long after the boy and his father settled into their quarters, there was a knock at the door. The innkeeper and his father talked in a low tone and the conversation ended with the innkeeper giving his father a pair of metal hooks with wooden handles. His father tossed the hooks on the bed, walked to the opposite door and out onto the balcony. The boy followed him. For a while they just stood, looking out over the rolling waters, watching the fishing boats bob up and down, the ships farther out seemingly sitting still.

Finally his father spoke. 'Been able to navigate the open ocean, one side of the world to the other and these town dwellers wont let me on a boat. Say I gotta work on the docks.'

'There aint another thing you can do instead?' the boy asked.

'Damn it, I jus said I got to work on the docks. It's the deal of that doctor man, that witch doctor.'

'He get us the room and clothes too?'

His father didnt answer; he just spat over the railing and wiped his lips on his sleeve. 'They say ships dont need a man like me. Say they got maps instead. Only thing I'm good for is hauling cargo like I'm some type of damn mule.'

Down on the pier a longshoreman rang a bell and the other dock workers came running. A ship was coming in. The men shoved at one another, trying to get to the end of the dock.

'Look at em,' his father said. 'Get paid per piece of cargo they carry. Fight like dogs to work.' He shook his head. 'Told me start tomorrow.'

The bell rang early, before either the boy or his father was awake. On the third clang, the boy roused his father.

'Bells ringin,' he said.

'Goddamn it,' his father said and swung his legs over the side of the bed. He pulled on his boots, pair of second-handers that came with his clothes.

In the early morning, without the sun risen, it was difficult to navigate the streets. Everything led to the docks though and as other longshoremen ran past him, the father picked up his pace. By the time he reached the dock, a dozen men were already there, one of them reeled the boat in and moored it to a piling.

'Got a fair amount a fish,' one of the men on the boat called.

The bell on the dock clanged again.

The father stepped forward, ready to take a piece of cargo, whatever form it might be in.

'You there, new hands,' a man said. He seized the father by the wrist. 'Wheres your hooks?'

'My what?'

'The hooks you was given. Dont act like you didnt know you was supposed to have the hooks.'

'I forgot em, I guess.'

Other men shuffled past the father and grabbed their sacks of cargo, piercing the burlap sacks with their hooks and toting them off the dock. A man on a wooden box at the end of the dock shouted and pointed frantically, directing the longshoremen where to carry their goods.

'Here,' the boss said. He handed the father a set of hooks with yellow handles. 'Take this off your pay. If you dont give em back to me when youre done, it'll cost you a week's wages.'

For a moment the father stood dumbly, the tools in his hand.

'Go,' the boss shouted.

The father turned around and stooped to grab a bag as he'd seen the other men do, but another longshoreman snagged the sack out from under him. He elbowed yet another man and sank his hook into the bag. He pulled and the sack came apart at the seam.

'Damn greenhorn,' a man on the boat said. 'Gotta loop the hook through on either side of the sack, keeps the bag from tearin.'

The father rehooked the sack and slung it up onto his shoulder.

'Salthouse!' the man on the block shouted. He pointed to the right. The father did as he was told and trod over to a grey stone building with a steep roof. A man stood outside, directing the organization of the sacks.

'You salthouse?' he asked.

'Yup.'

'Sacks torn.'

'Put my hook in wrong.'

The salthouse man shrugged. 'Might be, but I gotta charge ya.'

The father must have started at the statement because the salthouse man immediately gave his justification. 'When a sacks torn open, I dont know whether I got all my fish. You coulda stole one and hid it somewhere. Or you might have just made a mistake. But that mistake could mean you dropped some fish somewhere along the way. The dock manager'll take care of it.'

The father wanted to argue, but the other longshoremen were already dropping their second loads and running back to the dock.

By the time the father ran back to the dock, the first boat was gone and another was tethered to the other side of the dock. The cargo on this ship was larger and required two men to lift the sacks together.

'Still usin my hooks for this load?' the dock manager said.

'I guess I was planning on it,' the father said.

'Took so long getting back here, I thought maybe you'd run back to that inn the doctor put you in and got your own hooks.'

'Got held up at the salthouse because my bag was teared.'

The dock manager smirked and took out a notepad, made a mark on it. 'Gonna have to charge you for the hooks a second time.'

'Whys that?'

'Two boats, two jobs, two times you forgot your tools.'

'Grab this here end,' a longshoreman said. He pointed at the father. He did as he was told and the men lifted the sack. 'You go backward,' the old longshoreman said. 'Got bad knees.'

Walking backward with the cargo was cumbersome, forcing the father to waddle.

'Gonna have to pick up the pace there,' the old longshoreman said. 'Wont make enough money by dawdling along.'

'Smokehouse!' the director yelled.

The old longshoreman cursed under his breath, then looked at the father. 'That whore's sons gonna make us traipse all across the town to the smokery.' Despite having bad knees, the old man doubled their speed, nearly knocking the father down. 'Need another load after this and I'm a-set.'

'Set for what?' the father asked. He only responded with a question to get the old man talking in an effort to slow him down.

'Youre livin at the inn, aint ya?'

The father nodded.

'You mean you aint gotten in that pussy up there?'

'Didnt know there was any.'

The old man licked his chops. 'Whole lot of pussy there at night, ever woman in this village done a bit of whorin. Best way to make money aside from fishin.'

'That so.'

'Best to get em in the morning though, when theyre still fresh. By evenin it'll feel like youre stickin yer peter in a jar of jelly.'

The old man used his chin to point to the smokehouse. A man with an apron stood out front. 'Right here,' he said and they set down the sack.

'Come on,' the old man said and together they ran back to the docks. The sun was just breaking over the ocean and another ship laden with cargo was coming in.

The stranger lined the bricks along the ground, making outlines of the structures he hoped to build. The weather had begun to turn cold and he wanted shelter. While some of the bricks—the ones with crisp edges and evenly baked—could be stacked tightly, most still required some type of mortar.

The stranger dug an oblong hole, not unlike a grave. First he cut the hard-packed ground with the cow horn, then he used a plank of wood to move the loosened clumps of soil aside. The ground was solid enough that it would hold water should he be able to fill the hole. Rains were scant and short. He opted to waterlog his clothes and wring them into the hole. After his tenth trip, he recognized the effort to be futile. He formulated a new plan and drank more than his fill from the well. He did not work; he simply waited. Then he relieved himself in the hole. He made a few more trips to the well and soaked and wrung his clothes. Finally there was enough liquid to make a paste.

He focused his efforts on constructing a short, three-foot-high wall as long as he was tall. If he could make a wall this big, then he could build fires to cook by in the evenings. Once the fire burned down to coals he could kick the warm ashes into the soil and have a bed to protect him from the cold. Should the weather become colder, as it most definitely would, he could stretch some burlap over some sticks and trap some heat as he slept.

Such were his days, making bricks and mortar, then in the evening, trapping the varmints of this place, sometimes baiting one with the other. Sometimes he cooked them, sometimes he ate them raw. He threw the entrails either into the well or the mortar pit. When the weather turned brutal, the protection of the wall and the warmth of the fire were no match against the plateau winds, so he took shelter in the pit leading down into the well. Down deep enough, the temperature stayed above freezing.

Just as he himself migrated, other creatures began moving, making themselves apparent for the first time. The stranger found a coyote, not much bigger than a loaf of bread, sniffing at the ashes of the fire. Because he was feral himself, the stranger was able to sneak up on the animal without being smelt. With a single jab he pierced through the wild dog's backbone with the cow horn. It let out a single yelp, squirmed for a moment, but the stranger held fast to the horn and the coyote stopped moving. He picked up the pup, stroked where the fur was still dry. Then he heard a growl. A she-coyote with her mane bristling lunged forward.

The stranger received the attack with open arms. They rolled across the ground. The jowls of the dog clamped on the meat of the stranger's upper arm. With his free hand he took the coyote by the scruff and pulled her off his arm. A chunk of flesh pulled from his bicep and he began to bleed instantly. The coyote's snout waved back and forth, a flash of fangs and saliva. Her rear leg kicked, the nails scratching deep into the stranger's thigh. He let go of the scruff and grabbed the leg, gave it a quick jerk and it broke. The coyote let out a high-pitched whimper, gave another attempt at a bite, then began to scamper away, dragging the now clubbed paw behind her.

The stranger got to his feet. He was smeared in the grease of his own blood. Stumbling toward the wounded creature, he stooped to pick up a brick. The coyote, tongue hanging from one side of her mouth, tried to trot along faster. She whined as she limped along. The stranger caught up to the dog and brought the hardened clay block down on the animal's skull. A few other coyotes padded by, looking on at the wounded stranger and their dead kin without sorrow.

When the vultures came, the stranger flung stones and killed two of them. He drained the blood from his kills into the well, threw the feathers and brains into the mortar pit. From the coyote's pelt, he fashioned a loincloth. He used the much smaller pelt from the pup as a head covering, a tendon for a chinstrap. When the snow fell, he scooped it up in his arms and threw it into the well, knowing it would eventually melt.

IV

Years passed this way: with the stranger killing his way through the winter months and in the summer producing hundreds—maybe even thousands—of bricks. By his tenth year of making bricks, the stranger constructed a shanty, a place for him to stay during the winter. The well, now a noxious place festering with flies and forever tainted with rot, provided most of the mortar. As the water level in the well fell, it left mud rings scummed on the walls, making for the best paste. Meanwhile the liquid itself could still be used to make the base for the bricks.

And the bricks themselves had improved integrity in recent years. More often the liquid contained a fair amount of hair and bone and other unidentifiable fibrous materials. Just as the ancient Egyptians used straw to add cohesion to their bricks, the stranger used whatever he could scavenge.

When the first Indians came along, they were puzzled, studying the stranger's claim. They wandered around his shanty. One picked up the cow skull. Another crouched over a dried splatter of blood, now turned brown. The stranger himself came crawling up from the well, hauling a sack of sludge. The Indians stopped their respective activities and looked at the creature before them.

The stranger set the sack down and stood up straight. He looked from one Indian to the next, each one individually. There must have been a dozen of them.

'Amigos,' he said. 'You should see the place I'm creating.' The Indians' brows became collectively screwed at this foreign tongue. The stranger smiled and invited them into his shanty.

At dusk the man came to the slatwood building. The soldier in his limited counseling had told the man that people generally went there when they came into Fort James; he didnt understand why the man went down the side alleyway. Inside the structure whoops of laughter resounded. Men argued. Women laughed and made animalistic noises. The place smelled of smoke and urine.

The man walked around the room once, circling a long wood table.

'Got a new fish,' a youngin said. He might have been a couple years junior to the man, but gave the impression that he'd lived a hard life so far and the end was in sight. The man nodded his head to acknowledge the other men there.

The whore he'd seen earlier stood up from a table. She swayed as she spoke. 'Finalmente venha procura uma mulher?'

Some of the men laughed, but a drunk Mexican sitting next to her reached up her skirt. She let out a yelp, eliciting laughter from all in the building. She leaned over the table with her eyes closed, the skirt now halfway up her back. The drunkard pulled his pants down and mounted the woman from behind. Another wave of laughter and whoops rang out.

'Acted too late,' an old timer said.

'Pardon?'

'Wanted you,' the old timer elaborated. 'Got the Mexicano's prick instead. Wont even get paid.' The old timer gave the man a once over and added, 'Not that you coulda paid her anyway.'

The man took advantage of the impromptu conversation. 'Soldier from the fort sent me here. Said this is where all the people come.'

'Sure the soldier didnt say she was where all the people come?' the youngin said. He pointed at the whore now passed out across the table. Another youngin was pulling her leg straight back. A few whoops of approval went up, but not with the same exuberance as before.

The old timer laughed at the youngin's joke. 'Kids alright,' he said. He refocused his attention on the man. 'People used to come here. Aint much a reason to any more.'

'Why not?'

The old timer looked peeved at the further questioning. 'There just aint nothing to come here for.'

It didnt take long for the boy's father to become adept at longshoreman work. Within a couple weeks he adjusted so he knew when certain ships would come in. Often times the boy's father waited up, sitting on the edge of the bed, the metal hooks at ready in his fists. The bell sounded and he walked from the room as if called forth by a voice from the clouds.

Sometimes the boy watched from the balcony as his father worked, hauling sacks of fish, feed, tea and spices. There were odd times, when the boy—he'd adapted too—knew there were no regular ships, yet his father rose from the bed, grabbed the hooks and started for the door. Within a minute's time, the bell would ring. In the hours following the shifts, his father did not come back to the room. The boy took to looking through the footlocker, what few relics they had from before their time in the Sargasso. His father had long told him never to leave the room without him. Said that if he left the room by himself, he better not come back.

The boy could lay on the floor and press his ear to the boards and hear the muted voices of the people below in the common room. During the day it was mostly longshoremen talking, lying, making up stories, swapping tales about places not-here.

V

The Indians were hard workers. Together the number of bricks produced grew twentyfold, then doubled and doubled again. The stranger became the de facto leader of the cohort. Because the tribe was larger, it was harder to sustain. Some of the men formed hunting parties. They went out for several days at a time and when they returned they brought wild game, already skinned and smoked. They tossed the entrails into the well as the stranger instructed.

The well remained the central dumping site for the tribe. All excrement and waste went into the well. If women cut their hair, the hair was thrown in. Rendered fat from killings, if it was not burned, would also be tossed into the hole. A woman miscarried and the tiny stillborn with the umbilical cord was laid to rest in the pit. In the summer, the stink became unbearable and the women stretched some hides over a frame and covered the well.

The mixing holes were equally disgusting. Shallow things, like graves, the holes were filled with the muck from the well and the dirt was sifted in. Initially the Indians, eager to do their part in the construction process, danced in the pits, slogged the mud into the molds. But their enthusiasm faded and now the pits were a place where men went to be punished. The stranger or some elder might sentence a man who did not catch anything on the hunt to march in place in the confines of the pits. At first time frames were given—a man might have to walk in place in the pit for two days. Then the restrictions were forgotten altogether—the men having to do their time in the pits until another's indiscretion set him free.

Within a matter of a couple decades, the village was established, small crowded buildings hugging one another, a system of cisterns collected rainwater and stored it in troughs. Children were born and raised knowing nothing but this place. All traces of the fallen tower, the rambling rounded bricks of the ancient Indian settlement, were gone.

That night the man slept in a stable at the edge of town. He tied his mule to a post at the gate's edge. He crawled under a fence and lay down in a heap of dried grass. As he lay his head in the pillow of feed, he smelled manure. A goat bayed once. A chicken or two flapped their wings. Otherwise things stayed quiet.

He tried to study the sky, but the haze from the fires in the town drowned out the otherworldly lights, and only the brightest of stars could be seen. Soon his eyes grew weary of searching for things not visible.

He dreamt of his time in Port of Tobacco. He relived when he found his father's stash of bills wedged into a crack in the plastered walls. Without another thought the boy replaced the money and looked about the room. He was old enough to work, though he did not ask why his father wouldnt let him. Most nights his father came in late and did not want to talk. Some nights he brought one of the whores—the innkeeper's wife or a woman from the pub. No matter, it was always the same. He would make the boy watch while he had his way with the woman.

'This is how men do it, boy,' he'd say between thrusts.

Sometimes the woman would acknowledge the boy's presence; other times the boy just sat as a silent third party in the bed, trying to refocus his gaze out the window. Birds flocked about the harbor, screaming unto the grey skies.

When his father climaxed, he would stand up rigid, then slouch forward, loathe to take his member out. Depending on the woman, they might exchange some utterances. But the innkeeper's wife would look at the boy. Her brow wrinkled. She shook her head. His father strode across the room and pulled a pair of longjohns from the hook on the back of the door.

'Father told me bout the Sargasso,' she whispered. She stretched out one hand and stroked the boy's face. She was still naked, her pubis still wetted down, teeth marks still rankled around her nipples.

The boy didnt respond.

'He just tryin to show you how a man does.'

His father, appearing now as no more than a specter in the evening light, turned around. 'Whad you just say?'

The woman sat up and her breasts rolled forward. 'Tellin him how you was just tryin to be a good man.'

'You say something bout the Sargasso?' He grabbed a hook off the wall and walked across the room, toward her.

She put one hand out to deflect the oncoming blow. Her other hand held up the bedsheet. The hook gigged through the bones of her hand and split down between the index and middle finger webbing. She screamed. Blood trickled down off her elbow and stained the sheets.

'Get out,' his father said quietly. 'Youre just a common whore. Bitch with crotch rot, just like his ma.'

He pointed the hook at the boy, who cowered by the woman in the corner.

The innkeeper's wife pulled the sheet from the bed, wrapped herself in it and made haste from the room. Droplets of blood marked her path. She looked over her shoulder and cursed both the father and son, said theres no place in the world for either of them.

'You, boy,' a boot swatted the man across the posterior. He started awake and scrambled to his feet. It was morning now, though just barely. He turned to face his assailant. 'This aint no inn.' The stablehand was a darkman, skin like night.

'Needed a place to rest,' the man said.

'Places for asses, chickens—not people.'

The man nodded. 'Caint give you pay if thats what youre askin for.'

The darkman huffed. 'Dont make no difference to me. This place aint mine. I's here to keep up the place, git rid a the trouble.'

'Well, I'll get outta your way then,' the man sidestepped the stablehand. The hitching post stood solo. 'Wheres my mule?'

The darkman was already using a pitchfork to scoop up piles of straw and dung. He didnt give the man a glance when he said there wasnt no mule here when he arrived; it mustve been stolen while he was sleeping. 'Lucky the thief didnt cut your throat open too.'

'Who do I tell about my mule bein stolen?'

The stablehand's shoulders seemed to shake with suppressed laughter. 'Guess you could tell the old commandante,' he said. 'But it sounds like he might have his hands full with those injuns they spotted this morn.'

The Indians' efforts were impressive. Dozens of squared buildings were erected in a matter of years. The bricks, given their potpourri composition, held together rather well. In this place the sun could transform anything. A thicker wall of stones was erected. The stranger ordered it to enclose an entire section of the village. It needed to be twenty feet tall. The wall itself was actually constructed by building two parallel walls. The walls were braced with wooden beams, then filled with dirt and rock. If anyone were ever to attempt to blast through the wall, the insides would spill out on them, crushing them and burying them, leaving their bodies for speculative statements by archeologists.

The wooden beams were farmed from the banks of a river five miles south. Indian men whose arms rippled with muscles carried the trees in their entirety back to the village. From there, other Indians with tools hewed the trees into beams and supports. The wood shavings were either burned into ash or collected; either way they were deposited into the well.

The hunting parties were mostly younger men, still agile, but without the stout body muscle needed for hauling bricks and lumber. They stayed out for weeks at a time, whole packs of them. When they returned, the entire village feasted. They ate bison, bird and deer. The stranger kept an inventory of the kills and who did the killing. By his accounts, the stranger determined one boy did more killing than any of the others.

When the stranger asked the boy's hunting party how he learned to kill so efficiently, the other boys said he had no rules. The boy killed with whatever means he had. He preyed on weak animals, injured animals, bear cubs and sickly deer. He beat their skulls in with rocks, impaled them with spears, broke their necks with his hands. If he were to ask the Indian boy the same question, the boy wouldve simply responded that he had better rules for hunting. Nothing is sacred in this world. The taste of flesh and the feeling of a full belly is enough to blind any man to the horrors we create. Time, it is known, can heal all things, the layers of dirt and lies building up one on top of another like scar tissue.

It was in this revelation that the stranger knew when the time came for the slaughter of his village, he would have to wait for the Indian boy and his hunting party to be gone—the Indian boy was too much like him to be handled like a common man.

VI

When the time came, his father rose from the bed, dressed, took the hooks from the wall and went to the docks. The bell clanged. The boy knew that since his father cut the innkeeper's wife's hand, things would be different. It was one thing for the innkeeper to whore out his own wife; it was another to injure her.

A boat, as it sidled up to dock, blotted out the rising sun, making the immediate events clearer to the boy. The gangplank set down on the dock and the captain of the vessel met with the dock manager. Meanwhile the longshoremen huddled in groups. The boy watched as his father went from one group to the next, shut out of each. He went up close to the gangplank to claim the first spot in line. The manager and the father exchanged a few short words. Then, in going their own directions, the manager nodded to the old longshoreman.

Still, now with years passed and the images amplified in his mind, the man does not know why he did not call out. Yes, the sound of his voice may not have carried over the rooftops and over the din of the bustling dock workers, but at least he would have done more than witness his father's murder. The old longshoreman stood by a feedsack from the boat, awaiting someone to help heft the other end. His father, being without company, came over to the old man.

The old man made a gesture to suggest switching places. He pointed at his lower back. The father shrugged and walked to the opposite side of the bag. He stooped to lace his hook into the burlap. In one sharp motion, the old longshoreman threaded the hook into the nape of the father's neck. The boy saw the head spasm and fall limp when, with a final tug, the top of the backbone was ripped from the base of the skull.

Another dock worker came over to the corpse and helped throw him into the water.

The boy backed off the balcony and into the room. The sounds from outside seemed to filter in more loudly than usual. In haste, the boy took the money from the crack in the wall and threw the bills into the footlocker.

The man went to the gate at the fort. He waited for a soldier to open the great wooden door, but none came. Peddlers roamed the streets, selling whistles carved from sticks. Across the way, a man called out, 'Miracles and wonders, friends!' The man recognized him as the medicine salesman from the day before. 'Got one cure for everything. If you got a malady of the body, mind or soul, this here concoction is all you need…'

The man turned to the door of the fort again and pounded his fist against it.

'Niemand dort für Sie,' a beggar slouched by the door said.

The man only glanced at the beggar and pounded on the door again.

Then the man heard a bleating, a screech above the sounds of the village. He turned and saw the roofman riding on his mule. He pulled hard on the animal's reins, coercing another shriek from the beast. He circled around the medicine salesman. The man turned around and pounded on the door again.

A slot opened up and a man's face appeared in the framed opening. 'Whaddya knockin on this door for?'

'Want to talk with the commandante,' the man said.

The beggar, though of a different tongue, had heard the words before and now he laughed. The soldier laughed too. 'Sorry, partner, commandantes got a few other cards on the table right now.'

'You there,' the roofman called. The man spun around, thinking he must be the one being addressed. But it was not him; it was the salesman.

'Yessir,' the salesman said. 'Do you care to try a spot of the medicine yourself?'

'Ah, this should be good,' the soldier said from behind the door. Another face crowded the opening to watch the unfoldings in the public square.

'Dont think I want any of your nigger dust,' the roofman said. 'Got the niggers bein wiped out—entire villages of em—and here youre tryin to tell us this'll save us.'

The salesman began to stammer a response.

'Lemme ask you something,' he said. 'Wheres the dark boy you had with ya yesterday?'

Most everyone was quiet, the roofman commanding their attention from atop the beast.

'Well,' the salesman said. He licked his lips. 'He was a-blind and I poured the medicine into his eyes—'

'An wheres he now?'

The salesman's voice dropped when he said the boy was dead.

From behind the door, two howls of laughter went up.

'Dead?' the roofman asked.

'Yessir, when he saw the world for what it was with his very own eyes, his heart gave out,' the salesman explained.

The roofman yawed the mule in a small circle, pulled a shiv from his vest and planted it in the temple of the salesman's head. 'The world,' he announced, 'is God's greatest gift, right behind this life.'

The man turned back to the slot where the soldiers watched. 'Aint you all gonna do something?'

'Aint our call,' one said.

'You there,' the roofman called. This time he pointed across the square at the man. 'Wheres that shiv you come into town with yesterday?'

The man didnt bother searching his pockets; he turned and pounded at the door again. The sound of the hooves clopping against the dirt came on all too rapidly.

'This man out here stole my mule!' he called. But there was no answer.

'Show us your pockets,' the roofman said. He came closer.

The man's fist was raw from slamming into the door. 'I know bout those injuns,' he called. 'They followed me here.'

With that the roofman stopped approaching and the door to the fort was opened. The man dove headlong through the opening and did not look back even after the door slammed shut.

When the time came, the stranger went from one building to the next, killing the Indians in their sleep. More often than not he simply snapped their necks. He left the babies alone, letting them sleep. Only once did he wake an Indian. In one short blow, he ended the interruption. Then he went back and gathered up the babies, tossing them into a sack, then threw the bag with its contents still squirming and crying into the well. The sack floated on the scum of the well, the babies on top still alive while the ones underneath drowned.

Before the sun had risen, he'd disposed of all the corpses, leaving only the blankets and eating wares of the inhabitants. He moved those objects into the mortar pits, throwing some of the lighter livestock and some dogs in to mix the things about.

He waited a full week for the hunting party to return. There were four of them in total, each one carrying the dismembered prey he'd slain. As they approached, the stranger watched them slow, then stop, sensing something was amiss. The lead boy, a smallish one, held up one hand to his party. They waited until he entered the village. The stranger was waiting for him in the street.

The Indian boy asked where the villagers had gone. But the stranger did as was necessary and did not answer the question. He went out and met the remaining three. He killed the first two in one single action. Only the hunter boy was left. He did not tremble. And when the stranger went to shank him, the hunter boy deflected the blow with his forearm and ran past the stranger into the maze of buildings.

'Dont think we can avoid each other,' the stranger called out. 'Eventually one of these alleys will bring us to each other. You'll have to face your destiny.' He let the echo of his voice fade and heard a skittering of feet over graveled dirt. He changed direction. 'I knew it would be like this—just the two of us, chasing each other around a ghost town. Thats what people will call these places someday.' He stopped and listened again, but there was nothing. 'But you and me, we're a lot alike—too alike.' He laughed when he recited the old cliché: 'This town aint big enough for the both of us.'

A sharp jolt of pain stung the stranger's jawbone. The boy stood in a window, his arm already cocked back to throw another stone. The second stone blistered open the tight skin of the stranger's forehead. He dove through the window. The boy was gone, crawled out through the adjacent window. The stranger, being too big to fit through the other window, ran out the door. Blood came out of his forehead in an even sheet, rolling down over his eyes. He walked one of the wider roads, out toward the edge of the village. 'Every one you know is gone,' he said. 'You might as well be undone in time. This place aint a village any more.'

The boy stood by the well. He held a sharpened stick in one hand, a rock in the other. The stranger smiled until the pain in his jaw caused his lips to draw shut.

'What are you making?' the hunter boy asked.

The stranger was not surprised to hear the boy respond in a familiar tongue. It was his custom to converse in English with the villagers. He expected the laws of linguistics to hold true and for some of the boys to pick up the language. Enough time on this earth and every language becomes native.

'You cant even imagine,' the stranger said. 'It's unlike anything youve ever seen. Someday, when you see it, then you can imagine it. Thats the way imagination works.'

The boy launched the rock at the stranger. But the stranger brought one of his hands up and swatted the rock midair. They charged at one another, the hunter boy thrusting the stick into the stranger's torso. He yowled in pain. The boy tried to pull the stick back out, but the wood had splintered inside and lodged in the ribcage. He let go and swung. His fist caught the stranger on the ear. The stranger's head whipped around and his teeth clamped down on the hunter boy's wrist. Now he cried out. The stranger stood, wheezing, and picked the boy up over his head. Then he tossed the boy through the animal skin cover of the well. He waited for the sound of the boy's impact, but there was none. When he looked into the depths, there was no trace of him, just the sack of babies, and the stranger knew what had happened.

TWO

I

First the man was brought before the lieutenant of the fort. Outside the main curtain wall the noises of the village surged. It seemed a controlled pandemonium. The lieutenant stood in a courtyard in front of a brick cabin with glass windows.

'Sounds like the worlds endin out there,' the man said.

The lieutenant looked away, squinted, said it sounds about how it usually does. Then he asked, 'Whaddya know bout them injuns?'

The man opened his mouth to speak, but the soldier stopped him. 'If you lied just to git in the door, we gonna throw you back out, stripped naked with oil all on your body. Let you bake in the sun. If that old sumbitch on the mule is out there he'll make short work outta you.'

'I wasnt lyin,' the man said.

'If you lyin to me just to see the ol commandante, he'll a-sniff you out. Then youre worser off than dead.'

This time the man simply nodded. For a moment they stood, listening to the barking and bartering, the melee of the village.

'Bout these injuns,' the lieutenant said.

Inside his mouth, the man welled up some spit and swallowed it. He didnt want his voice to sound hoarse like those wandering desperate men who try to barter favors. 'That sumbitch out theres ridin my mule.'

'Dont give a goddamn.'

'That mules my one way to get outta here. Tried to steal him from me yesterday when I first got into town.'

'Bring up that mule again and I'm a-gonna cut out your tongue and feed it to you,' the lieutenant said. He made eye contact with the man. 'Brought you in here cause a the injuns. Whaddya know?'

The man swallowed again. 'They follered me a while now,' he said.

'From whereabouts?'

'Down cliffside there back a piece, an old village place—maybe their grandparents lived there or somethin.'

'Howd they find you there?'

'Well, they mighta been follering me before that too.'

The lieutenant spat. He didnt need to ask the next question.

'Follered me from first mountain valley I come on when I rode in off the plains.'

By the gate of the fort, the two soldiers were opening up the slot and yowling with laughter. They took turns shoving each other out of the way and watching whatever spectacle of the streets was unfolding before their eyes.

'You come all the way from the plains?'

'Yessir.'

The lieutenant dragged the heel of his boot through the dirt over the stretch of spittle. 'Problem is I dont rightly believe you.'

The man rubbed the back of his neck, shifted his weight from foot to foot. 'It's the truth.'

'Whyd a sumbitch like you ride burroback into the mountains?'

'For the century—I mean census.'

The lieutenant chuckled. 'Alright there, pardner,' he said. 'I'll be goddamned if youre a-lyin to me.'

He turned around and opened the door to the brick cabin, ushering the man to follow him.

Quite some time passed before the stranger saw anyone come near the village. Once or twice, well past dusk, when Ursa Major and Ursa Minor battled for the heavens, a fire would go alight in the dark horizon. The stranger gazed upon those encampments from afar, knowing those men huddled around the flames. They traveled together out of fear, not daring to go into these darkest of places by themselves. President Polk gave them vision, a sense of mission from his east coast house, saying this was it—this place was the destiny of the revolutionary grandchildren. A hundred years later another president would send men to the dark side of the moon, shadowed from even the glow of earthly lights. In a hundred more years, men would talk again around fires, telling stories of their grandfathers' heroics. This is our history: periods of darkness with flares of light to gather around and build into myths.

Another time, a whole season later, two men passed on horseback. One pointed to the village, the other looked, holding a hand over his brow as if in a salute. The stranger, hidden in a tower, peeked out from a slitted window. In his mind he made a mental inventory of the buildings. Every blanket was folded, turned down. What straw he had was forked into neat piles by the stableyard. The well was now a sinkhole filled in with dirt. Any evidence of previous inhabitants was gone. After the two men rode off in the same direction whence they came, the stranger crawled out of his hiding spot, went to the shanty by the well and began digging at the floor. In his mind he calculated the folds in time, the movement of the earth's crust—the things that would later be termed as plate tectonics. From the hole he extracted a clay pitcher. Though dusted over with age, the edges chipped and the handle long gone, it felt like it was a mere week ago he'd buried it. In a single action, he broke the pitcher and pulled out the garments from within. He beat the dust out of them until they resembled the shade of blue he recognized.

The boy took the footlocker and his father's money down to the livery at the opposite end of town from the docks. The livery owner eyed the boy.

'Youre the castaway,' he said.

The boy nodded.

'Without your pa?'

The boy didnt need to think when he said he didnt have

a pa no more. Whether the livery owner understood what he meant or not wasnt apparent.

'I got some money,' the boy said. 'Need a horse.'

The livery owner laughed gently, then stopped when he saw the boy pull out the stack of bills. 'Well, I could get you a horse, sure,' he said. 'Just you headin out of here?'

'Yessir.'

'All by you lonesome?'

'Guess so.'

The livery owner rested his knuckles on the counter and weighed a proposition in his mind before he spoke any further. He peered over the counter at the footlocker next to the boy, then examined the stack of money. 'Tell you what, bub,' he said. 'Do this—go off by youself and you aint gonna be no boy. You'll done be a young man.' The boy liked the way that sounded. Up to this point running away was a mode of survival. But here, now, it made him into a more mature being. 'You gonna need more than a horse.'

The boy nodded though he didnt know exactly what he was agreeing with. The livery owner said to follow him and together they went to the stables.

'This'll do you real fine,' the livery owner said. He stroked the mane of a mule hitched up to a wagon. The animal seemed docile enough. The wagon was not in total disrepair. 'Could make it quite a ways,' the livery owner said. 'Make it all the way to the ocean on the other side of the country, I'd wager.'

Finally the boy asked how much it would all cost.

'Everything you got, bub. Thats the cheapest I can let it go for.'

II

The Indian boy came to and his first breath sucked in dirt. He coughed and tried to move his arms, but they were pinned to his sides. When he tried to open his eyes, granules of dirt fell into them and he blinked rapidly to clear them from his vision. Through the tears that welled up he could see a white haze he took for daylight. Everything in his periphery was dark. He quickly assessed that the only parts of his body he could move freely were his feet. Over and over he flexed his ankles, dug his toes into the soft ground and pushed. A fraction of an inch was gained. More dirt fell into his eyes. He gasped another breath, the weight of the world literally pressing on his chest cavity. For hours he repeated the action. Toward dusk the Indian boy thought he had stopped making progress, then realized it was an illusion: with the darkening of the sky, the progress was not readily evident.

All through the night he continued to dig his toes into the ground and flex his ankles. By morning he could barely move. As the sun rose, he felt its glow warm the top of his head. That gave him motivation enough to press on. An hour later he emerged from the burrow. He collapsed on the ground and sucked in the fresh air.

In his mind, he sorted out the events. He remembered being thrown by the stranger into the well. The impact of the fall was momentary. He remembered hitting the sack full of babies and infants, hearing some abbreviated cries from the ones that managed to survive afloat in the muck.

The Indian boy figured that such a fall into a pit that no longer contained a proper liquid must have broken every bone in his body. But no bones were broken. And now that he was conscious, he was here—in a foreign place altogether. He rubbed the dirt from his eyes the best he could—for his hands were also filthy. As far as he could see in every direction there was nothing except grass. Mountains, the natural border scrawled across every sky he saw growing up, were gone.

Teachings from the elders of his tribe allowed for another life beyond this one, but in another form. And to all appearances, he was still the same Indian boy. Whatever spirits were at play here, they did not abide by the laws of men.

The ground rumbled some and the boy widened his stance. He looked to each side, waiting for a stampede of animals to crest the horizon. The rumbling grew, yet nothing appeared in any direction. A wisp of steam came from the hole he'd just struggled out of. Timidly, he leaned forward to peer down into it. Then a bigger plume of steam belched out and it stung the Indian boy's eyes. He fell. The ground surged with tremendous force and he clamored backward. A geyser shot up into the air, hissing as it went. Whatever place the Indian boy had come to, it was primal and struggling still to take shape.

★ ★ ★

The man was shown to a room the lieutenant called a parlor. Chairs like the man had never seen—leather so shiny it reflected the lampglow—sat on a bearskin rug.

'Commandante wants his visitors waitin out here for him,' the soldier said. 'He'll a-call you when hes ready.' He promptly left the room.

The man stood awkwardly in the center of the room, unsure of what he should do. The walls themselves were the only things resembling the rough-hewn look of the rest of the fort. He touched one of the bricks and it crumbled into the man's fingers. He sifted the grains of dirt. Then, in the dampened light he examined a larger chunk of the brick. It felt like a tooth. He shook his head at the thought.

He hesitated, then sat in one of the leather chairs. He'd never felt something so soft. It wrapped around his body, seeming to hold him like a woman. Naturally, he thought of his own woman. He thought how this was it—he would legitimize her and the child, bring them into existence during this very meeting. He closed his eyes. Few times had he felt a peace in his life this deep. The last time he could recall was in leaving Port of Tobacco, the footlocker and some rations the only cargo in his newly purchased wagon. He set off, north and west—more west than north. He glanced only once over his shoulder and watched as the glimmer of the ocean ebbed out of view and the land of grasses swelled around him. If any traces of his past life remained, they were bones and timber lost to the sea.

Like the pilgrims and zealots, the exiled mormons, the sooners and Okies who would descend on this place in incremental fashion as if Moses himself declared they would come, the man made his way into a land void of promise.

As he suspected, the two men returned with greater numbers. The stranger was ready for them. He stood at the entrance road to the village, his feet spaced a shoulderwidth apart, his hands clasped behind his back. Most of the men approached on horseback. A few wagons toted cargo. All the men were dressed in blue. A man in the front raised a hand to signal the company to halt. Another man on horseback trotted up next to the commander. They conversed, taking turns pointing to the stranger. Several of the subordinates passed around a canteen. Everyone studied the stranger. Finally the two men—the commander and his lieutenant—rode forward.

'Howdy there,' one said as they came within speaking distance.

The stranger returned the greeting.

'Couple of scouts saw this village here,' the commander said. 'Maps dont show any such place.'

The stranger nodded, said yessir.

'Mind if we ask what this here place is?' the lieutenant asked.

The stranger feigned surprise by raising his eyebrows. 'This here place,' he said, emulating the man's speech, 'is Fort James.'

'Fort James?'

The commander said he'd never heard of it.

'My job was to ready the fort for inhabitation,' the stranger said. He stood as a soldier for inspection.

The commander leaned forward on his horse and glanced over the plain blue uniform of the stranger. It was devoid of insignia and rank. But it was remarkably clean. 'Your job?' the commander said. He clarified: 'And what is your position here at Fort James exactly?'

The stranger turned his head and smiled so his teeth showed. 'Well, sir, I'm this here fort's goddamn commandante.'

III

The young man drove the wagon across the plains, navigating as he knew best. He drove the wagon during the night, guided by the stars. In the daytime, he crawled under the carriage of the wagon and slept. If the night grew too brisk, he might take some of the sailcloth from the footlocker and drape it over the wagontop to make a tent. Though food was scarce, he did well enough for himself catching small game and scavenging the rare fruit or patch of tubers. Should he catch a mouse, he would use it to bait a hawk, then kill the predator bird with a sling. Occasionally he went a couple days without food before happening upon something to sustain himself. There were no rivers to speak of, just mere trickles. He had a talent for living that few people have ever possessed, especially now.

In all his life he had never been alone. As he rode, he tried to recall a time when he could find no trace of another person. He could think of none. There had always been someone's voice, his father's presence. It struck him as odd—him in this vast place all by himself. The world is so big, the young man knew. He'd sailed half of it, seen more than most old men had ever seen. Yet this was the first place unaffected by people. He wondered how long it might be before this place he traversed became infected with people. He wondered if there were places human eyes had never seen.

'Come,' a voice called from the office.

The man opened his eyes, his reminiscences interrupted by the instruction. The door to the interior office from the parlor was ajar. He entered.

The commandante stood behind a large wooden desk, the top stained and lacquered. He shuffled papers into a stack. His hair was white, pulled back into a ponytail. The hair on his face was also mostly white, though a grey streak ran down from his lower lip. The man did not recognize the aged commandante as the stranger.

'Sit down,' the commandante said. He continued to busy himself, then eventually sat. The man looked around the office. In all his life, in all the places he traveled, he had never seen a place so polished and new. What parts of the desk were not hidden by paperwork had designs inlaid. A set of fully stocked bookshelves with glass doors covered the wall behind the commandante. And the old military officer, despite his age, looked fresh—his uniform dark blue and creased.

The man's observations did not go unacknowledged. 'Made a nice place for myself here,' the commandante said. 'Took some time, some patience and planning, but I made this place my own.'

'Looks to be the nicest place I ever been in,' the man said.

'Probably true,' the commandante chuckled. 'This could be the apex of your existence.' The man faked amusement at the comment, though he didnt know what the commandante meant. After the chortles died, there was a silence.

'Youre not from around here,' the commandante said.

'No sir, caint say I am.'

'From out on the plains?'

'Thats right.'

'Come in for the census?'

The man seemed to exhale for the first time in quite a while. 'Yes,' he said. 'Yes. Thats why I'm here. Need to register my family.'

The commandante stood and turned to the bookcase. From a lanyard around his neck, he took a skeleton key and opened one of the glass doors. He pulled an oversized book off the shelf and set it with a thump on the desk. 'Be happy to register your family,' the commandante said. 'But first I want you to tell me about the Indians you saw.'

The man stared at the great book, several swathes of parchment thick, the commandante's hand resting lightly on top of it as if he were about to swear an oath of truth. 'Only saw three or four of them,' he said. 'One was on a horse—white horse like I never seen. He wore this outfit all made of bones.' The commandante nodded knowingly. 'They done follered me a long ways—since I first come into the mountains. They had a couple chances to kill me, but they never did.' Then the man asked if these Indians might not be the murdering kind.

'Didnt know there was another kind,' the commandante said. 'And from what I know of them, this one in the bone armor could be the end of us all.'

'One injun?'

The simplicity of the question amused the commandante. He held up an index finger, then took another key from his breast pocket. He opened a desk drawer and took out an oblong box with a small padlock on it. He used another key to open the box. 'Got to keep this one quiet,' he said. 'Call this Pandora's box. You know Pandora's box?'

The man shook his head, said he didnt.

The commandante smiled, said Pandora was the name of the place out east of here. 'Place where I purchased this. Names Greek in origin, I believe.'

'Oh.'

For a moment the commandante sat with his shoulders quaking in suppressed laughter. 'Forgive me,' he finally said. 'Cant take it back now.' The box opened with a click and he lifted the lid. Inside a cloth was wrapped over something. He lifted it from the box and set it on the table. Then he unwrapped the revolver. 'Know what this is?'

The man said he didnt rightly know, looked to be some type of tool.

'Indeed,' the commandante said. 'It's a tool for building empires. This here is a revolver, a sort of gun.'

'I know about guns.'

'Ever seen one this close?'

'Caint say I have.'

The commandante opened the chamber and exposed the hollow spaces where bullets were stored for use. 'This is the most efficient way to kill men,' he said. 'You can take this gun, load it with six shots, kill six men. Give a man a belt with two of these on it and hes his own damn army.'

'Dont reckon that injuns got a gun,' the man said.

'I wouldnt think so,' the commandante said. 'Most men alive right now will never see a gun. Someday people will think differently. They'll tell stories of the old west and gunslingers, showdowns and shootouts.'

The man's brow furrowed. 'Why'd they do a fool thing like that? If we aint got guns, why'd anyone tell a story like that?'

The commandante smiled like he'd led the man to ask the question. 'Because they will have guns. Children will have guns for play, our heroes will carry guns. And us—the history of the future—we will be assigned our stories based on the present.'

'You done got me thinkin in circles, sir.'

'Best you do since everything tends to be cyclical.'

The man didnt bother to ask the meaning of that statement. 'So you gonna go out and kill that injun with the gun?'

The mere suggestion seemed off-putting to the commandante. 'No,' he frowned. 'Thing with a gun is you cant take it back. All I do is press a trigger. Then, somewhere farther off, through a different chain of events, the bullet collides with a body. Once that bullet is out of the chamber, the path it's on is already set. If you think this place is hard country now, fire this gun off in the public square. Watch what this place will turn into.'

'So how you gonna get rid of them injuns?'

The commandante leaned back in his chair as if pondering the statement in some philosophical fashion. 'Figure I'll ride out there and smash their skulls with a rock.' The man wanted to react, but he sat inert before the military officer. 'Someday people will call it cruel—the way we dispense with life. By that time we'll have mortars that can traverse an ocean. A gun could hold a thousand bullets and pump them out in a minute's time. We'll have bombs to level cities. Killing will be tidy. Industry usually streamlines itself. But right now we have to make do with what we have. I could take a strapping from an old wagon wheel and pound it into a blade, slice open a human head with it, you know.'

The man tried to decipher what the commandante said, but it might as well have been spoken in another language altogether. He took a moment to collect his thoughts. He studied the officer, realizing that a man like him didnt make it to old age without cutting others' lives short. He needed the commandante for protection.

'Can we talk bout registerin my family now?'

The Indian boy wandered through places without borders or names. If there was a division between man and beast, he did not see it. What life there was milled about, nearly blind, covered in vellus hair, grunting and snorting. At first these beasts gave the Indian boy cause to worry; he had never seen anything like this before. Then he realized the animals were harmless, too dumb to inflict any harm. They rooted in the swamps and bogs, digging out mudfish. Some of the swamps boiled, sending dollops of steamy mud into the air. The beasts, dumb as they were, might wade into the bog. Feeling the intense heat they began shrieking. Flooded with some rudimentary chemical resembling adrenaline they would begin thrashing, usually sinking them deeper into the hot muck. The other beasts upon hearing the shrieks began to panic themselves and they too might run into the bog.

Plants, those scrag things that held too little promise in his past life, were alien things blooming with giant flora. Insects as big as his hands and feet scuttled to and from the plants, feasting on pollens and nibbling at the leaves. The boy took a stick and chewed it into a point. He used it as a spear and stabbed a beetle through the back. Its legs kept moving as if nothing happened. Its wings, now pinned by the stick, attempted to flutter. The serrated pinchers at its mouth opened and closed rhythmically. All this the boy observed before taking the beetle to the edge of a bog and turning it on the stick over the steam. The steam made the exoskeleton of the bug easier to crack. He pulled the meat—if it could be called that—from the creature's thorax.

At night he lay naked on a rock in a darkness greater than any known to any human who has ever lived. He did not dream; he simply slept and awakened. When you are a stranger to a familiar world, even the imagination cannot manufacture an escape.

IV

The commander remarked that the stranger had made quite a place for himself. 'How'd you manage?' he asked.

'I enslaved an entire generation of Indians,' the stranger replied. Both men laughed heartily. They sat at a table in the cantina. The soldiers, tired from their trek, bunked at the garrison inside the fort. The two men passed a bottle of amber liquid back and forth.

The commander belched, letting his cheeks balloon when he did so. 'I gotta say this is the damnedest place I ever come across.' The stranger pretended not to understand what the military man meant. He took a light sip from the bottle, then handed it back. 'You say you got orders to take in my entire company—that we're gonna be quartered here.'

'Yessir.'

The commander glugged two fingers' worth of liquor, smacked his lips. 'It's a wonder I ever found this place. Scouts near missed it. And I didnt rightly believe them when they told me bout it.'

'Hard to imagine a place like Fort James,' the stranger conceded.

The commander stood, swayed a little until he regained his balance, then sauntered over to the window looking out into the street. 'Dont know what to make of all this,' he said.

Again the stranger feigned ignorance, said he didnt know what the commander meant.

'Left out of Santa Fe near about four months ago,' he said. He still looked out the window, slid his hands into his trouser pockets. 'Left there with close to three hundred men, six months of supplies. We were scheduled to arrive in Denver within three months.'

'But you got attacked by some Apache.'

Slowly the commander turned around to look at the stranger seated at the table. 'Yeah. The Apache, a whole horde of em. Ever single one of em swingin a club or an ax, fighting like dogs. Saw one nigger bite right through one of my men's necks.'

The stranger whistled.

'Couldnt tell my men what to do. They all just tryin to stay alive. Cant call no retreat cause we aint got nowhere to go.'

The stranger chuckled and took another sip from the bottle, said that type of situation is bound to happen when youre in a land that isnt yours. 'But thats why we got this here fort now.'

The commander leaned against the window frame. 'How do you mean?'

'Fort James is a place to guard against the Indians,' the stranger explained. 'My job is to take in the troops that need shelter. This land is rough. Its inhabitants are rougher. This fort's job is to take in anyone who didnt originally live here.'

For a moment it looked as if the commander had fallen asleep standing up—his eyes were deadened with the weight of alcohol. 'When we met, out there at the edge of town, you told me what you were,' he said. As he had been doing, the stranger looked beguiled by the statement. 'You said you were this fort's something.'

'Commandante.'

'Thats it,' the commander said. 'Aint no rank I heard of in the American military. Who you say you get your orders from?'

'From the top,' the stranger said. 'The Commander in Chief, you might say.'

The commander stood a long time studying the stranger. 'And what does a commandante do?' he asked.

The stranger shrugged, said the job was a bit open-ended. 'You can say I am in charge of the fort itself.'

This made the commander stand up straight as if he was called to attention. 'I'm the ranking officer in the company,' he balked.

'Certainly,' the stranger agreed. 'The company—all those men—are yours. Fort James is my responsibility.'

'The buildings?'

'The whole place.'

'Except the men.'

'The men are yours.'

The commander nodded—more to himself than in agreement. 'Alright then,' he said. 'You take care of this place and I'll look after everything military.'

The stranger took a swig from the bottle and handed it to the commander. 'Good way to do it.'

The young man's wagon trundled on during the day. In his quest to go ever deeper into the unknown country, he had forsaken sleep. He rode through the night and back into the daytime, alternating his methods of navigation: first using the scattered lights of the stars; then following the concentrated glowering of the sun. At times he fell into momentary slumber, the reins wrapped around his wrists so as not to lose control of the wagon altogether. Every once in a while he awakened to find his mule stopped and eating a tuft of grass. He rubbed the crust from the corners of his eyes and stood in the bed of the wagon. Slowly, he turned to look around him. Spread out in every direction there was nothing—not a tree or river, a building to speak of. There were no green and white signs with reflective lettering telling him it was two hundred and fifty miles to Tulsa, a hundred-fifty-mile straight shot on Old 40 to Amarillo. If he waited and held his breath, there was no sound. When the wind blew it did not make a noise, for there was nothing to obstruct it and make it call out like the chopped cries of a propeller pulling an aircraft across the skies.

Like those dark places surrounding the world we've since created, this country was not yet a frontier, a mystery or a destiny. It simply was. Not until the young man came upon the freshwater stream and the grove of saplings did this become a place for humans. Laughable now to think he felt ownership over the land. Funnier still to hear people talk about the infancy of the nation, how young the country was then. Buried under the grass and topsoil, under layers of shale and granite, the footprints of the Indian boy were fossilized, the bones of the early mammals also preserved in a muddied mixture heated into a brick solid state.

What plants there were would be covered in ash and the delicate leaves ribbed with veins and dimpled with spores, their countenance inked into time and also buried. The Indian boy had wandered for some time now. He'd seen the blind beasts die out, replaced by other more competent things with eyes that provided only slightly better vision. The insects proliferated. Lizards as big as men, some bigger jetted from rocks, snapping at the bugs. Fear of these things had left the boy a hundred years ago; centuries of fear take time for recovery.

He looked to the sky, the canopy of orange and blood that did not change from morning to evening. Only in the night did it stop glowing. Some days—some decades—smoke blotted out the day and all wandered in the dark. The insects died and so did the lizards. Plants withered. The ground rumbled constantly, shaking rocks down from cliffsides, loosing the soil. Trees crackled and crashed. Winged things—not yet birds or bats—fluttered from the branches. The ones that flew into the smoke fell from the sky. The boy picked up the winged creature, pulled the feathers from its body and bit into it. The cindered air had cooked it already.

Forests gave way to rocked canyonlands. The ground there was hot. But millennia of diaspora calloused the boy's feet and he walked amongst the fissures glowering the furious colors of the primordial sky. Another earthquake rattled the land and the calliope of vents screamed out. The stone slab under his feet buckled and gave way. There was a rush of steam. Around him, the winged creatures rained from the darkened sky. Somewhere distant, over the hisses and squeals of this continent's subduction, a herd of lizards quarreled over the carcass of one of their own.

The commandante opened the book, looked at the man. 'Need your surname,' he said to the man.

'Surname.'

'Yes,' the commandante said. 'Family name, last name. It's how I go about recording your existence.' The man shook his head. 'You dont have a last name?'

'No,' the man said. 'Never had any call for one.'

'Well,' the commandante said and closed the book. 'You'll need to purchase a surname.'

'I can buy a name?'

'In a manner of speaking. It's an administrative fee. Cost of creating a new person.'

'But I dont got any money,' the man said.

'Nothing?'

The man shook his head. 'Caint you just write my name in the book? I gotta get back to my woman. She was done set to have a baby when I left for here.'

'Surely you have some sort of collateral,' the commandante said. 'Anything you can leave with me in good faith.' He took a moment to gather his thoughts. 'What'd you ride in here on?'

'Had a mule,' the man said. 'But that sumbitch out in the village stole it from me. Thought he might try an kill me too.'

The commandante sighed. 'That leaves us with one option,' he said. 'You can work off the debt.' The man didnt know how to respond. He wasnt sure if this was charity or part of a codified system of this fort and the census process. 'It's just as well,' the commandante said. 'You wouldnt want to be outside these walls right now. Those Indians are coming and they aint going to leave much standing.'

THREE

I

Some miles farther north and even farther west, the young man's wagon broke. For a while now he had taken to tying the reins of the mule to the bench seat during the day. He'd say yah to get the mule to go, then he'd climb into the back of the wagon and fall to sleep with the swaying of the wagon. He awoke when they stopped or hit a bumpy patch. He might take the reins for a time to correct the mule's path or he might let them stop for a break. Nighttime was still his preferred time for travel.

He sat on the bench clucking at the mule, promising a break come first light. He looked to the sky, saw Cepheus, the zigzag of Lacerta snaking to the foot of Perseus. For a moment he recalled his father telling him of the love between Perseus, a fearless warrior, and the beautiful princess Andromeda. Their love was great enough that the gods placed them in the stars. Because he was young and naïve, he asked his father if that really happened. But his father laughed as did the other sailors and he said it was as true as any other stories told on this boat.

The memory came to an abrupt end as the wagon lurched and tilted back to one side. The mule neighed and the young man nearly fell out of the wagon.

'Whoa, whoa,' he said. He jumped down and stroked the mule's mane. Then he crouched to inspect what the problem was. In the pale moonlight he saw the wheel canted at an unnatural angle. He swore to himself, stood and unhitched the mule. He tied it to the back end of the wagon with a length of rope. 'Caint have you wanderin off on me,' he said. 'We'll solve this one come morn.'

In the light of the full morn, the young man could see the predicament for what it was. The front axle of the wagon splintered apart on the right side. The cracks in the shaft ran through the coupling all the way to the left side. It was a wonder both wheels hadnt given out. The young man figured that if he moved the wagon even another wheel turn, both wheels would be laying flat on the ground.

He threw a blanket over the mule's back and rode a short ways out. There he found the grove of saplings by the stream. He let the mule water there and inspected the trees. Grasping one, he gave it a hard shake. It still had some give to it, but it was sturdy nonetheless. Once the mule drank its fill, he rode north a short ways and surveyed the land. It was flat for the most part—a slough in the land just west of here might break some of the wind, make the wind, when there was some, blow more gently. From here he could see out in every direction, see out a dozen miles at least. He'd build up here, a short piece from the stream—close enough to fetch water, but far enough not to worry about flooding. Out here nobody would be able to bother him.

★ ★ ★

Next, the lieutenant took the man to the bunkhouse where the fort's other workers were housed. 'You'll get a few changes a clothes,' the soldier said. 'Keep the grey ones for workin in the mines. Rest is your day clothes.'

'Day clothes?'

'Cause youre new, you get the night shift: evenin to mornin.' They crossed the compound, the riot outside the fort swelling, plumes of smoke going up in the air. The lieutenant shook his head. 'Villagers gettin all worked up over a few niggers, want us to stick our chicken necks out of the fort.' Inside the curtain wall, what the soldiers called the compound, was much larger than the man imagined. They came to the stoop of a bunkhouse. 'You'll get every eighth day off. Get paid on that day. Best to go to the cantina, buy up some rations for the week. Dont want to take to spendin your money like an outta-luck whore.'

The lieutenant opened the door to the bunkhouse, yelled down the row of stacked beds that they had a new worker. A couple men grunted responses. A few men who had been sleeping roused long enough to belt out some curses. Then the soldier was gone.

The place smelled of urine and sweat. Aside from a crude lantern constructed from a frying pan with lumps of flaming fat, the light only showed through a sheet of paper stretched over a window frame and made translucent with grease.

'Open bunk over this a-way,' a voice said.

The man stumbled toward the voice, came to a bed where a man with a crooked back sat sucking on his lower lip. 'Got a bed,' the cripple said again. 'Gotta take the top though. Arent makin it up there myself.'

'¡Callate la boca!' a man from the neighboring bunk said.

'You Mexicano animal siestaing all day,' the cripple called back. 'Shut your trap.'

Other men stirred in their beds, grumbled about the noise. 'Best to git some sleep,' the cripple said. 'Long night ahead of ya.'

'I start workin tonight?' the man asked.

'Think we'd let you stay here if you wasnt?'

The man pulled himself up to the top bed and lay down. The middle of the straw mattress sagged. As he rested his head, he smelled mildew.

The Indian boy walked out of the cave. He had awakened in there and was guided to the mouth of the place only by the faintest glow of lights. He stepped gingerly; soreness pervaded his body, ached in his bones. Once the light was strong enough that he could see where he was stepping, he paused near a stalactite. He touched it and the rock was smooth, slick with water. He put his mouth to the end of the pointed rock and suckled as a newborn might on his mother's tit. It took some time to satiate his thirst; but once it was satisfied he wandered out into the daylight. His vision fogged at the edges and he rubbed his fingertips across his eyelids.

That was when he noticed how rough his fingertips were, how long his nails had grown. He felt at his face and let his fingers rove over the ruts now cut deep with age into his brow and around his mouth. He felt smaller than before, his back now hunched. Skin on his forearms sagged. When he turned his head, the bones in his neck crackled, the loose skin under his chin flapped. No longer could he be properly called a boy—if ever such a title fitted a child who saw the birth and death of an epoch. He was simply the Indian—a fossil of bygone times, produced in an era yet to be had and set free through the brutish powers of the metamorphic process.

Overcome with thoughts he couldnt begin to interpret, he sat on the ground. The hard ground hurt his buttocks. He covered his face and cried, each sob jostling a joint he never knew to ache until now. Snot poured out of his nose and over the cleft of his lip. He used the back of his hand to wipe his nose, finding the bridge to be another sore spot. He ran his other hand through his hair, which had grown long and wiry and considerably thinned out. He let out a cry, alien to those who have never imagined themselves in unimaginable scenarios. It was a long sustained yowl, and once his lungs were drained of the cry, he panted as a way to build up to another.

In the third round of panting, he felt another presence. In the fleeting moment before he looked, he assumed the presence to be the stranger, but it was not. A creature, not rightly a man, but a man-looking beast with a thick brow and muzzled mouth stood looking at the Indian. The pseudo-man opened his mouth as if to speak and made a yelping noise. His arms flew up from either side and swatted at nothing. The old Indian rose from his seat and backed away, keeping his eyes on the caveman. He kept one hand on the ground and felt for a rock to throw. He found one no bigger than a human fist. The caveman yelped again and began sauntering toward the Indian. In one swift motion the Indian threw the rock as if he were still a boy. Glancing off the skull of the caveman, the rock ricocheted into the cave, sending off a flurry of sparks. The half man let out a series of yelps and tripped. Blood squirted from the wound. He rose onto all fours and ran for a short distance that way before regaining his balance on two feet.

The agreed division of power between the commander and commandante was this. Inside the fort proper—the compound—the commander reigned supreme. The surrounding village and the few civilians who worked inside the fort were the jurisdiction of the commandante. In most every case requiring either of their attention, the proper party was easily discernible. The commander sent small bands of soldiers out on a regular basis with a single mission to kill Indians. This country, he told the men, belonged to their cause alone. 'Exterminate the niggers,' he said. 'Any way you can. No method is too barbaric for their kind.'

Over time the village became populated with waywards who were too weary for further travel. The commandante gave them shelter, assigned them occupations. Wages were negotiated. Women could always whore themselves out to the soldiers to bring in some extra funds. A whole bunch of workers with slitted eyes and dark hair from a defunct railroad company bunked in a two story structure. They chattered together, rarely conversing with anyone else. The commandante assigned them to maintaining the streets.

From time to time, the bands of soldiers came back, toting with them the bodies of slain Indians. Their fellow soldiers were laid to rest wherever they had fallen. Indian bodies were taken to the Arab, a young man with dark features. He examined the corpses, taking their hands in his and inspecting the fingernails. He opened the Indians' mouths and pulled at their teeth. 'Hatha kharaz gayed,' he murmured. He inspected their scalps and eyes, prodded at their abdomens with his fingertips. He paid the soldiers accordingly, then set to work piecing out the bodies and turning the various body parts into trophies and jewelry. Many times the soldiers, while they were out wandering the village, used the money they were given to buy a necklace with beads made from Indian teeth or a vial of crushed Indian bones. 'Wa tajaloka kawi la tohzam,' the Arab said. He made a motion to show them to mix it in a drink and imbibe it. He sold candles with wicks woven from human hair, the stock made from melted fat.

II

'Wake yer shit-splattered sorry ass up,' the cripple said. The mattress thumped the man from underneath. He started awake. The room was darker than before, more silent than before. Yet all who lived there were moving—silently dressing, pulling on their grey working outfits. 'Got to git outta bed fer the first shifters,' the cripple said.

The man slung his feet over the edge and jumped down. He undressed and pulled on his working greys. Bits of sand and grit combined with the canvas cloth of the uniform would rub his skin raw. No sooner had he pulled on his boots than the men began to file out of the bunkhouse. The cripple waved over his shoulder, beckoning the man to follow.

Outside it was only slightly lighter, the evening already setting into night. The man looked to the sky, expecting to locate a constellation, but found none. The entire sky was awash in black. The line of workers meandered between more buildings and through an archway. The girth of the passage would have become near impossible for an obese man—fortunately no such condition existed in the walls of this fort. At the end of an alleyway, a staircase steep as a boat ladder ascended up to a catwalk. Above him, the man could hear footsteps trooping across plankwood. He followed.

Once up on the catwalk, the man could see the fort for its vastness. They were high enough he figured he could see as far as he could on any mountaintop. Then he saw the fires set out far on the plateau. He looked to either horizon. There were more fires.

'Keep movin,' a voice said behind him. He felt a hand press against his back. Rather than argue he kept walking.

'Tis the niggers,' the cripple said, half turning around while he hobbled. 'Lettin us know they there. Old injun trick, a fire every five hundred feet, you in the middle.' He giggled like a child, covered his eyes with one hand, then removed it. 'They can see us, but we cant see them. Clever pricks.'

'Keep movin,' the voice shouted from up the line.

The men continued along the catwalk. The man could see the catwalk encircle an opening, the scaffolding descending into the depths, engulfed by shadows. A faint light showed from the hole. As seconds passed it grew brighter. For a moment, the man thought it might be a miracle of types, a sign like a falling star. Then the source of the light became evident: a shift of miners on a lift gathered around a lantern. They unloaded and the next group stepped on. Ropes began creaking and the lift—the light with it—descended into the shaft. As his night vision righted itself, the man looked out to the fires on the horizon. In the dark, the men shuffled forward, awaiting their turn to enter the mine.

As he awaited his turn to be lowered into the earth, the man surveyed the size of the structure—not necessarily the fort and village, but just the scaffolding alone. Such a thing must have taken years to construct. He tried to imagine the process, but could not.

Like we do, he related it to his own experience. He thought of his own time building his abode out on the plains, how he scrapped the wagon for parts, using the yoke as an upright. He pulled the boards from the wagon bed, then used a rock to pound the nails out of the planks. On the last plank, he became hasty, swung and missed the nail and sliced his finger open. Out here there was no call for him to cry out. Instead he sat on his haunches and sucked until the blood slowed to a trickle. Then he resumed his work.

From underneath the wagon, where the axle had splintered

apart, the man scrapped the iron fitting. He took the bolt from the hitch. In the evenings, when it became too dark to work, he sat running the bolt against a rock, attempting to file it down into a shiv. The coarseness of the iron rubbed his palms raw so he wrapped the handle in a scrap of cloth.

Finally, after some weeks disassembling his wagon, the man had constructed a frame of sorts for a hovel. He opened the footlocker and pulled out a bundle of sailcloth. Though one of the smaller sails, it still weighed a considerable amount. He stretched the sailcloth over the frame and used cord to lash it tight. Then he took the extra stretches of the cloth and stuffed them into the footlocker thinking perhaps he could use them later—who knows what this place would bring.

Tracking the caveman was easy enough. He lacked the cunning of most beasts the Indian had hunted over the years. Before the Indian set out, tracing the droplets of blood to their source, he ambled over to the mouth of the cavern to retrieve the rock he'd thrown. Not seeing it—for his eyes were cloudy with cataracts—he looked for any other implement he might use. He found where the throwing stone struck a stalactite, knocking it from the ceiling of the cave. Upon impact, the stone cone split laterally, creating a sharpened club. The ancient Indian took up the club, his elbow popping. He rested the weapon on his shoulder like a prehistoric Paul Bunyan.

Droplets of blood—bright against the flat stone of the ground—led the Indian to the wounded caveman. The protohuman sat on the ground, amidst his own feces, in a puddle of his own urine. He whimpered, held the side of his face and rocked back and forth. Blood matted down the fur on the back of his hand.

The old Indian squatted down to study the caveman. Only half aware of who the Indian was, the caveman peeked through his fingers at his assailant. He kept yelping, whimpering. This thing did not cry tears; it only called out in misunderstood pain. For he did not realize how imminent the danger really was.

The Indian stood, raising the stone club in the air. As he brought it down, the caveman, through some innate sensory system of danger, thrashed his arms. But it was too late. The club built too much velocity and broke on his forearm. The broken half continued on its path and bludgeoned the caveman. He fell backward, his eyes frozen in a wall-eyed fashion.

The last-second affront to the assault left the Indian sprawled out on the ground. He still held the stub of the weapon. He tried to let it go, but his hand wouldnt move. The Indian, aching more than when he first awoke, sat up. His arm dragged across the ground. Those two bones that make up the human forearm—the ulna and the radius—were snapped clean through. The skin bulged where the break occurred. Already blood pooled underneath, coloring the skin dark purple and stretching it into an unnatural sheen.

The commandante and commander met on a regular basis under amiable circumstances and conditions. They took turns inviting each other to their respective quarters. First the commander would invite the commandante to the fort. A lieutenant would show the officer to the headquarters, as it was termed.

'New bookcase,' the commander said as they took their seats. 'Brought in on that wagon we found out there on the far side of the plateau.'

'Fancy,' the commandante said.

'Next time we come cross a good find, we'll move it to your office,' the commander said. He took a green bottle and two short glasses from inside the bookcase and set them on the desk, poured some yellowed liquid into them.

'I wouldnt want anything that nice,' the commandante said. 'End up getting stolen, broken.'

The commander took a sip of his drink, asked if things were really that bad on the outside.

'Afraid so,' the commandante said.

'Should rein that in,' the commander said. 'Cant have anarchy surrounding my fort.'

The commandante looked down into his glass, swirled the beverage around into a whirlpool. 'Thing is,' he said, 'think the problem might be from your fort.'

The comment took the commander aback. He gulped down the rest of his drink and refilled the glass. 'That so?' he asked. 'What makes you figure?'

'It's the leave you give the soldiers, the freedoms. They come into the village and wreck the saloons. If they cant find a decent whore, they end up raping the girls. Lot of upset fathers out there.'

The commander nodded knowingly. He pursed his lips together after sipping at his drink. 'You have a solution.'

'Ive been thinking of one.'

'I figured as much.'

'You have to give me jurisdiction over the soldiers when theyre out in my village.'

'That can be done.'

'And if they commit a crime outside, I want to be able to get them after theyve gone back in the fort.'

'Believe thats called an extradition clause.'

'Call it what you like,' the commandante said. 'I need some justice to restore order.'

For a moment, the commander looked dissuaded. He took another sip of his drink, finishing this glass, then said, 'Alright. Fine.'

III

It took some time for the lift to descend the full length of the mineshaft. The man looked up as they descended. The stars were still blotted out by the smoke of the Indians' fires. Around him the air grew cold and damp and smelled of dirt and lichen and sulfur. Whatever system of pulleys and ropes they used to lower the men—ten in each load—the clamoring of the metal facets ceased once they passed the halfway mark.

'Tis a deep one,' the cripple said, tugging at the man's arm. 'Dug ourselves right under hell, thats what we say. One of these days we're goin to knock a support in place and knock the devil right off the jakes.' He laughed at the joke, but the other men on the lift paid him no mind.

Finally the lift came to rest by a horizontal shaft. The way was lit with oil lamps backed with tin plates. The man squinted against the light. 'Come on,' the cripple pulled the man by the arm. 'Got to walk from here.'

The men could walk upright, two abreast in this shaft. The floor was fairly even, the walls squared up nearly true. As they proceeded, the shaft became narrower, more stooped, and the men again fell into single file. Their path doubled back on itself and the man expected to re-enter the elevator shaft from another angle. But they did not. He conjectured after walking so far that this shaft cut underneath the lift. The oil lamps became fewer and farther between. Without question each man placed his hand on the shoulder of the man in front of him. The ceilings dropped even farther and the man readjusted his grip on the one in front of him. Now he held onto the man's pant waistband.

The line of people slowed. This particular space allowed the men to stand. At first the man thought they had finally come to their worksite. In the dim lamplight he saw what slowed their progression. The men had come to a shaft that descended at a sharp diagonal angle. A rope ran down the shaft and the men grabbed it and backed down the shaft slowly.

'Whatre we diggin up here?' the man asked the cripple as they waited.

'Nothing. Everything. We send the carts up through the vent shafts farther on. Those men get the privilege of sortin the goods.'

The man took the rope and stepped backward. He looked over his shoulder, trying to gauge how deep this shaft went. Some distance away he saw a lantern flit off and on; it was growing farther away as if he gave chase to a falling star.

Setting a bone was not a difficult task to perform on others. The Indian found it considerably more troubling to set his own bone. And seeing as he'd hurt his dominant arm, he lacked the dexterity needed for such an operation. For a while, he lay next to his slain predecessor. He thought about dying, how it might bring a closure to everything he'd seen. He thought better of it after a few minutes. Death only contributed to this world, creating yet another pocket in the earth of broken down carbons and fossilized remains. To die is to become a part of the world indefinitely. Fools will talk of achieving immortality through their works—they tell stories and create as if they were God—but in the end it all turns to dust. The places where your wondrous creations entertained others' imaginations become hollow spaces, cavities, for the world to fester.

The Indian rolled over. He felt cold, laid on his side. He curled into the fetal position and pinned the hand of his broken arm with his knee. With his good arm he felt the break in the bones and aligned where they needed to go. He gritted his teeth and gave his body a sudden jolt. The bones in the arm shifted, locked into where they had broken. Pain seared up his arm into his head; it clouded his vision and he howled in agony. A grease of sweat rolled out across his entire body. He lay on his back, chest heaving and howling until he could not catch his breath and he chomped at the air with futile gasps.

He knew what he had to do next. He tried to clear the pain from his thoughts and concentrate on bracing his arm. He rolled back over to his good side and threw his weight forward. His vertebrae cracked as he leaned forward. He blinked a few times, breathed through his nose. After a million years of existence, he still functioned. Few things are as resilient as the human body.

He looked to the slain caveman and the shard of rock that struck the deathblow. The Indian shuffled in a hobbled crab-walk fashion to the corpse. He took up the rock and set to work on the body.

At first the commandante merely fined the soldiers who caused disturbances in the village. If they started a fight in the saloon and broke a chair and tables, they were told to pay on the spot or expected to provide restitution. In the beginning the soldiers balked at the ultimatum and went back to the haven of the fort. But the commandante pursued them, found them. The commander went with him.

'Cant make me rightly pay,' a soldier would say.

'Take it right out of your wages,' the commander said.

The commandante had another method of assuring payment. 'Arab would pay good money to have a tuft of your ginger scalp,' he said. 'You pay the saloon four dollars for the furniture or I'll take it in hair.'

The soldier paid.

'Cant say I approve of threatenin the soldiers,' the commander said as they walked from the fort back out into the village.

'Take something from a man he never had,' the commandante said. 'That wont affect him, just feels like he never earned it. I wont take deducted wages.'

The commander weighed the logic and nodded his head. 'Some of the soldiers feel like theyre bein cheated out here in the village. Feel like theyre bein charged higher prices because theyre soldiers with a steady wage.'

'Hardly blame a business owner for meeting the market demands.'

The commander laughed. 'Just think it might be best to show some gratitude for the soldier's commitment to protectin the fort if they were a bit more reasonable in their barterin.'

The commandante weighed this statement and agreed. 'Done,' he said. 'The village will treat them as one of their own.'

The commander smiled. 'Appreciate it.' His smile faded quickly and he confessed that affairs inside the fort were almost more than he could bear.

'Hows that?' the commandante asked.

'Bein here,' the commander said, 'makes my men edgy. We do the excursions, sure, an they kill up a fair amount of injuns. But my numbers are dwindling, got fewer men than we came in with.'

'I see,' the commandante said. They walked past the Arab. 'Ayugad ladayka seyada?' he called out. The Arab waved and yelled back in his gibberish speech. He held up a jawbone on a leather lanyard, feathers stuck between the teeth.

The commandante responded in equal measure and laughed.

The Arab laughed in agreement. The commander, not being privy to the conversation, forced a smile.

The two officers kept walking. 'Didnt know you spoke other languages,' the commander said.

'A few.'

They strolled to the commandante's office, a cubby with a flapwood door, single latch on the outside. A thinned and scraped-down animal hide stretched over a window that set a good ten feet off the ground. They entered and sat on wooden chairs with rope backs at an old saloon table.

'Cant offer you anything but water,' the commandante said. 'Dont have liquor.'

The commander took a flat bottle from inside his coat. 'Not to worry,' he said. 'I got my comfort here, next to my heart.'

'Wish I could offer a solution to your personnel shortage,' the commandante said.

The commander threw his head back and slugged down some of the flask's contents. 'Could recruit from the village,' he said.

'You could,' the commandante agreed. 'Cant say many of the men would want to enlist.'

'Might be able to contract them out so theyre not full soldiers.'

'Make them mercenaries? Have them go out and hunt down the Indians?'

The commander shook his head. 'I know, it's a poor idea,' he said. 'Dont rightly know what to do.'

'Want a suggestion?'

'I would, yeah.'

The commandante leaned forward, rested his elbows on the table. 'Have the villagers take care of the fort like they do the town.' He held up his hand to keep the commander from interrupting. 'You probably got fifty, hundred soldiers tied up in keeping that fort running. Let my villagers do that work and pay them well.'

'And theyd be my men then?'

'Its only fair,' the commandante agreed.

Most all the young man's meals came from scavenging. Down near the grove of saplings—what he left of the saplings after constructing the hovel—he set up snares made of baling wire and twine. He watered the mule, carried back a canteen from the stream each day. Once or twice he rode the mule out a ways, studied the horizons, listened for anything not of this place. But there was nothing.

At night he lay outside the hovel, maybe building a small fire from twigs, grass and dry mule shit. When the flames dissolved into little more than glowing coals, he looked at the sky, found Andromeda, then located Cassiopeia. She was hanging upside down, his father would have noted. He sat up, intending to change the direction he was laying; he wanted to correct Cassiopeia, set her free.

But when he sat up, he saw a light on the horizon—another fire. This one glowed large as if a pyre meant to signal an army. The young man went to his hovel and found the shiv, placed it in his trouser pocket. Then he walked south and lay in the grass, waiting for morning, waiting for whatever was out there to come.

IV

The caveman's arm bones provided an adequate brace for the Indian's own arm. He lashed the skeleton pieces to his own arm with braids of the caveman's hair. He moved his arm. There was still considerable pain, but the brace of bone immobilized the broken point in the bones. It was as he had speculated—the skeleton of the protohuman, hard enough to crack the stalactite, would offer him decent protection as well as support. The Indian marveled at his own ingenuity.

Given this boost in confidence, he took the stone he'd used to sever the arm of the caveman and scrape the meat off the bones, and began cutting at the other arm. He cut the hand off at the wrist and set it aside. Then he cut the arm off at each joint, filleted the muscle. Strings of tendon clung to the osseous matter and he allowed them to stay. Stripping the body of flesh exhausted him. Blood and guts spilled out across the flat rock and he was covered in a viscera of bile and brains and sludge. He pulled the innards of the chest cavity out. When the work of emptying the gizzards from the body became too involved, he rested by using a corner of the rock to slake the skin off the severed hand.

For two days the Indian worked on the caveman's body—removing the bones, cutting muscle and tendon, twisting the skull free of the neck bone. He stopped only briefly to eat of the only food supply available. He set back to work, strapping the wet bones to his body—femur against his thigh, ribs wrapped around the trunk of his own body. He even took the skull, now void of brains, and chipped the crown away and made a helmet out of it. He laced the vertebrae together using long sinews taken from the protohuman's leg. It was a clumsy suit of armor, but it could take the load off his arthritic joints, relieve the ache in his bones soft and compacted with osteoporosis.

When he walked down from the mount, he carried only the lower jawbone of the caveman as a weapon. Other cavemen caught sight of him and hooted in displeasure. They ran hysterically through their horde pointing at the Indian as he approached. The bones clanked together disharmoniously. A rock flew up from the horde and was deflected by the ribcage of the armor.

The Indian paused and noted the suit's effectiveness. Then he flung himself, jawbone raised, into the crowd with a vengeance he'd not felt since he was a young man thousands of years from now.

⋆ ⋆ ⋆

Come first light, the young man assumed the hovel to be safe. Whoever was on the horizon in the night must have passed on. He walked toward the hovel.

'Hello,' a voice said. The young man spun around. Two men dressed in burlap sackings stood side by side. One had a stripe of a scar running the length of his neck and up into his hairline. The other used a walking stick.

'Crept up on me,' the young man said.

The men nodded. 'You have eat?' the scarred one asked. He made a motion as if feeding himself from the palm of his hand.

'No,' the young man said. 'No food here. Best if you an yer brother here move long.'

'Bitte, seine Sie gnawed if, Herr,' the one with the stick pled. 'Soldaten haven ins alles genomes, was wir hatten. Sie haben ins nackt zurueck glassen.'

'Caint rightly help you,' the young man said. He slid his hand into his pocket, grasped at the shiv. 'Just go on and git.'

'We coffee,' the scarred one said. Now he made a drinking motion, his fist acting as a cup.

'Verhoekere niche das einzige, was wir haben! Du machst einen Fehler,' the one with the stick cried. He slapped at his companion.

'Womit werden wir es brauen?' the scarred one asked. He turned his attention back to the young man. 'Please, Herr, good coffee.'

It had been some time since the young man had any coffee; since he'd smelled it. He figured the last time to be over in the bird islands, on the other side of the ocean. His father had traded a gunnysack of hogs' feet for fifteen pounds of beans. Some of the sailors boiled the beans whole, others smashed them and boiled them. The young man's father told him to take one bean at a time and suck on it; doing so would make it last longer and keep his piss from turning brown.

'Alright,' the young man said. 'Yeah. Lets see the coffee.' He nodded so the men knew what he meant.

'Ja gut,' the scarred one said. 'Good.' He reached into a sack slung across his back and pulled out a white bag, smelled it and closed his eyes. He staggered forward to hand it to the young man.

'Set it down,' the young man said. He pulled out the shiv and menaced the visitors. The scarred man dropped the bag and backed away.

'Nein,' the one with the walking stick cried. 'Das ist alles, was wir haben.' The rest of what he said became lost in sobs.

The young man edged forward, the shiv extended in front of him. He crouched and picked up the sack. Holding it to his nose, he inhaled deeply. The coffee might have been a little old, but it still had an aroma that reminded the young man of civilized places.

'Food,' the scarred one pled again. He placed his hands over his stomach and began to cry. 'Vor einer Woche haben wir mien Pferd des Fleisches wegen getoetet,' he said between sobs. 'Schönes Ding. Ein weißer Hengst.'

The man with the walking stick sat down in the grass, his legs stretched out in front of him. He sat and stared at his feet. 'Vielleicht wird er sich unserer erbarmen, wenn wir tot Sind, und uns begraben,' he muttered.

At that moment, the young man realized the error in his thinking. If he simply stole from these men who had nothing to lose, they would have no issue with returning later to kill him. They thought he was hoarding food, eating well. They must have not seen his mule by the stream and when they did there would be little to keep them from taking it. The young man pocketed his shiv. 'Alright,' he sighed. 'I got enough wood to build a fire, boil us up some leather straps. Give you somethin to gnaw on at least. Then you go north.' He pointed and repeated the word north.

That evening the young man took some of the reins he'd cut from the wagon and boiled them with grass and leaves. They each held a strap, sucking and chewing on it. The guests, wherever theyd come from, had not been on their own for long, and they would die soon enough. It was as the stranger would say in a couple months' time: this place is hard country.

'Coffee?' the scarred man asked.

The young man laughed and wagged his finger. 'Clever prick, aint you?' he asked. 'No. No coffee for either of youse. Done traded for it an I aint sharin.'

The lame man was already asleep, the wad of leather in his cheek, a hand over his belly. Not long after, the scarred one also fell to sleep. The young man lay across the doorway of his hovel, hoping that the beggars passing one way or the other might disturb him into wakefulness. He fell to sleep, his hand gripped around the shiv.

In his dreams, he was in a darker place than he'd ever been—a cave of some kind, a manmade cave. He was far from alone. In the shadows, men toiled away, hauling buckets of rocks and lengths of lumber in. An old man, a cripple, took him by the hand and led him ever deeper into the mineshaft. They passed oil lamps, which brightened the shaft for a minute's time. Then all went black until they came upon the next light. They traveled in this fashion—an alternating of light and dark—for a long ways. All the while the cold and damp of the mine became more pervasive.

'We all the way down here in the bowels of the mine,' the cripple explained. 'Dig, dig, dig. Thats what the commandante wants. Drought? Dig. Niggers on the horizon? Dig. Always digging.' The cripple took a lantern from a cross beam and when they came to an intersection of shafts they went into the darkest one. The cripple stopped briefly and held the lantern to illuminate a pile of tools on the floor.

'Grab yerself a spud bar,' he said. The man did as he was told and hefted up the iron rod. It was a simple instrument, three feet long with a flat end and a beveled end. The cripple grabbed a sledge hammer leaned up against the wall. 'First ones in this part of the shaft today,' the cripple said. 'Means we get first pick where to dig.'

He set the lantern down and wandered a short distance to where rocks and boulders cluttered the tunnel.

'Looks to've fallen in,' the man said. 'Caint say I want to dig there.'

'This shaft,' the cripple said, 'aint ours. Go through here an we're in a different place altogether.' He chuckled and his laughter echoed in the shaft. 'Come now,' he said. 'We have work to do.'

It didnt take long for the commander to summon the commandante to his office. He appeared more haggard than a few days before, when the commandante last saw him. Bags were under his eyes, his hair and uniform unkempt.

'Your men,' he began. Then he paused and uncorked a bottle, held the bottle at ready. 'Dont know a goddamned lick of English.' He drank.

The commandante nodded. 'It's a common thing out in the village. We got all types out there. They speak a common language though.'

'An whats that?'

'Barter. Money. Trading—whatever means they have to survive.'

The commander sniffed. Set the bottle down. It was mostly empty now. 'Money,' he said to himself, then directed his gaze at the commandante. 'And whats this bout chargin my men a tax?'

The commandante feigned a moment's worth of confusion. 'Thought we had agreed to treat your soldiers like my villagers. Remember, they were being charged an exorbitant—'

'I recall,' the commander interrupted. 'What I dont rightly remember is you addin a tax.'

'It's what the villagers pay.'

Leaning forward on the desk, the commander asked what happened to the villagers who welched on the tax.

'It's a loss in revenue,' the commandante explained calmly. 'As the officer of the village, I have to collect on the loss. I send the people to the Arab. He takes what he thinks is fair.'

The commander slugged back the last of the bottle's contents. 'Explain that part,' he said. 'About the Arab. Tell me why he cut the heart out of one of my men for failing to pay a tax he didnt know existed.'

'That soldier was a half breed. Part Mexicano. A Mexican dried heart on a chain is said to be good luck.'

For a time, the two men sat quietly—the commander staring at the floor, his eyes bloodshot, beads of sweat rolling down the back of his neck, dark spots under his arms. The commandante watched. Often times, and usually at death, people speak of plans. They saw whatever happened, no matter how heinous, that it was part of some otherworldly schema. The commandante could have lied, said it was part of some plan. The truth was worse though—this was simply the way of the world.

'Probably could have saved your man if you spoke either language,' the commandante said.

'You speak the Arab's language,' the commander said. 'And it aint savin him.'

'Hows that?'

The commander smiled. 'Soon as you stepped in here my men—the ones who speak English—cut that Arabian nigger to pieces.'

The commandante was not surprised. He raised his eyebrows and sighed. 'I didnt come in here looking to start a war,' he said. 'I think it might be best to say we reached a balance.'

'You plannin on lifting the taxes on my men?'

'No,' the commandante said. Then he asked how the commander planned to talk to his civilian workers.

'Maybe I should talk with them through money,' he said. 'It is their common language.'

The commandante feigned amusement. 'Very good,' he said. 'But if you wanted to sidestep the payment part, I could speak to them.'

'Know ever tongue of ever man in the village, do ya?'

'Yes.'

As he opened the side drawer of the desk, the commander did not take his eyes off the commandante. He pulled out another small glass flask. This one only had a couple fingers of liquid in the bottom. A drag of backwash hung suspended in the alcohol. He waited a good long time, studying the commandante. He swigged down the alcohol.

'Alright,' he said. 'Suppose your jurisdiction will expand since youre interpreting for my troops.'

'It would make sense.'

Under his breath, the commander cussed.

The commandante interrupted. 'Place like this cant have two minds—cant be two things,' he said. 'Let me give out the orders over all of the fort and I'll make certain theyre your commands.' He placed a hand over his heart. 'Be your words spoken through me.'

Conversation had worn on the commander, he slumped forward in the chair as if fending off sleep. From around his neck, he pulled at a lanyard. There was a key on it. He unlocked another desk drawer, took out a box and used another key to unlock it. He pulled out the pistol. 'Know what this is, dont you?' He pointed it at the commandante.

'I do.'

'Got this from a general at the fort before we were sent out,' he said. 'Only one in the whole company with a gun. Armys going to issuin a gun to each soldier. We were told to pick up rifles at a place up north, a big fort with plenty a rations.'

The commandante shifted in his seat. 'Suppose you have one gun,' he said. He made a gesture like he held an insect between his thumb and forefinger. 'You take it out of the box, it's the same as firing a bullet. Everything happens so fast you cant possibly chase it down, cant put a bullet back in the chamber.'

'Aint gonna want to take my bullets back,' the commander said. He put the gun back in the box, the box back in the drawer. 'Just remember when youre speakin for me, who has got the power.'

V

Anything that resembled a human, the Indian laid waste to. He found families huddled in caves and set a fire at the mouth. If they ran through the flames and smoke, he cut them down with the sharpened jawbone. From a mountain ledge he watched nomads pass by; then he dropped rocks on them, watched their bodies buckle and fall.

Every few years he stopped and made repairs to his suit, tightened the bones fast to his skin. Any hair he had prior to the suit was now worn away. He took strips of hide and made intricate coverings for his hands, a chin strap for the skull cap. Neanderthals saw him coming and they either ran and hid or hooted, fists pumping in the air. The Indian slayed them with indifference. He wandered to one side of the known world and looked out on the black and tumbling sea, mist flying up the air. Far out a whale curled to the ocean surface and spewed a plume of water into the air. The Indian picked up handfuls of sand and let it run through his knotted knuckles. Then he walked back through the mountains where someday strip mines would peel away the countryside. He went through a pass not yet discovered by Lewis and Clark and wandered deep into a murk of forest and glade. Alligators, bigger than any man, wagged through the swamps, slept half submerged. When one reared up at the Indian, its mouth scissoring open, he moved swiftly to one side and brought his jawbone dagger down through the animal's eye. He paused for a day and extracted the teeth from the alligator, strung them with a strip of its hide and wore them across his chest like a bandolier.

Ever farther west, he encountered great wooled tusked beasts that trundled through drifts of snow. He watched the Neanderthals attack in packs and wrestle them to the ground, hacking at the baying beasts with clubs and spears. They pulled the muscle out from under the fur and ate it while the animal still writhed. When the Neanderthals were finished, the Indian killed the hunters as they had killed their prey.

He came to an edge of the plains fenced in by mountains that jutted from the earth with sharp fury. Instead of walking into their depths, he turned and walked their length, keeping them in the periphery of his right eye. The farther he traveled, the warmer it became. He ate scant meals of whatever he could find—insects and cobwebs, leaves and compost. He did not stop to defecate, preferring to shit as he walked. For weeks he did not sleep, progressing through night and day alike. Above him the sky spun like a pinwheel out of control—stars rotating and moving, swarms of stray stars streaking across the night, the sun blazing away on the same terminal path day after day.

The mountain range merged with his path and he climbed hills populated with conifers. As he walked, he pulled the pinecones from the boughs and licked the sap from the barbs. What few humans he saw here he also killed, in one fashion or another. Some time later he camped in the woods, made a territory for himself. He wandered there a good many years, waiting for a proper man to appear, waiting for the stranger to come. He took bundles of sticks and sharpened the ends, made a fence of pylons to ensnare a hasty invader. But none came. He constructed perches in the highest trees so he could see out for miles in each direction. Still there was nothing. Eventually he came to expect his body to give out. No body—even with a suit of human bones—is expected to last a billion years. He lay in his encampment, letting the moss grow around him, letting his body sink interminably into the topsoil. He closed his eyes like the stranger would so many years from now in his mineshaft bed. He tried to think of another lifetime before this one. But he could not; his own life covered everything now.

A screech pierced the night and the Indian opened his eyes.

The sky, more than ever, swarmed with flitting fleeing stars. Close on the horizon a concussion arose and the sky went awash in what looked like a sustained flash of lightning. Trees blew over and the forest rumbled. The Indian pulled himself up from the soil and ran toward the source of the pandemonium. He ran through trees that stood like pillars of fire. Flames reached out and lashed at his skin. His skin melted and fused with the bone suit. He sloshed through a steaming creek, dead fish floating atop the bubbling water. The hillside he climbed on all fours felt as if the soil had been tilled and left to dry. When he reached the top of the bluff he looked down into a crater as big as the base of any mountain. Screams seared from the center of a giant hole, a ring of fire belted out in every direction. Other meteors pelted the distant skies. The immense heat from the center of the hole radiated the Indian's body, blistering his skin and shriveling his nipples and penis into nothing. What hair he still had—his eyelashes and pubis—turned to cinder. The constant rush of wind and sirens of heat deafened him. His eyes felt roughened as if sand was thrown into them. This, he imagined, is what it is like to watch the world end. In the recesses of his mind, he compared this to his childhood and knew that no, this was not the end of the world; this was the beginning of the modern era. He dropped the jawbone dagger, backed up and ran headlong, leaping into the crater.

The young man awoke before the beggars. He rifled through their burlap sacks and found nothing except a lock of hair and a child's shoe. When they finally awoke a couple hours later he told them to go. 'North,' he said and pointed. He signaled they would find food out that way. 'Lots a food,' he said.

'Thank you,' the scarred man said over and over again. They took their sacks and tottered off into the north country.

The young man resumed his daily rituals of checking snares and gathering mule dung. He practiced throwing rocks he had pulled from the river at birds. More often than not he hit the fowl. He rode his mule up the slough to the south and let it graze while he scanned the horizon. Weeks passed without incident.

One day on his return trip from the slough, he came to a creek, where he hitched his mule. Several burros drank from the creek, a dark-skinned man with a mustache stood next to them.

'Hola,' he said and smiled.

The young man slowed his step and looked at each of the Mexican's animals. Their backs were piled high with bundles and wicker baskets. 'Afternoon,' the young man said.

'Vimos a tu casa arriba,' the Mexican said. He pointed north, toward the man's hovel. 'Varios hombres—uno débil—dijo que venga aquí.'

A few wagons trundled in on the horizon with more Mexicans. They had dogs. A few women, clad in rags, rode on the back of one of the wagons. When they saw the creek, they jumped down and ran to the water. One stripped down to nothing and jumped into the stream, screaming. Another did not move from the wagon. '¿Usted piensa que ellas nos traerán a un buen precio?' He raised his eyebrows at the young man. When one of the women stood, he groped at her breast, said bien over and over.

'Yeah,' the young man agreed. 'Bien.'

'Le daré una de mis mujeres aquí,' the Mexican said. 'Si usted nos da comida.' He made the familiar eating motion.

'Aint got any food.'

'¿No hay comida?'

'None.'

The last woman finally slid from the wagon and began to waddle over to the creek. She was with child. A couple wagon hands chided her, followed her, exaggerating her gait. One man spat on her. She came to creekside and bent with great difficulty to drink. 'Esta cabrona se lo dió a un hombre gratis,' the Mexican said. He made a motion like he was humping the air. 'Le digo a mis mujeres que chupan a los hombres. Pero ella lo hizo entre sus piernas.' He looked down on her with contempt.

The woman cupped her hand and slurped up some water. She rubbed her face. One of the other women sat next to her and felt her swollen belly. The young man studied her. 'What'll you do with her?' he asked, pointing to the pregnant woman.

'La perra está dañada,' the Mexican said. He made a face like he ate something bad. Then he smiled. 'Pero todavía funciona la boca.' He made a motion like he was performing fellatio. He laughed.

The woman heard the words and understood them, but she continued washing her arms in the stream. A couple tears rolled down her cheeks. The young man, even confronted with the nude whore bathing in front of him, could not look away from the pregnant woman. 'I'll give you food,' the young man said. He did not take his eyes off the woman. 'I have meat and roots—I could make a stew. Have some coffee too.'

'¿El café?' the Mexican asked. He smiled, then his eyes sharpened. ¿Qué desea usted?'

'I just want her to stay here with me,' the young man pointed to the pregnant woman. 'This is a better place for her—better place for a child.'

Chiseling at the rock was a two man job, the cripple explained. One man needed to hold the spud bar in place—one hand on the shaft, the other near the flat end. The other man swung the hammer into the spud bar. The motion was repeated over and over. Chips of rock flew up amidst sparks. The racket came from all around, echoing through the corridors and amplifying off the walls.

'Signal to stop?' the cripple asked. 'If youre holdin the bar, you place your thumb over the hammer end.' He laughed and shook his head. 'Remember though that we switch places every half hour. Smash my thumb and it'll be my turn next.'

The man nodded. They commenced working. The cripple swung the hammer into the spud bar. Vibrations shot up the man's arms and pulsated into his head. He opened his mouth so his teeth wouldnt clap together. The cripple swung again and the rocks splintered, sending shards of stone at the side of the man's face.

'Stop,' the man said. The cripple swung again. The joints in the man's wrists and arms clapped together violently. His eyes seemed to shake in his head. He scrunched his eyes shut and placed his thumb over the butt end of the bar. He held his breath and waited for the next blow.

'Quittin already?' the cripple asked.

'Think we could switch places?' the man asked.

Initially there was some opposition to the commandante's rule of law inside the walls of the fort. Soldiers talked in the saloon of how commandante wasnt even a recognized rank in the American army.

'Where'd this fella come from?' one asked.

'Heard he was here all by hisself, like a hermit,' another said. 'Commander let him stay round just to make him happy.'

'I say if he lived out here like a nigger, we shoulda killed him same as a nigger.'

A chorus of agreement rose up from the saloon.

'Hes crazy,' one soldier shouted.

Another chorus more adamant than the first resounded.

'Why's he got all those villagers diggin a mineshaft here inside the fort?'

'Gave em our bunkhouse too.'

'Cause he done killed half the soldiers round here for breakin rules.'

The more the soldiers drank and the more they told stories, the more enraged they became. 'Figure we should go out and string that commandante up by the flagpole,' one suggested. 'Skin the sumbitch alive.' Soldiers nodded, pretending to agree with this approach soberly. 'Least a hundred of us left; no way he can overpower us.'

'Thats right,' a new voice said from the doorway. It was the commandante. The room became quiet. Men sat with their eyes downcast at their drinks, their hands cupped round their mugs. 'Here I am,' the commandante said. He held up his hands to show that he carried no implements. 'You'—he singled out the last soldier to speak—'could stand up right now, break that mug and use a shard to cut me right here.' He traced his finger down his neck. 'Major vein right there—the carotid artery—bleed to death before I could even curse at you.' He walked amongst the tables, looking down on each man, each soldier avoiding his gaze. 'I never did nothing without your commander's approval,' he said. 'Not a tax, nor a decree. I never gave an order on my own. If I did, this world would be a different place. You could kill me, yes. But it wont make a difference.'

'Our commander is doing this?' one very drunk soldier asked.

'Yes.'

'Our military commander is treatin us like commoners, while the villagers live like kings.' It was half a question and half a statement. The commandante did not answer directly.

'I am in charge of civilian affairs—village dealings you might call them,' he explained. 'If you want to be treated as I treat my men, perhaps you should institute a change in command.'

FOUR

I

The Indian awoke and coughed. He tried to move, but found his arms and legs to be pinned. He could see nothing—not because his eyes did not work, but because, like a billion years ago, he was buried somewhere. The smell was familiar enough; although everything becomes familiar after so many years in this world. He wiggled his fingers and found whatever his casing was to be pliable. He shifted his body and pressed his arms against the sides of his packed container. There was a splintering and finally a prolonged crack. Mulched wood scattered as the hollowed log split apart. The Indian pushed one half of the log aside and stepped out. He still wore his skeleton armor and he noticed how the bones fitted better now. His body was more filled out, muscular, younger and taller. He could not remove these bones if he desired. The flames from the crater had fused them to his skin.

After he stopped marveling at himself, he looked up and found a tribe of Indians watching him in amazement. This log was in the middle of an encampment. Men, women and children all stood frozen, watching this man who emerged from a rotting log examine himself.

First the Indian addressed them as friends, then he told them in their tongue how he was sent here on a quest to destroy a stranger. A billion years is a long time to stew on vengeance. The Indian smelled the air, fresh with conifer resin and light smoke. Hes here, the Indian assured them. In this time, the stranger walked amongst them. Then he asked who would join him and if they had a horse.

It felt like a lifetime had passed when the man and the cripple rode the lift to the mouth of the mine. They were soaked through with cave dew and sweat. The man's arms were numb from swinging the sledge and holding the spud bar. A throbbing pain swelled in his head. When they reached the top, the world was bright and the light stabbed at the man's eyes. He placed his hand over his face and groaned.

Once his eyes adjusted, he removed his hand. Veils of smoke hung limp in the air around the entirety of the fort. Soldiers stood at ready by the gate, sabers drawn from their sheaths. A lookout was stationed at the highest point on the scaffolding.

'Places still standing,' the cripple said. 'Good news, I suppose.'

'This a common thing?' the man asked. 'Injuns attackin the fort, I mean.'

'Cant say it is,' the cripple said. 'We usually keep them farther out. To them this place is death.'

The next shift of men, awakened not long ago, walked past them on the catwalk. The cripple grabbed one man by the sleeve and asked what was going on. 'Hell out there, brother,' the miner said. 'Commandante said we'd all be safer in the tunnels—said to go as deep as we could.' The miner kept walking.

Once they reached the bunkhouse all of the miners were abuzz with speculation. 'Redskin niggers finally gonna have their way with us,' one said. 'Done killed too many of em.'

The cripple limped over to talk with the man, telling him stories of Indians he'd met in his time. The man climbed up to his top bunk. Warmth from whoever was sleeping there minutes before still radiated in the straw mattress. He closed his eyes and blocked out the din of the returning miners. He thought of his woman—of the boy she was sure to have birthed by now.

He recalled the day the band of Mexicans left, taking with them the wagons and the women, the burros stuffed full with rations. They took the last of the man's coffee and a few rodent pelts as a payment for the pregnant woman. She sat on the ground, used her fingers to comb through her hair. She hummed to herself. The man walked over and offered her some boiled roots. First she smelled the thin soup and then wrinkled her nose.

'Not much a life out here,' the man said. 'But it can be alright sometimes. It's quiet.'

The woman avoided looking him in the eyes. She nodded. 'Por favor no duela al bebé,' she said, sliding her hand over her womb. A tear welled in her eyelashes, gained mass and trickled down her face. 'Este bebé es mi salvavida.'

The man, as if he understood the words of the woman, knelt and stroked her cheek with his thumb. 'I'll do whatever I need to do to protect that child,' he said.

* * *

The soldiers found the commander cowering in the village office of the commandante. They brought him back to the fort, barely sober and shackled. Rumor had it the soldiers were searching for him and they intended to hang him in the courtyard. He had fled and hid in the only spot of the village he knew intimately.

'Youre a son of a bitch,' he said. He spat on the ground just shy of the commandante's boots.

'This sumbitch'll treat us better than you,' the lieutenant said.

By now the soldiers—albeit fewer in number—had gathered around. The civilians were also roused and came to the opened gate of the fort to inspect the scene. Bystanders related what they thought to be the case to those who sidled up. The commandante held up his hand and a quiet settled on the crowd. He smiled at the commander. 'This man has done nothing wrong,' he said. 'Hes not done anything right either.' A few people laughed. 'We cant kill him.' Now the crowd stirred, the soldiers murmured to each other. 'We will turn him out into the village and he will be treated like a stranger. Let him scavenge for food and make his life by taking from others. Here, in this fort, I am now the ranking officer.' A few weak cheers resounded at this last sentence.

The commander tried to plead his case, but the crowd jostled him back out of the fort into the open space before the gate. They took turns beating him and urinating on him, kicking dust onto his wet body. He coughed and cried, lay curled up on the ground. They stripped him of his uniform and left him naked.

II

Order fell on the fort in the most natural of fashions. The power of the commandante remained a mystery to his own men, yet they dared not to explore it. He would make a decree and the men did as they were told. The role of the soldiers was reduced to the level of hired help—cleaning the barracks, overseeing the construction of the mine, tending to the commandante's personal needs. The gate of the fort was ordered to stay shut, only to open to those who knew of Indians' whereabouts.

He obsessed over the Indians. It had been years—decades even—since the Indian boy disappeared. Questions of time nagged at his mind. He wondered if the Indian would be cunning enough to figure a way back; if the boy possessed the lack of humanity necessary to survive the throes of history. He wondered if the Indian had seen all the things he saw, if he saw the world for the beautiful heap of bones and flesh and blood it was.

Outside the walls of the fort, the village degenerated into mayhem. The commandante refused to extend his rule of law over them. They can establish a government, law and order, if they wish, he told the soldiers. At one point they had a system of government; they have chosen to give it up. Somewhere amongst them, the commander trifled, stole and begged. He took to wandering from rooftop to rooftop and marauding the newcomers to town.

In the streets, children ran and played, scamming outsiders with gimmick trades. Vendors and buskers crowded each other, fought and argued. At the bar, women whored and the men drank. Waste filled the streets, stinking in the height of day and sinking into a low stench at night.

Because the village had become such a place of madness, the fort itself became more self-sustaining. The men, civilian residents and soldiers alike, had their jobs working in either the mine or the day to day fort operations. Most days they only worked and slept. The miners with their twelve hour shifts were notably routine. Then, on payday, the men of the fort rejoiced.

Fort James had its own commissary and saloon. As it was the only store within the fort's walls, the men had to go there to buy anything. Rarely did they ever see cash; everything was bought on credit and recorded in a ledger by the saloonkeeper. He shared his book only with the commandante.

The men sat and drank, told stories. They might dance. Since there were no women to speak of inside the fort, some of the men would drink their fill then fornicate in the jakes. Often times, the men who enjoyed sitting and drinking would recall the history of Fort James; of the commandante's career.

'Fought in the Injun wars,' a miner might say. 'Thats why he done got injuns on his mind. Cant stop killin em.'

'This place is built on some injun burial ground,' another said. 'Found some nigger's bones down in the mine—down about twenty rods.' Jeers of disbelief rose up from the bar. 'You could ask my partner, if he spoke American, that is.'

The men laughed and the first miner joked that the commandante built the fort here just to piss off the niggers. There wasnt any other earthly reason for this place.

★ ★ ★

The Indian and his pack of men roved the western lands of America. They went through areas unchartered and unnamed. They crafted crude weaponry from petrified trees and arroyo rocks. At night, when the stars spun in a kaleidoscope menagerie in the sky above, the Chief—as he had been dubbed—told stories of the world to come. He told of a time—and now was the dawn of that time—when beasts in the body of humans would massacre their tribes. The men, he told his fellow Indians, would look decent enough: their clothes were fine and cut to their bodies; their hair and teeth would be cleaner; their eyes would be vibrant shades. But underneath, these people were feral animals. Do not let them speak, he warned. Dash their brains out with a stone. Rap them in the backbone with a stick. Rip their throats out before they can cry for help.

One of the tribesmen asked if the Chief wore the bones of a white man. The Chief shook his head, said the bones were of a common ancestor. He thought that if he killed the men who came before him, it could change the world. But it did not.

Another tribesman asked why they lived as they did then. If history could not change the world, why did they roam the mountainsides looking for white men? The Chief sighed, said there would be a man—a stranger—who called those he encountered friends. He held up his index finger, the boned finger flexing with it, and warned that this stranger was no friend. But this animal of a human, this stranger, he could shape history.

Still another tribesman asked how they would find this stranger. The Chief seemed to anticipate the question. He simply replied that the universe was a small place and there was plenty of time.

The man wasnt asleep but an hour when the clamor of the other men in the bunkhouse woke him. The cripple pulled on his boots.

'Niggers done attacked the village,' he said. The men shoved past each other to exit the bunkhouse. Outside, in the courtyard, the soldiers braced the gate with wooden beams. Up along the top of the walls more soldiers kept watch on the village below. Plumes of smoke bellowed up into the air. The tips of fire lapped at the side of the fort.

'Cant tell how many there are,' the lieutenant reported to the commandante. 'Smokes too thick to see.'

The commandante nodded and walked to the gate. 'Open the slot,' he said to a sergeant. The soldier did as he was told, standing clear of the porthole. The panel slid open and an Indian's face, teeth gritted, looked back through.

'Goddamn!' a soldier yelled. Another stepped in front of the commandante and ran his saber through the opening, through the throat of the Indian.

With the view now clear, the commandante studied the melee. 'Yes,' he said to himself, nodding. He held his coat by the lapels. 'This is what I thought it was.'

A woman ran through the street, naked from the waist up. A rock on a rope intersected her path and crushed her skull.

She collapsed dead. Another villager, the black stablehand, was maimed, but still alive. He took a knife from his boot and slashed his wrist and looked to the sky.

'What'll we do?' the lieutenant asked.

'Let the village burn.' The commandante walked to the opposite side of the courtyard and, before entering his office, he turned around. 'Might want to head down into the mines and dig. Probably our only hope of salvation.'

The men from the bunkhouse heeded the commandante's words and fled to the tunnels. In the narrow alley leading to the scaffolding, several men were trampled to death, including the cripple. A few more fell from the scaffolds. As the man passed by the wall on the highest scaffold, he could see the village below. Like the other men, he slowed to see the destruction. Indians, no more than a dozen, leapt from rooftop to rooftop, trolling the alleys. Bodies of villagers lay strewn in the streets, half hanging out of windows. Fires everywhere chugged black smoke into the air.

'Hurry up,' a miner called from behind. He shoved at the man and they kept walking.

Men loaded onto the lift until it creaked under the weight of its burden. They descended rapidly. Some men, braver and dumber, slid down the cables or scaled the walls. As they descended, the men on the lift debated what they should do.

'Commandante says tunnelin is gonna be the only way out,' one said.

'Dont mean anything, we're too far down to poke our heads out elsewhere.'

'Theres an old mine shaft farther down—looks to be from another mine,' the man volunteered.

'You was workin with the old fool, the man with the crooked back.'

'Thats right.'

'Old fool found an old shaft, eh?'

The man said it was so. 'Looked to be all caved in on itself,' the man said. 'Wasnt keen on workin on it. Figured it might bury us alive.'

'God willing,' the miner mumbled. Then said to the rest that they were going to find this other tunnel. 'One thing for certain—we aint gonna come back out to the same place we done left.'

III

Life on the plains was never easy. It never would be. Years after the man died, the Dust Bowl would torment the land. Tornados would funnel down from strange skies and assail the earth—some coasting by established farmhouses, some uprooting whatever lay in its way.

For now though the man and the woman cohabitated in peace. He fixed her meals and fetched water. He dared not to touch her for fear that the baby inside of her might somehow become damaged. In the evenings he built small fires so he could look at her. They each spoke in their respective languages, though neither knew exactly what the other said.

'No hay razón para que usted me detiene aquí,' the woman said.

'Havin you here is a godsend,' the man said. 'I was content to live out the rest a my life alone.'

They sat in the hovel and the woman inspected her surroundings—the pan with the low light of a grease wick, the slat and dirt floor, the canvas walls. Outside night had long since fallen. 'No debemos quedarnos aquí,' she said.

'Someday I'll build you a place right here,' the man promised. 'Place with walls and a proper door—a couple rooms.'

The woman reclined and rubbed her abdomen.

'Everything alright?' the man asked. Any action denoting pain prompted this reaction from the man. The woman closed her eyes and laid her head on the wad of sail that served as her pillow.

'La mayoría de los hombres no les importan si estoy embarazada,' she said. 'Me dicen que soy una mujer suelta.'

The man scooted across the floor and stroked her forehead. 'That sounds good,' he said.

'Dijeron que a los hombres todavía les gustan los cenos. Dijeron que sería mi especialidad.'

The man nodded knowingly and shushed her. Then he lay next to her, watching her breathe until the flames in the pan flickered and extinguished altogether.

The Chief led the men through smelters and deserts, gulched places where cacti lorded over them like structures of ancient men. He took them in and out of the folds of mountains. They waded across streams, swam across rivers. When they encountered a wagon with a light-skinned family riding into the steppes of the mountains, they rode in from all sides, the Chief on his white horse. With nowhere to go, the man driving the wagon stopped, reached under the bench and pulled out a bullwhip. The woman touched her forehead, stomach and each shoulder, clasped her hands. She hurriedly said a few words. The children covered their faces.

When nothing was left of the family, the Indians burned the wagon and continued on. They trooped deep into the woods and found a duck trap—a contraption of thin sticks bound together with cord. The Chief ordered the Indians to watch the creek. The next day a man dressed in furs, wearing a beaver tail as a bib, came and checked the trap. The Chief stood on the opposite bank of the creek.

The duck trapper hardly started when he noticed the Chief. 'Je peux échanger,' he said and showed off a vest of deerskin. 'J'ai obtenu...'

The Chief watched in mild amusement as the man twirled like a dancer and pointed to his moccasins, saying they were made from coon hide. He watched the facade of the duck trapper crumble. He looked at the trap in the water. 'Si vous me permettez de m'en aller, je vous,' he said, 'donne tout ce que j'ai.'

In time all languages sound the same—in a million years the hooting and baying of a caveman sounds the same as the romance of a European tongue.

'Il ne travaille pas comme ça,' the Indian said.

The duck trapper looked up just as one of the tribesmen crept behind him and dropped a rock on his head. His eyes bruised over immediately and blood spilled out of his ears. He smelled of shit. The Indians undressed him and floated his body down the river.

Killings of this sort became more and more common over the years. Every now and again, a fellow might put up a fight and mortally wound one of the tribesmen. For the most part though, men realize when their time is up and they simply resign their last living moments to degradation—always crying and begging, their bowels letting loose and them laying face down in the dirt.

Such was the case with the cabin near a mineshaft deep in the mountains. A few men bunked inside and cursed at one another. Had they not kept a lantern burning inside, the Indians might have passed them by. Now they circled the cabin. The one with an ax knocked the door from its hinges. The men inside, who until a moment ago were bragging about their hunting kills and how many women they had bedded, shrieked. One covered his face like the children of the wagon and peed himself. When they were finished with the cabin, the Indians laid what they could of the men in their bunks, shut what was left of the door and shoved the cabin over the precipice.

Some time later, the Indians watched from a ledge as a man on a mule passed below. They rode down from the ledge and crept up on the man. He rode with his eyes closed, seemingly asleep, then momentarily waking. The Indians stalked him for days and watched his paranoia mount. On their second day of following the man, he hid in the woods, then scrambled up a steep slope to sleep on a perch.

When the man awoke and came down to his mule, the Indians were waiting for him. The man bumbled and made the usual pleadings, saying he wasnt worth killing. He was right, of course. Most people, as the Chief knew, didnt deserve anything they received. Then the man called them friends—amigos. The Chief drew near and examined the man as one might examine their destiny in the stars. The words that passed from the man's mouth were not his own, but borrowed from another person in another time. He signaled to his tribesmen to take the mule; they would follow this man to the ends of the earth.

In his office, the commandante sat in the chair at his desk. His time was near. He took the box containing the pistol from the desk drawer and the census book from the bookcase. Without much time he had to work quickly. He drew the knife from his boot and cut vigorously at the pages in the book until he had hollowed a spot big enough to house the box. After concealing the box in the book and placing it back in the bookcase, he removed the lanyards with the keys from around his neck and put them into the desk drawer. The usual thoughts of a man in his final hours circulated through the commandante's mind. He told himself that it wasnt supposed to be this way. There was a plan for him.

Outside he could hear the muted pandemonium. He exited the office and the noise grew. The others atop the wall shouted down a blow by blow account of the village's destruction to their comrades. One foolish soldier opened the slot in the gate to watch the mayhem himself and an Indian slopped a bucket of hot oil through the hole and scorched the man's face. He collapsed to the ground, screaming and clawing at his eyes. The Indian ran away and the others shut the slot. A fellow soldier took out his saber and lanced his burnt comrade through the heart.

The commandante walked up to the lieutenant. 'Place looks empty,' he said.

'Most all the civilians is down in the mine, diggin like you told em.'

The commandante sighed, said he wished they would hurry up. Then he ordered the soldiers to open the gate, let him out. No one moved.

'Ya dont wanna go out there,' the lieutenant said.

'I know it.' The commandante stared straight ahead as if he could see through the gate. 'Let me out and bolt the gate behind me.'

The lieutenant exchanged glances with his fellow soldiers. 'Alright, sir,' he said. 'Whats the password gonna be to git back in?'

This made the commandante chuckle. 'Wont be comin back in,' he said. He waved his hand and the soldiers hefted the doors open. The world outside—the noise, dust and smoke—blasted through the aperture like a blast furnace. The commandante readied his dagger and stepped out from the fort.

IV

In the mines the men toiled—clearing boulders and shoveling the graveled remains of boulders. Wisps of dirt feathered down from overhead. They moved without regard for the integrity of the tunnel, without care of taking their loads atop. Soon they had nearly sealed themselves in the passage. The man used his spud bar to knock a path through the rocks in case they needed to retreat.

'Hurry up,' a miner yelled.

Another shouted for them all to be quiet over and over again until they lowered their voices to groveling and the miner tapped on the sheet of piled boulders with his hammer. Somewhere in the depth beyond an echo called out its hollow message, each time repeating lower and lower until it disappeared into the abyss completely. As soon as the noise faded, the men snapped back into action, working at twice the pace they had before. Some men, upon finding a pocket of loose-packed rocks, straddled their find and dug with both hands like dogs. One man in the backswing of his hammer clubbed a man in the back of the head, killing him instantly. Another, who had worked and become a brawny fellow by slaving in the mines, wedged a spud bar into a crack, gripped a mallet with both hands and brought his entire force down on the tool. The hairline fissure scattered and spread. He struck it again and pebbles fell like rain on all who worked. He struck the bar a third time and the stones gave way. A hollow rattle of rocks falling into the sealed corridor brought on another sustained silence amongst the men.

Suddenly there was a concussive blast—first a flash of light, then a gust of wind and finally the roar and heat. The men near the opening were shredded by the force of the air and vestiges of their flesh flew back on the other men. The walls buckled and the ceiling caved in.

The Chief and his men followed the man at a distance. The man seemed to know he was being watched. He traveled incessantly, at all hours of the day, at different paces. The Indians pursued. From distant perches, the tribesmen signaled one another, triangulating the man's whereabouts. They kept a distance substantial enough to ensure the man peace of mind. Still his actions grew more paranoid.

He climbed a steep cliffside using handholds and footholds left by ancient Indians—now all extinct. He wormed through the tunnels of the plateau, the Chief and his men circulating through the forests below, straining to catch a glimpse of their prey. They finally spied him, a good long while later, when he fell from a hole in the cave wall into the abandoned Indian village.

The Indians camped without a fire. The tribesmen asked their Chief what they should do. Without an inflection in his voice, the Chief said they would return the mule to the man; he would need the beast to arrive at their destination.

One Indian asked when they would know they had arrived. It had been a billion years since the Chief had seen his home.

When we all converge, the Chief said, scratching at the edge of his skullcap—thats when we've arrived. I'll take the mule to the man and see if he is alone.

Another asked what would happen if the man was not alone.

He may be in the worst position out of all of us then, the Chief replied.

As soon as he passed through the gate of the fort into the village, the commandante turned to his left and stabbed an Indian through the back of the hand. The Indian cried out in pain and the commandante pulled the blade out and swiped the blade in a long arc, nearly decapitating the man.

Around him most of the village was already in ruins, bodies, parts of bodies strewn in the streets. Fires contained and dying now put out more smoke than light. Somewhere in a distant reach of the city a baby wailed. A dog tramped down an alleyway. The commandante turned around and looked up at a soldier keeping watch from the top of the wall. The soldier pointed to a building, made another gesture with his hand.

Without any further exchange the commandante went to the building, kicked in the door. There was no one inside. He looked up at the slatwood ceiling, saw the shadowed feet standing above him. But these were not the feet of the Chief. Quietly he exited through a window. He slunk down an alley, stepping over a rotten corpse—only a rag of a scalp and leathered skin covered the skeleton. Whatever organs the man died with had long since been harvested. The teeth were already pulled from his mouth.

The baby stopped crying. It was a sudden thing. The commandante turned onto a main street, stepping over the body of the former commander. It looked as if he had bled out from the leg. The dog that passed by once doubled back and sniffed at the corpse's crotch, lapped at the congealed blood.

'Git,' the commandante said and the dog loped onward, stopping at another corpse briefly and then continuing on.

He came to the edge of the village, where it opened up onto the flat pan of the plateau. The commandante scanned the horizon, then looked back toward the fort. It blurred in the fans of the flames, a gauze of smoke muted the febrile blast of the sun. The commandante cleared his throat and called out, said there wasnt room for the both of them in this here town. He thought he would laugh at his own joke, but he didnt.

'Cant say you look the same,' the Chief said.

The commandante spun around. The Chief squatted beside a pile of bricks that used to be a shed of sorts. The bone armor was less white than it had been, stained now with blood and soot.

'You look different too,' the commandante said.

The Chief stood, gripped a broken adobe brick in his hand. The skeleton hand wrapped around his hand. 'It was about right here, wasnt it?' the Chief asked. 'The pit, I mean.'

For some reason the commandante found himself unable to speak. His mouth was dry. He cleared his throat again, blinked until his eyes watered. He asked in a foreign tongue if the Indian knew what happened next.

'Ja.' The Indian gave a single nod. 'Doe u?'

'Nro,' the commandante admitted in yet another language.

'You thought you did.'

The commandante nodded. The two men sauntered toward each other, both moving disjointedly—one because of his armor, both from age. When they came close enough the commandante jabbed the knife at the Indian and the blade glanced off the arm bone. The Indian countered by striking a blow to the head with his skeleton fist. The force was enough to break the bones free of the lanyards. The commandante tried to stab the Indian between the ribs, but lodged the blade into the ribs of the armor. The Chief brought the brick down on the commandante's face and slaked the flesh clean from his cheekbone, exposing most of the ball of his eye. Whatever noise the commandante made it was not a scream, nor was it a moan—it was something in between. The Chief struck him again; this time a more direct blow. He felt the bone of the skull give and turn mushy. The commandante's body began to shake and his one good eye spun around.

Then the Indian realized that the commandante's body was not the only thing shaking. The ground rumbled. From inside the walls of the fort a plume of smoke rose up. The scaffolding around the mine lift collapsed.

'Querido dues,' the Chief cursed. He looked down on the commandante. What was left of his mouth turned up in a smile. The Chief struck a third blow and killed the commandante.

LAST

ONE

I

Deep in the mine the stranger had been sleeping as he had for decades now. He lay recumbent in his bed of dynamite, thinking of the man. He had lived the entirety of the man's existence in his head and replayed his favorite parts of the man's life. He recalled how the man lay next to the woman, listening to her whisper in her sleep, watching her brow twitch and her limbs deftly move, her eyelids fluttering as if she threatened to retreat from the dream. In his mind the man tried to imagine what she was dreaming, if she was thinking of him. She wasnt of course.

Another memory: the woman undressed by the stream. The man had taken her there as he was afraid to leave her alone. At first the fear was that she might run away. Then, after some time, the fear of her leaving under duress became the mounting anxiety. They spent their days with each other. When the man walked to the stream, she walked with him, her hands clasped under her protruding belly.

'This here,' the man said, pointing to the slough. 'This was where I decided this was a good nuff place to settle. I went to the top a that hill there and looked out in all directions. Didnt see nothing cept grass. Like bein out on the ocean.'

The woman let her fingers slide apart, leaving only her right hand under the womb. She grabbed the man's hand and laced her fingers into his. The man started for a moment, thinking she might be trying to convey something urgent. He looked at her, but she kept her gaze downcast and a dimple welled in her cheek.

'It's like the ocean,' the man said again. 'Cept here you can walk on the water. Aint no place for you to get stuck, caint fall in.'

They came to the stream's edge and the woman let his hand go. He stood dumbfounded for a moment, watching her wade shin deep into the water. She bent over and pulled out some pebbles, examined them in the sun. The man went to the mule and untethered the beast from one of the saplings. When he turned around, the woman pulled her tunic over her head. She stood completely naked in the creek, cupping water and washing her body. She hummed.

As some people do in confusing situations, the man froze. She lifted her hair back, exposing the nape of her neck. It occurred to the man that this was a part of her he had never seen. Strangely enough, he did not think this of her breasts, full and sagging, the nipples brown. Nor did this thought occur when he saw her rub her sex with handfuls of water.

After she washed, she put the tunic back on and walked toward their hovel. The man followed, running to catch up with her. He nicked his ankle on some driftwood and the woman patched his wound that evening, kissing the mark after the blood had dried.

The couple weeks that followed were filled with more touching and kissing. The man eventually placed his mouth on hers. As he was unsure what to do, she took over, her tongue roving over his teeth and tongue. She whispered to him in her strange language, her eyes avoiding his.

The man said he loved her too.

'Usted me puede tener si desea,' the woman said. She took the man's hand and moved it over her body, down under the womb and between her legs.

The man pulled his hand away. He was shaking. 'Whats gotten you riled up?' he asked. 'We caint do that with a baby in there.'

'Es fino,' the woman assured him. 'Metélo. No le va a causar daño al bebé—lo he hecho antes.'

The man shook his head. 'Dont want to be one a your misters. I wanna be your husband. We could raise that baby like it was ours—yours and mine.' He didnt know what else to say, if the woman even understood what he said. He threw the blanket door aside and went outside to look at the stars. The woman followed. The lantern within their hovel illuminated the structure. It could be seen from a dozen miles away.

It was in the middle of this memory that the men in the mine struck the stranger's dynamite and blew him back into existence and buried themselves alive.

The man tried to open his eyes, but found it too difficult. The weight on his chest made breathing a chore enough. He parted his mouth and inhaled, but loose granules of dirt flooded his mouth. He coughed and pain shot through his ribs, seemed to stab at his backbone. For a few moments he concentrated solely on breathing—inhaling through his nose, though one nostril was packed with dirt, and exhaling through his mouth. After a few breaths he moved his arms. He had some mobility. With all the strength he had left he shoved at the weight on his chest and felt it give way. He kicked his feet and freed himself from the immediate imprisonment.

It was completely dark. In this darkness, the quiet of this place, the man wondered if he had died. Having never pondered what comes after death, this seemed plausible enough. Those who die become subducted into the earth. But how doubtful we are when it comes to a life after this one. As he lay contemplating his death, the man's hands roved over his body, inspecting the rash of wounds he sustained during the implosion. A gash ran from his shoulder blade to his backbone. The little finger on his left hand was broken. One of his ears was half torn from his head.

He began to crawl. It made no difference whether he was living or dead. Either fate would suffice. Indeed though, the man was alive. Little did he know just exactly where he was in relation to the rest of the world. The labyrinth of tunnels the miners had constructed spread out under the fort like tree roots that have a farther reach than the branches have above ground. At this moment, fifteen hundred feet above him, a wall of the fort, now on unsteady ground, had collapsed, spilling out the loose fill. No more than a thousand feet from there the Indian Chief and three of his tribesmen hunched over the corpse of the commandante. A vengeance that stews over the course of a lifetime is always unfulfilling. Killing the stranger was no different.

The Chief turned to a tribesman and ordered him to cut the commandante's hands off. Cut up his entire body, the Chief said. Scatter the pieces, cook some pieces and feed others to the vultures. Burn his uniform and hair. Grind his teeth with a mortar until they are nothing but flour. No sooner had he given the command when a tribesman grabbed the Chief by the arm. He pointed out across the dry open ground, past where smoke and dust swirled in dirt devils. A man approached on a vector not from the fort, not from the village in the cliff. He was a ghostly white. The Chief took the dagger from the commandante's hand and began walking toward this new stranger. The tribesmen followed at a trot.

'You there!' the Chief shouted. The man on the horizon kept walking toward him without regard for the Chief's words. Some soldiers gathered at the fallen portion of the wall and readied themselves. But neither the approaching stranger nor the Indian paid them any mind.

The stranger stepped over a body, sidestepped a pile of burning dung. As he drew nearer, the Chief could see this stranger's skin was without any color. What clothes he had looked to rot right off his body. The tribesman in the stovepipe hat took off in a sprint toward the stranger, bringing his hatchet over his head. The other tribesmen followed. The stranger—the Chief knew at once that it was him in the flesh—seized the Indian by the wrist and grabbed the hatchet. He brought his elbow into the back of the Indian's head and used the blunt end of the hatchet to crack the next Indian's skull. He ducked the spear the third Indian threw and launched the hatchet at the retreating tribesman. The blade buried in the Indian's back and he fell dead.

Only the Chief was left. The stranger kept approaching; he yanked the hatchet out of the back of the Indian as he passed. The soldiers at the fort watched these figures, small against the backdrop of the desert land and the rubble of the village, obscured by wafts of yellow smoke.

'Didnt figure on it happening this way,' the stranger said. He came close enough for the Chief to see the blood veins tracing blue lines through his face. This was him—the stranger of the Chief's youth. His hair was longer and darker, his skin fairer. The stranger smiled so his teeth showed. 'How'd it feel to kill me?'

The Chief could not stand any longer; he sat on the ground and stared out past the stranger, past the fort. 'Felt the same as any other of the million men I killed,' the Chief finally said.

'Good to know,' the stranger said. 'I figured I would have to be the one to do it when the time came.' In the short time the stranger had been out of his mine, the sun had taken a toll on his skin, reddening it into blisters, popping and glistening now. 'Did you follow the man I sent out this way?'

The Chief nodded once, the tincture of the skullcap reflecting the sun overhead.

The stranger said he figured it was so, said time was a cruel thing. 'Spend a whole lifetime pursuing a thing constructed in your dreams,' he scoffed. He gestured with his fingers like he was crushing a bug, then opened them up like whatever it was had vanished. 'Then you find out that the world is… this.'

'I used to be a much older man,' the Indian mumbled.

'Hows that?'

'I woke from the earth,' he said. 'Like I had been buried there. Woke and found the earth a younger place, and me a much older man—shrunk with age.' He sat hunched, the humerus bones, resting in the femurs. He sighed. 'I suppose you are going to tell me my time is up,' he said.

The stranger examined the edge of the ax. 'I dont decide such things,' he said.

For a moment, the Indian almost laughed in spite of himself. 'You didnt decide to throw me—my entire village—into the well?'

The stranger looked over toward the bloodied mess of the commandante's corpse—his corpse. 'Commandante there thought he did,' the stranger said. 'But Ive had a while to think. Most men dont live in their heads enough to understand the universe like I do.'

This statement did make the Indian laugh. 'When you cut me up, cut my ears off first.'

The stranger returned the laughter. 'Suppose it wont make a difference. You'll be dead here a few minutes. Just thought you'd want to know what the future looks like.'

The Indian laced his fingers together, the boned ones and the ones of flesh all folded around each other. 'Dont need to know,' he said. 'Seen the past clear enough.'

'Yes,' the stranger said. 'Thats how you can tell. Thats how I knew the commandante—that old fool—would die and I would be here now.'

The Indian turned his head to look at the stranger and call him a fool, a charlatan. But the ax came down and severed through the bridge of the Indian's nose and cleaved a wound wide and deep. Brains spilled out with blood. As if he were still alive, the Indian's body shook and a puddle of urine flooded the ground around him.

The stranger stood over the body until it stopped writhing. Then he turned about face and walked toward the fallen portion of the wall. The soldiers rankled their blades and shouted in cacophony. At the edge of the spilled fill, the stranger knelt and scooped up a handful of the till, he examined the gravel and sand, the bone meal and teeth. Then he looked up at the soldiers watching him. He dropped the fill and extended his arms. 'Friends,' he said. 'Ive been looking for this place for quite some time.'

II

As he crawled through the mines, the man tried to calculate his direction best as possible. He reached forward, feeling the ground in front of him, trying to feel if his body had slid over the dirt, if he had passed this way before. He had been crawling for some while now. Hunger growled deep in his gut and he ate a few pinches of dirt to fill the void. He'd slept just as he was crawling, taking care only to sleep in a passage narrow enough that he couldnt turn around while he slumbered.

In the complete dark, he had little room to deviate from whatever he supposed his course was. When he had to shit he pulled down his pants and crapped in the middle of the passage.

He came to the end of a tunnel and the overhead opened enough that he could sit upright. The obstruction in front of him was a pile of rocks, something wooden too. He figured it to be a collapsed ceiling. Knowing this was an unstable area, the man loosened a rock and waited, listened for the grumblings of another pending cave-in. When there was none, he grunted and rolled the rock aside. In his mind, the man strategized, thinking if he could clear the rocks under the wooden beam, he might be able to make safe passage by using the beam as a support. He spent hours wedging his fingers into the fissures between the stones and clawing them out. Dirt packed in under his fingernails and flakes of the nail began to lift from the finger itself. Twice a stone, loosened by the removal of another stone, fell on the man—the first time on his hand, the second time on his shoulder.

Before the man had burrowed his way through the caved-in portion of the tunnel, he fell asleep. In his dreams, he kissed his woman, grabbed at her breasts. She laughed and held him close to her. A baby, swaddled and cooing, lay in a crib made from a crate. In this dream the woman spoke his language and she told him to stay here with her.

'Why would I leave?' the man asked, kissing at her neck and down onto the exposed tops of her breasts.

The voice she spoke in this time was not her own. 'Because you already have, you son of a whore.'

He looked up into his woman's eyes and she cried, looking out the door over his shoulder. The man turned and walked out of the hovel. As he walked past the threshold, he realized he held a jawbone, sharpened down into a shank, at ready. He stepped outside and the world was a different place. Giant mammoth buildings blocked out the sun, though one constructed of glass panels reflected it in a mosaic fashion. The ground was flat and hard, scraps of paper, flimsy white cups blew down the streets. The man turned around to look back into the hovel and his abode was on fire.

He awoke with a start and lay in the darkness of the tunnel, gasping for air as if he had been running from something.

The stranger was met with a mixture of distrust and admiration by the survivors of Fort James. For some he was a folk hero—able to vanquish the last of the redskinned niggers; he had killed the ugly cuss with the bone outfit. Some of the soldiers, to save face, dismissed his actions as insignificant. 'We wouldve killed em when they came after us,' they said. 'He was just there first, thats all.' Still a few more, both soldier and civilian, wondered what he'd said to the Chief. 'They looked to be friends,' the lieutenant said. 'Chattin it up.' Others rebutted that the end result was the same—a dead nigger and no more injuns.

When he first entered the fort, the soldiers stepped back and let him through the passage. He drank from a trough in the courtyard, asked where all the villagers had gone.

'Done bin killed by the niggers,' a soldier said. 'Few went down into the mines. Few come out, but there was a cave-in and most all them was buried alive.'

The stranger nodded knowingly. 'Anyone in charge?'

'That was the commandante—the old soldier.'

'No one else in line?'

The soldier exchanged glances and shrugs with the other soldiers. 'Cant say there is.'

'Then youre free,' the stranger said. He smiled. 'You dont have to answer to anyone.'

The lieutenant walked over. 'Need to stay organized,' he said. 'Those Apache niggers is bound to come this way agin.'

The stranger shook his head. 'Not if there isnt one to tell them to. We killed every last one of them. No need to stay enlisted. This is our place now.'

'Our place?' the lieutenant asked. 'Where'd you come from, stranger?'

A smile, big and toothy, curled the stranger's lips. 'Ever had a dream so real you woke up confused?'

The soldier's brow screwed and he said he supposed he did, least he thought he might have when he was a child.

'Thats how I woke this morning,' the stranger said. 'Dreamt right into existence.'

'You always talk in riddle?'

III

Above him the space was vast and endless, stretching out into nothing but a depthless black. The man outstretched his hand and touched the ceiling of soil and rock. He imagined the stars spiraling around the stratosphere, blips of comets and meteorites. He opened and shut his eyes and saw no difference.

He burrowed back into the pile of rocks, a space only wide enough for his torso. Air did not circulate readily as he worked and the space became hot and stuffy, the stink of wet earth and sweat. He backed out by wiggling his hips and pushing with his elbows, taking care not to hit his head against the ceiling above. Once free of the tunnel, he sat up and gasped for air. Even the cave air, stale and mortared, seemed fresh now. After a couple minutes, he sighed and crawled back into the narrow passage. He did this a number of times, even sleeping briefly between digging sprees.

Finally he felt a tumble of stones give way on the other side and his hand stretched out into a void of much cooler air. Though many men's eyes play tricks on them when there is nothing there, this man thought he saw a wash of light spill through the tiny hole. He dug more feverishly, no longer concerned about breathing with the channel now properly vented.

Soon he had scooped and pushed enough of the earth aside that he could fit through. He pulled the lower half of his body, confined by the narrowness of the passageway, by walking forward on his hands. Pressure from the tunnel he'd dug seemed to be pressing down on his legs. He kicked. Some stones rattled and fell. He pulled himself free and listened to the thump of the tunnel falling in on itself. A mist of dirt rushed through the air, covering the man in a fresh and even layer of grit. Still, he lay gasping on the floor of the mine. Dirt stuck to his teeth and gummed up his tongue. He used the back of his hands to rub the sediment from his eyes. But it was to no avail; his hands were too dirty. He blinked rapidly.

Yes, there was a difference now—something not easily distinguished: there was light in here. Not much, but light, in the way it can find the most desolate corners of the world, had found this place. Though it was much cooler in this section of the mine, the man thought it to be much warmer. He laughed out loud and it echoed in the stone corridors. Then he called out for help, asked if there was anyone who could hear him. He waited for a reply after the echo and its many iterations had faded into nothing.

He stood, one hand over his head in case the ceiling was too low. He straightened up tall and realized this was the main shaft, the only one with a height great enough to accommodate the average miner. For a moment, he tried to figure out how this was possible. He and the other miners had gone into the farthest recesses of the tunnels to make their way into the old mine the cripple had found. Surely there was no shorter way to go. The man called it quits and began staggering toward the source of the light. He imagined it must be a short ways ahead.

* * *

The office of the commandante remained untouched. While the survivors of what was now called the Injun massacre looted the homes of the dead and burned the bodies in pyres, they did not disturb the officers' quarters. Not a single soldier so much as thought to step foot inside the commandante's office. Perhaps it was superstition. The stranger knew where the quarters was located. His first night in the fort, when he slept in the bunkhouse, in the very same bed the man had occupied just a day before, he fell to sleep examining the ceiling. The wood was darkened a bit. Any layman could tell it was a water stain. The stranger looked at the stain, at the swirled grains of the wood, the warp and weft. He examined the head of a nail popping out from where the beam and slat met. Then he closed his eyes and followed the trajectory of the nail, how it held fast into the wood, held in by forces of friction. Beyond here was the roof, a tin roof rusted through in spots by the rain which came only in short spurts, the dust snow of winter lasting much longer. When the snows melted, they trickled off the low edge, pooled in the divots and ate at the metal.

From this one point in time and space, he calculated what the entire rest of the fort looked like. He could see the foyer of the office with its great leather chairs and bearskin rug. In his mind he saw the shape and make of the desk, each drawer. He traveled into the keyhole and saw the pins and tumblers within, knew how to unlock the contents inside. The glass cabinets with their brass knobs where the books were stored. Each book with its own story. Instantly he knew every word, he knew the characters and where they came from in the author's life, when and where the writer sat when these things first spawned into existence.

But there was one book that, as the stranger lay thinking about it, caused a dark spot in his mind. Whatever this book contained, it was not a story, nor words. No, this was something different. He resolved to explore it in the morning.

He shifted in the bed, in the spot the man had worn in the mattress. It caused him to wonder about the man. He tried to postulate the man's location. Like all the other civilians of the fort, the man had gone down into the mines. That much the stranger knew. Again he interpolated what the world looked like. The darkest corners of the manmade caves were illuminated in his mind. He could easily see each crevice, every fold in the stone. Then he came to a place where the laws of geology and physics broke down, where he could not imagine what lay there. The limits of the expanded mind are still confined to this world; the worlds we imagine beyond this one are built from the bones and waste of the places we've already used.

The stranger sat up and looked around the bunkhouse. Some men murmured in their sleep. Some simply just dreamt. At the far end of the house a pan with a twisted rag as a wick burned melted fat. The stranger pulled on his boots and went out into the night.

IV

The door of the commandante's office had been left unlocked, the things inside untouched. For as long as any one of them could remember, the commandante had been there. He existed before anyone ever came upon Fort James. Even though they saw him killed, saw his body cut into pieces and burned, the soldiers who worked under him refused to believe he was dead.

'No,' the lieutenant said to his fellow soldiers. 'The commandante is more than a man.'

'What is he?' another asked.

'Cant rightly say. Whatever he is though, he dont die.'

Whatever acts the commandante had committed in his lifetime became amplified in the recounting. As the men drank and talked, they built a new image of their slain leader. In doing so, they sanctified what he did and hallowed the places he occupied. Years later, men would do the same to the likes of Custer and Jackson—great men known for attempted genocide. Years earlier entire nations were wiped out by heroes like Cortés and Pizarro. They were beatified by history and elevated into a status of savior.

The office was as the stranger had imagined it. What little light there was came from starlight radiating in through the windows. The stranger circled the desk and sat in the chair. He opened the drawer with the keys and took them out. Then he turned to the glass-doored bookcase and unlocked it. His fingers ran along the cloth bindings of the books and stopped on a wide-spined tome without a label.

He pulled the book from the shelf and laid it on the desk with a dull thump. His eyes adjusted to the dark and he could see there was nothing written in the way of a title. Digging his fingernails into the stack of pages, he opened the book and found nothing. The center of the pages had been cut out to accommodate something. Whatever it had been, it was gone now. He swore to himself. For some time he just stood, leaning, hands flat on the desktop, staring down into the vacant sockets of this book.

Then, as metanoias happen, he came to understand what had been set before him. He stood up straight, rolled up the sleeve of his shirt and reached down into the hollowed space of the book. Inside it was cool and damp. He reached in farther, past his elbow. He stifled a burst of laughter and thrust his arm deeper, until his ear pressed against the desktop. He strained his arm and stretched his fingertips. In his mind, he imagined what artifacts of the world the commandante created he might find. He felt something soft, almost furry. He pinched part of it between his index and middle finger and pulled it from the book.

He set the dead bird on the desk. It was half decayed. For a moment, he stared blankly at it. Then his shoulders began to shake. Hiccups of laughter spilled out and soon his whole body shook.

He reshelved the book, locked the cabinet, and put the lanyards of keys around his neck. All these worlds, all these places that all of him had been to, were so beautiful he could hardly contain himself.

The man thought what he might say to his woman when he saw her again. He practiced words over and over again.

Knowing that she understood little of his language, the man practiced what he would do with his hands, where he would direct his eyes. He spoke out loud and practiced his intonation.

'I done been round the world,' he said. 'The only place worth comin back to was you.' He thought he would take her hand, squeeze it. If she understood, she would lean in and kiss him.

He stumbled over some loose stones that made for poor footing. After a few more steps he said, 'I wont ever leave you again.' The echo of his voice resounded in resoluteness.

He tripped again and noticed the footing here was different than it had been. The clamor and scattering of stones was not present. He reached down and felt something cold and wet. What light there was barely exposed the vestiges of a miner, the wet flaps of skin and scalp. Nearby a wooden beam was splintered so the end flared out like the bristles of a broom. Bones and hair tangled in the fibers. The man vomited on the remains. He apologized, shook his head and staggered on.

He came around a bend and the light amplified. He squinted and his head pulsated in response to the surge of brightness. After letting his eyes adjust, he opened them and realized he stood at the bottom of the lift shaft. Ropes and timbers, bodies and rags of clothing littered the shaft. At the top the scaffolding obscured most of the daylight beyond. What shafts of light that did appear cut through the dust and vapor. It looked like the man could reach out and grab a hold of one.

'I wanted to give up,' the man said. 'Wanted to lay down an die. But then I'd think of you. I'd keep on goin.' He imagined the woman would understand, tears might well up in her eyes and she would say something back, letting it tumble out in that Mexicano language of hers.

He grabbed a rope that dangled from a beam about fifty feet up. He placed his foot into a pocket in the rock. He began climbing. He used the ropes and supports. Once or twice he trusted an unsturdy foothold and nearly fell. After he ascended a couple hundred feet, he wanted to stop. His shoulders ached from being raised for so long. His fingers cramped and went numb. The closer he got to the surface, the colder it became. At one point, he highstepped his foot up onto a beam that stretched from one side of the shaft to the other. He shoved all his weight onto the booted foot and heard the nail pop through the sole before he felt the blister of pain. He howled in agony. But he had already begun this motion and he shifted the rest of his weight forward, the nail remaining stationary while his foot shifted forward.

Once he had enough support, he lifted his foot off the nail, the thin sole of the boot now greased with blood squeaked as it slid free of the nail. The man looked down, but he could see nothing. Wherever the bottom was no longer mattered. He knew the fall would kill him.

He kept climbing, the wound in his foot throbbing. He came to a point where there were no longer handholds—not a rope or beam—just a sheer face of rock for a good ten feet. The man craned his head round, saw a metal rod with a pulley on the end sticking out of the wall. He summoned up what strength he could and lunged for it.

He caught himself, wrapping one arm around the rod. The metal cut into the soft skin of his armpit. His feet dangled freely for a moment. He kicked. The toes of the boot scraped against the wall and eventually caught on something to help propel him farther up. So the climbing went for the next couple hours.

The man reached the clutter of the collapsed scaffolds at the mouth of the shaft when the daylight had begun to fade. He pushed up through the boards and beams of the fallen structure, sliding a planked tress aside. At last he was free of the mine. The fort looked different than the man remembered it. He stumbled off the heap of broken frames and stood staring back at some spectators. He opened his mouth to say something, but only a hoarse whisper came out. Then he collapsed.

TWO

I

At first the soldiers—and the few miners who hadnt entered the mine when it collapsed—wanted a leader. Without any real consideration, they appointed the stranger, the folk hero and savior of Fort James. He resisted the private offers of leadership from the lieutenant, the subsequent offers from the sergeants. By default the men listened to each other in ranks. Only a few resisted.

Despite this return to militaristic order, the stranger remained the dominant force of reason in the fort. When he spoke—usually over drinks at the saloon—the men listened and his words became law. In rebuffing yet another offer to act as the lord over their desert manor, the stranger addressed the crowd in the saloon.

'Why would I want to lead you?' he asked rhetorically. 'I have no power, no responsibility to anyone except myself. It's a good life.'

'Give you anything you want,' a drunken soldier said.

The stranger shook his head and raised a finger. 'Right now I can have anything I want. Empower me and then you'll scrutinize everything I do.' The drunk soldier raised his cup in a toast of agreement and began jabbering at another soldier. The stranger looked around the saloon. Men danced on the tables, lay on the floor. A couple old timers—miners who never considered fleeing the Indian attack—aggregated in the corner. One soldier in the center of the room rested his forehead on a table and vomited on the floor. Two more men stood behind the counter of the saloon skinning a jackrabbit with a dirk. 'You all look like a bunch of goddamned prisoners anyhow,' the stranger said.

The few men in proximity heard what the stranger said and they set down their drinks, ceased their conversation. The stranger repeated himself and more fell silent at the words. Soon all but a few men stared at the stranger.

'Look to be a jailhouse,' he said. 'All you wearing the same color, taking orders and staying bound to a single place.' He shook his head, remarked that it was sad. 'Owning this world means you make up your own code and live by it.'

'Truest damn thing I ever heard,' a young soldier said. He patted the stranger on the shoulder and raised his cup. A murmur of agreement spread through the saloon.

'Dont pretend to agree,' the stranger said. 'Not while youre all dressed in the same garb. Stop being soldiers.'

The young soldier pulled his navy blue coat off, then stood on the bench and ripped the gold stripe from the side of his pants. The other men in the saloon cheered and began to disrobe. Some of the men stripped down to their skivvies. Others ripped the sleeves from their jackets and pieced out their uniforms, traded one man's kerchief for another's belt. One man dropped his pants and underwear and began masturbating. A few men hooted and watched intently until a former officer broke a bottle over his head and he fell naked and bloodied to the floor.

'Lets burn the rags!' a man yelled. And the men with a gathered heap of clothes went out to the courtyard. The moon above was big and jaundiced as if it reflected the flames of the burning clothes. The men danced around the fire until the moon disappeared and the sun broke over the horizon.

Some men slept on the ground, despite the patches of snow and the early low-hanging bands of fog. The sun already reached its apex and began falling by the time some of the men started to stir.

One roused and stood, his head still heavy with ache. 'Look there,' he said to his comrade. He pointed toward the scraps of scaffold. Some pieces of wood shifted and a man emerged. However haggard these former soldiers were, they remained in fine shape compared to this newcomer. The man who emerged from the hole looked as if he might say something, but then fell to the ground unconscious.

Before he woke the man dreamt of his woman again. He dreamt that he walked a path of tiled stones back to the hovel. For miles out to each side, great sleek-looking structures sat on parcels of green land. The windows of each home had glass and walls of brick. They all had doors with locks. It was a strange place. Out in the distance he could see his woman. She was in the middle of a wide path. The path was made of billions of stones pressed together and coated in tar. Markings like Indian war paint decorated the path. As he came closer to the hovel and his woman, he noticed it was located in intersection with another pathway. Above the misshapen tent and frame a yellow light suspended from wire blinked on and off. The woman went about cleaning the hovel.

The man kept walking on the sidewalks, his gait building to a steady trot. On the adjacent running road he spied a vehicle of sorts barreling down it. Exhaust streamed out of a stack in the top.

'Es mi único amor en esta vida,' he shouted, though his waking self would never know what these words meant.

The woman appeared to be deaf to his shouting and the truck plowed over the hovel with her inside.

The man started awake.

'Thought you'd never come to,' a voice said.

The man blinked rapidly until his vision cleared and he saw a face staring down on him.

'Tended to the horses, when we still had some. Castrated a few. That makes me the closest thing to a doctor round here,' he said.

'I'm at Fort James,' the man said.

'Fraid so,' the doctor said. He changed a compress on the man's head. 'Been watchin you for a day now. Bossman wanted me to tend to ya. Said it was a goddamned miracle you survived like you did.'

'The injuns,' the man said.

'Theyre all dead,' the doctor said, said it was thanks to the bossman. 'Mean sumbitch he is, smart too.'

'The commandante?'

The doctor snickered. 'Commandantes been dead now,' he said. 'This bossman is someone else entirely... Miracle you made it like you did.'

'Whos in charge then?' the man asked.

'No one,' the doctor said. 'Aint no one in charge. Bossman refuses to be the boss.'

II

In two days' time the man sallied forth from the doctor's quarters. He went out into the courtyard of the fort and looked around. His breath was a vapor cloud. Piles of wetted snow huddled in shadowed places. Where the wall had fallen, snow dappled the rubble. What was once the village looked to be the ruins of a long forgotten civilization. The doctor had followed him outside.

'Got your strength back?'

'Yessir.'

'Good. Hate to say it, but I aint a goodwill worker. Used to getting paid.'

The man dragged the toe of his boot through the dirt. 'I owe ya then?'

But the doctor replied with a no sir, said the bossman ordered him to do it. 'Besides you dont got money on ya. I checked your pockets when I took ya in.'

The man understood. Nothing in this world is free. In this case the cost was a horse doctor searching his pockets. 'How long was I out?' the man asked.

'Been sleepin now for a day, day an a half. On an off.'

'No.' The man shook his head once. 'The snow, the cold. How long was I down in the cave?'

'You probably know better than anyone else. When you go in there?'

The man let a sustained pause in the conversation take place to see if the doctor was funning him or if he really was a dunce. Finally he said it was when the mine collapsed; he'd been trapped when the injuns attacked.

'Fine then,' the doctor said. 'If you is a looter, jus say so. Dont give me some made up story.'

'I went down on the lift, went to where—'

The doctor walked away.

As the sun rose up farther, the earth warmed. Shadows not shaped as they had been before betrayed the snows that hid. In some spots the snow melted away altogether. Perhaps he had not been down in the mines that long, the man thought. Cold snaps happen. He came around the corner of a building and found a group of men sleeping on the ground. A few of them groused and stirred in the early morning sunlight. One such sleeper's eyelids barely opened. 'Whatre you lookin for?' he asked.

'Wantin to know whos in charge here,' the man said.

'No one.'

'Got to be someone. What about the census?'

The sleeper grunted and rolled over. The man walked on and came to the bunkhouse. A skinny fellow lay on the stairs leading up to the entrance, his head pillowed on his folded arms.

'Cuse me,' the man said. He tossled the skinny fellow by the shoulder. The body slumped over and the shirt opened. An entire side of the fellow was black and shiny, bruised from neck to waist. The man put his hand on the man's sternum and he felt nothing in the way of life. He stepped over the body and into the bunkhouse.

The fire in the pan at the other end of the house had gone out. It smelled musty in here now. Surprisingly only a few of the bunks were filled. He could see his bunk, saw someone sleeping there, laying on his back like he fell to sleep studying the stars.

'Anyone here wake yet?' the man asked.

'Wasnt til you open yer yawp.'

In the dark another added he would close up the man's mouth with a couple timber nails—put them right through his lips.

'Just late in the morn,' the man said. 'Figured I might find someone—'

'Found some men who'll cut the voicebox right outta yer throat if you keep it up.'

The man backed out of the bunkhouse, nearly tripping over the limp body of the skinny fellow. He went back around to the courtyard. A few men had finally risen, milled about. Then the man walked to the office.

* * *

The stranger lay in the bunk. In his mind he repeated what the man had asked: Is anyone here wake yet? He slowed the words down, broke them apart and listened to how the man's voice wavered when he spoke. In his mind he could see the events leading up to the question—the man talking to the sleeper, finding the skinny fellow. The stranger then could see how the skinny fellow died too; he could see his childhood, conception and birth.

The man had backed out of the bunkhouse. The stranger thought of those footsteps, tentative and small. He plotted them as men would plot points on a map and figured a course. As the man walked back across the courtyard, the stranger saw what he did.

He could see what the man saw at this moment. The office was as the man had last seen it, only dark now without the wall sconces lit. Again the man called out in a child's voice, asked if anyone was here. When no reply came, he went into the office. It looked as if the commandante was still here, maintaining this place. The man went to the desk and examined the papers scattered thereabout. Circling around the desk, he tried the doors to the bookcase. They were locked. He looked through the glass at the spines of the books. Then he saw it—the census book. If he could just write his name—any name in there. He rattled the knobs of the bookcase doors and sighed.

He searched through the drawers of the desk and under the desk, but found no keys. The man took a stack of papers from the desk and held them flat to the glass of the bookcase, then punched it. The glass pane popped and broke. Carefully, the man pulled out the remaining shards. He tried to reach in and pull out the giant book, but found that breaking one pane would not suffice.

When the stranger witnessed, through the man's eyes, his struggle to obtain the book, he sat up in the bunk. This must not happen. Since he slept in his clothes, he neednt dress and he stalked out of the bunkhouse, trooping over the body of the skinny fellow. At first he walked briskly, then he flat out ran. He threw open the door of the office and made his way inside.

The man was already gone. Shards of glass lay on the floor. The giant book lay open on the desk, the hollowed pages exposed. He noticed droplets of water soaked into some of the papers. He touched the spots and closed his eyes, trying to extrapolate the events from the evidence. But there was nothing he could see; this book had opened up too many possibilities. Then he noticed something shiny—a copper disc on the floor. He picked it up, examined the coin in the low light. On one side there was a profile of a man who was not yet president, just a fellow building log cabins. The reverse side had two shafts of wheat, the words one penny inscribed between them.

III

After the man opened the book and found the pages hollowed out, he stood, much like the stranger had: hands on the table leaning over the void of text. For all the man in his limited wisdom knew, this was the only record he could have of his existence. He thought momentarily of his woman, of the baby she must have birthed by now. He grabbed the book by the cover and flung it shut. As he did so, a couple objects flew out. A spittle of water dotted the desk.

His curiosity was roused and he located the objects that seemed to just materialize from the book. They were coins. He gathered them in his hand hurriedly. They were cold and wet, smelled of chlorine and fluoride. Men would kill for money. He put them into his pocket and ran from the office with his new-found fortune.

By now many of the fort's inhabitants were up and moving. They acknowledged each other with nods and grunts. The man walked with his hands stuffed deep in his pockets to keep the coins from clinking together. Without a task being assigned to him, the man did not know what to do with himself. Most of the other men also seemed to have this problem. They gathered in groups and talked. One fellow upon awakening swore, stood up and urinated on his still slumbering companion. Those who were already awake howled with laughter. The incident of course turned into a fistfight that ceased only when both parties were properly bloodied.

The man continued on, walking behind a building. Finding a private place was proving difficult. Everything here—including the jakes—was communal. Without boundaries each man kept an eye on the other.

'Hey,' a voice called. The man turned and saw a big man stalking toward him. 'You the pile a horse shit that come into the bunks this mornin?'

The man kept his hand in his pocket and gave a single nod.

'What you run outta words now? Use em all up by the time the sun done rose.'

'Sorry,' the man said. 'Just wonderin who was in charge a this place.'

The big man blinked, then leaned back. 'You the fella who come up outta the mine a couple days back?'

'I am, yeah.'

The big man nodded. 'Maybe you aint familiar with this place. I'll give you a pass this time. But next time you come into the bunkhouse with questions when we're still sleepin, I'll rip your head off.' He didnt wait for the man to respond, he stalked off after another man and began berating him.

Suddenly it occurred to the man that if this fellow was up and about, there was a good chance the bunkhouse would be vacant. He started back across the courtyard, walking as fast as he could with his hands in his pockets. Before entering the bunkhouse he looked left, then right, stepped over the skinny fellow.

As he thought, the inside was vacant. He went down to his bunk and sat on the bottom, where the cripple used to sleep. He sat facing the door and took the coins out of his pocket. It was dim in here, but there was enough light filtering in through fissures in the structure so he could examine the coins. He held one up and turned it. The edge had tiny grooves; the front had an embossed portrait of a man. On the reverse side an eagle with its wings spread. Another had a man with a winged helmet, a pillar and a bush on the other side.

He sifted through the coins—just shy of a dozen of them—and found one with an Indian one side, a buffalo on another. Another piece of the same denomination had an anglo man's countenance. On its opposing side a set of two hands clasped in a symbol of brotherhood, a set of tools crossed above them like the bones of a jolly roger. Wherever these coins had come from, the man figured it must be a place quite unlike any he'd ever seen.

The stranger emerged from the office and paused on the front step. He looked out over his creation—the fort with the collapsed scaffold heap, the fallen wall that opened up into the rubbled village. He'd remembered telling himself long ago that the world was a beautiful place. If only he knew now what his other self had known then.

It was in the moment when he touched the coin, picked it up off the floor. He knew of the children, who believed in the myth. 'Stand with your back to the well,' a grandparent would say. 'Close your eyes. Think of a wish. Now toss the coin in!' And he thought the thoughts of the children: the anxiety of moving into a new home, the desire to own new things, the wish to be somebody else entirely.

These were the issues solved with loose change.

The stranger chuckled to himself. He thought of the legends about paying a boatman in the land of the dead. He thought of the Irish family begging for two coins to cover their child's eyes. Magicians who, through sleight of hand, could make the coin vanish, then seemingly reappear. He paused, gauged the sun—now past peak in the sky. Night fell earlier and dusk would settle in a few hours' time. He figured the path of the man in his head and decided on the intersection point. Then he walked to the saloon.

THREE

I

The man went into the saloon—a place with cracked adobe walls, open windows and filled with long plank wood tables. When he came through the door, the man stopped and looked about the room. Small groups dotted the floor. Some groups kept talking without paying the man any mind. At least one other group ceased their conversation momentarily to gawk at the newcomer. To his left the man saw a group of older men—men whose hair was grown white, their skin sagging. He took a seat with them.

One nodded when the man sat down, another gave a curt greeting. The bartender leaned over his counter and asked what the man would be drinking.

'Whatever you got,' the man said. 'Glass a anything strong.'

This request sent a round of snickering through all the men who heard it. The bartender poured something from a green bottle into a clay mug with a broken handle. He patted the counter. When the man came to fetch his drink, the bartender intervened. 'Hold on there, friend,' he said. 'Gotta pay before ya drink. Aint any of this payin when you done had your fill.'

The man nodded, said he understood. He slid one hand into his pocket and took out a coin, placed it on the counter. He hadnt taken more than a step back to his chair when the bartender asked just what the hell this was.

'Coin,' the man said. He sipped his drink. 'Figured it to be enough.'

The bartender walked out from behind the counter. 'I wanna know just what kind a coin puts a redskinned nigger on it.'

'Lemme see,' one of the old timers said. The bartender handed it over and the old men passed it one to another, some holding it farther away, others holding it close to their eyes.

'Dont know where the hell you come to find a coin with a nigger's face on it,' the bartender said. 'But I wont take it.'

Upon hearing this, one of the old timers pocketed the coin, then folded his hands on the table.

The man pulled another coin from his pocket, looked at it, then gave it to the bartender. 'Hope this ones better.' This one had a woman in a long flowing dress walking in front of a sunrise. The bartender studied the coin for some time, using his free hand to rub at his crotch, before remarking this one had a beauty on it.

'Coulda gotten two drinks with this one,' he said.

The man sat back at the table with the old timers.

'Got money from all over, do ya?' one asked.

'No,' the man shook his head. 'Dont got a whole lotta coins. Just enough for a couple drinks.'

'You rob someone to get those coins?' another asked.

The man looked at his drink, shook his head. 'Aint a robber,' he said. 'Just come this way to take care of some business dealings.'

This made the old men laugh.

'Got some matters a business proper to take care of in old Fort Jimmy, do ya?'

'I does.'

The old timer to the man's right set his hand on the man's shoulder. 'What kind a business you in, son?'

The man sipped at his drink again. He let the heat of the alcohol flare through his nostrils. 'Dont own a business myself. Come out this way to take care a some family business.'

'If you lookin for a wife, you done come to the wrong place,' an old timer said. 'Place got as many women as we got bottles a decent drink.'

Everyone murmured in agreement. Two of them clinked glasses and duffed the remainder of their drinks.

'Got me a wife,' the man said.

'That so?'

'It is.'

'What she look like?'

For the briefest of moments the man could not recall the face of his woman. He closed his eyes in a long blink and pictured her. 'Pretty,' the man said. 'Prettier than the woman they put on that coin.'

'Got tits on her?' one of the old timers asked.

The man nodded, said yeah, sure.

'She still all tight down in the holes?' another asked.

The man finished his drink. 'Dont rightly know what you mean.'

This admission from the man elicited the biggest laughter of all.

The old timer to the right explained it to the man: 'When you stick her with your pecker does it feel like shes grabbin it or does it feel like youre priggin a bucket a cornmeal?'

No one waited for the man's reply, they simply howled with laughter. The bartender came over and poured the man another drink. The man paid with a smaller coin—this one had a man with a winged helmet.

Once the laughter subsided, the man said he came this way to register his woman. She was with child.

'Whaddya mean register?'

The man drank to wet his mouth before speaking. This drink was much more sour than the last. He coughed.

'For the census,' he said. 'Register my family so they dont get taken away.'

'Whats a census?' an old timer asked.

'It's a—the thing I gotta do here at the fort for my family,' the man said. 'If I dont get em registered then the government can take em away.'

The old men exchanged looks, one shrugging and another raising his eyebrows. One said he never heard of such a thing. Then he asked where the man had been told about this census.

'Fella came to my house I built out on the plains,' the man said. 'Told me bout the census.'

'You leave him there with your wife?'

The man nodded. 'Said he was a doctor. Said I could make it out to Fort James an back and I would miss the birth, but not by much.'

'You left a stranger with your pregnant wife?'

'He aint a complete stranger,' the man said. 'He done built a house a his own a piece down from mine.'

'Hate to tell you this, friend,' the old timer to the right said, 'but we bin here a while ourselves and we aint never heard of a census.'

The man looked from one old timer to the next. Each avoided eye contact. 'Why'd a doctor lie about that?'

'Maybe he aint a doc,' one old timer offered.

'Be best if you get on back to your woman,' another added.

The man's mind tried to process the information he'd just been given. He hadnt drunk that much, but he felt the dizziness of excess. 'How do I get back?' he asked.

'Dont know how you came in, son.'

'Came in yonder way,' the man said. He pointed out the window, toward where the village used to be. 'Came up the cliff-side, kind of circled the whole place before making it in here.'

'And you come from the plains?' one old timer asked.

'Yessir.' The old timers all exchanged glances. 'What is it?' the man asked. 'Whats the quickest way outta here?'

'Goin west, then cuttin south, take a pass in the mountains—probably the same pass you come through to get to this place.'

'Theres a way to cut a day off, son.'

The man turned to the old timer to the right. 'What is it?'

The other old timers said it was a bad way to go and implored their friend not to tell the man.

'Youre a hearty boy,' the old timer said. 'You'll make it alright.'

Then he told the man about a patch of desert. 'Gotta cut through on the diagonal,' he said. 'Bout ten miles a nothin but sand. You good with navigatin?'

The man said he was.

'Good. Bear south and east, straight line. Cut at least two days' time off your travels if you cut through the desert.'

Another old man interrupted. 'If you decide to go that way, make certain you do it in a day. Any longer than that and you'll end up as vulture droppins.'

A third old timer sniffed. 'He done went on one fool's errand, of course he'll go through the desert.'

'Might actually be best to cut through the desert,' the other said. 'Gets cold this time a year. At least it might be warmer out there in the desert.'

'Could consider leaving tonight,' a new voice said from the far end of the table.

The man did not recognize the stranger. Time spent crossing whatever spandrels they encountered had aged them both. His voice too changed with the consumption of alcohol. They sat at opposite ends of the long table. Between them men told jokes, stories, one sang to himself as he slugged back another shot.

'The return is always something jarring.' In the air the stranger traced an arc with his index finger. 'We go these great distances and carry memories. And when we get back—' he spread his fingers open as if the trajectory he drew exploded into nothing '—the world is a different place altogether.'

'Care to tell us where you from, stranger?' one of the old timers said. 'Always talkin bout walkin.'

It took a moment for the stranger to swallow his drink, let his tongue run over his palate and answer the inquiry. When he did answer, he simply said he came from beyond the horizon.

'Whereabouts? Eastways? Farther west?'

A few more men ceased their conversation and looked to the stranger for an answer.

'I come from all over the place,' he said.

A couple men snickered. By this time everyone in the saloon stopped talking and listened.

'You a drifter then?'

'No.'

Finally the man spoke. 'Dont I know you from somewhere?'

'From some other time, probably. From right now.'

One old codger sighed, scooted back in his chair and left the table.

'Listen good,' said one of the old timers. 'We just tryin to be friendly like here. Aint a need to be coy with us.'

The stranger stared at the man for what seemed like a long time. Nearly all the men stayed quiet. 'I walked through the graveyard where you are buried on my way in here,' the stranger said. He turned his head and stared at the old timer.

'What the hell does that mean?'

'Did you have dreams last night?'

The old man cursed the stranger, took his drink and left the table. Other men feigned to restart the conversations they had been carrying on.

'I had dreams last night,' the man said.

'They were of your wife—of your woman.'

The man's brow furrowed. 'Yeah. They were.'

'You some type a magic man,' another asked. One man replied he knowed the stranger was a magic man when he done saw him slay that boned nigger.

The stranger chuckled and shook his head. 'I'm a man of science and of history.'

'And you can tell me what my dreams were by usin science and knowin history?'

'When you woke this morning, you lay in a bed that wasnt yours. Your pecker hard in your drawers.' A few of the men cracked smiles. But the stranger did not break cadence. 'You dreamt of fucking your woman, or at least you recognized her as your wife in the dream. But you woke too early, woke to another voice calling you back into this world. And when that person left the room, you closed your eyes and tried to redream what you had just lost, do what you needed to do.'

The man looked puzzled.

'What did you do after that?' the stranger asked.

'I got ready to go out into the day.'

'But you must have sat up in bed, ran your hand through the scratchy side of your beard. You must have stood up and walked across the room to where your boots lay next to a makeshift basin.'

'Yes, but—'

'Or perhaps you didnt. You dont remember. It never happened.'

'No,' the man said. 'Youre right. I did do all those things.'

The men who still listened exchanged grumblings.

The stranger shook his head. 'You didnt do any of those things until I said them.'

'No,' the man insisted. 'I did. It just didnt seem important.'

The stranger broke his gaze with the man and looked individually at each man still seated at the table. 'Lived a bunch of years and you be authorities on this world. Vast majority of our lives are driven by survival, by the basic functions—shitting, pissing, eating, sleeping.' He sighed. 'You all think the quickest way from here to wherever is a straight line. Could be a line through a mountain, crossing the plains, traversing the desert.' He clucked his tongue. 'Clever clever humans. So easy to predict. Someday a locomotive will have a set of tracks running just a quarter mile north of here.'

'Youre a surveyor for the rail companies,' a bystander exclaimed. 'We're goin to be a train stop!' He raised his mug. A few men smiled and clapped.

'No.' The stranger held up his hand. 'You'll be dead by the time the train runs by here. This whole place will be dead.'

The bystander set his mug down hard so the grog inside slopped out onto the table. 'Now wait a second.'

'No,' the stranger said. He looked to the other side of the table. He posed a hypothetical question: 'The train is moving and a man walks backward through the cars. Is he in the same place for longer?' No one answered. 'Thats fine,' he said. He looked back at the bystander. 'You dont see everything like I do. Your life is just a few memories stitched together. Even right now, your existence is just me. I am what you will remember. You'll select what you want to remember, what you will construct into what you call yourself.'

'I'm a fur trapper.'

Again the stranger chuckled. He drank. He set the cup down. None of the men gathered therein spoke. 'How much time you spend trapping furs?'

'Pardon?'

'Those furs, do you trap them all the time?'

'Not now.'

'But you call yourself a trapper.'

'Thats right.'

'But at this very moment you are a liar and a drinker—'

'Now wait a minute—'

Several of the onlookers guffawed. The stranger seemed unaffected by the outburst. 'I'm not saying that you dont—or havent—trapped some animals and skinned them. But for the most part youre traveling, going from one place to another. Blank spaces between each location.'

The trapper gave a sullen nod, said he supposed that sounded right.

The stranger smiled, held up his glass in a toast. The trapper did not reciprocate. 'Most people dont want to hear that their lives for the most part are empty. They identify themselves by trade, the families they rarely see, but are constantly constructing, reconstructing in their minds. A gravestone is fitting. It exists in only one place, reminding others that you at one point were somewhere.'

Two of the old men exchanged whispers and stood up together and left the table. Most of the crowd, confused by the exchange, also dissipated. Just a few remained—the stranger, the man, an old timer and the fur trapper.

The sudden loss of interest in his speech did not deter the stranger. 'These great empty spaces, scientists will grow to love them. And because science loves them, so will all of you. The great emptiness. It can give the illusion of movement, of progress. Didnt we all come west because it was empty?' When no one responded right away, the stranger said, 'Thats why I'm here.'

The trapper nodded. The old timer too.

'It is a happy foolishness, this life.'

'You aint a man a God is ya?' the old timer asked.

'Cant say I am, no. I'm not a man of the earth either.'

'Just science.'

The stranger shook his head. 'You havent been listening. Theres history to consider too.'

The trapper said that he'd drunk his share, tipped his hat and left.

'What history you mean?' the man asked.

The stranger drank the last of his grog. 'This morning when I awoke—it was the last significant moment in my story—I went to the mouth of the mineshaft.'

'You slept in a mineshaft?'

'It's where I woke up. But thats not important. I went to the mouth of the mine.'

'So youre a miner then?'

'No, I only woke up in a mine.'

'But you had to've gone into the mine. Did you fall into the shaft an wake up after hitting your head?'

The stranger went to drink from his cup again, then remembered it was empty. He looked at the man. 'Youre heading out into the sand desert tonight?'

The man nodded, said that was right.

'You should be getting on then. Night comes on fast this time of year.'

The man stayed seated. But after looking at his company—now just the stranger and the old timer—he nodded again and left.

II

The man walked out into the courtyard of the fort. The first lights of Aries were poking through the twilight and signaled the oncoming night. In his head, the man calculated his path, a south bearing until he came to the great swathes of sand that drifted up against the mountainside. The few coins he had left jangled in his pocket. He had nothing else. To stay alive he would walk clean through the night. When morning came he would sleep in the shadows of one of the dunes. Any respite would have to be short lived. Sleeping too long would mean another walk through the night—a full night with no water and no food.

In a few hours' time the man reached the edge of the desert. A stream with silted water bordered the edge and he drank his fill. Then took care to soak a handkerchief and wad it into his pocket. Under the lights cast down from the heavens, the dunes looked to be cut of two shades of blue—one nearly white and vaporous, the other an indigo darker than the purpled skies.

The walk into the foothills of the dunes took longer than the man had anticipated. Darkness and the size of the dunes had deceived his vision. Gradually the sand lifted and sloped. Soon he took steps and watched the grains of sand give way under his feet so every step he took gained him little ground. He leaned into the slope and breathed heavily. The inside of his mouth became coated in dust. He stopped briefly and found a pebble, much larger than the grains of sand. He put it into his cheek to stave off thirst. Then he kept walking.

Once he reached the ridge of the dune he figured he should walk along it until he came to the first peak. From the peak he could gauge his path across the wasteland. He walked some way with considerably more ease and then the wind blew. The granules of sand pelted and prickled his exposed skin. Sand had worked its way into his boots and down into his shirt and pants. His eyes teared up as the wind kept blowing. He pulled the soggy handkerchief from his pocket and squeezed the moisture from the cloth. He had intended to use it later, but circumstances had forced him into this other spot. After unwadding the cloth, he tied it as a bandit might, with a triangle covering his mouth.

A couple hours later and the temperature had plummeted into a brutal cold. No longer could the man feel the sand whip against his legs; they had long gone numb. The cloth of the handkerchief stiffened with frost. He kept moving, knowing full well that to stop in the darkness meant resigning to death.

As the first peak came into view and he slogged one footstep after another, spillage of sand emanating with each step, the man felt a renewed sense of purpose. He closed his eyes and took a few more steps. In his mind, he thought of his woman, wondered if the baby had been a boy as the stranger said. He opened his eyes, then looked back down the slopes, out into the pan of the plateau, where Fort James lay against the shroud of night like a votive for the dead of this place. For a moment he pondered the stranger, felt as if his eyes were upon him. The man shook his head and trudged to the top of the sandy mount.

He looked out over the formless land, at the menagerie of shadow and shifting sands. The mountain pass hulked some dozen miles off, a hollow space in the ether of night.

III

For some time the stranger and the old timer sat quietly. Each seemed to be tending to his own thoughts. Then the stranger asked where they had been in their conversation.

'You was answerin that man's question—the man you jus told to get up an go.'

'Yes.' The stranger spent a minute recollecting the course of the conversation. Then he began speaking again. 'The return:

how each time we revisit the past it becomes something else.' He sighed, then continued. 'I went out from the mineshaft and I watched the sun cut through an old scrag. I stretched. I felt like a newborn. It was at that moment, when I looked at the ground and I noticed a bird, a common bird—nothing too grand—lay dead in the dirt. Most of the flesh was gone. Little bones, white from the sun stretched out in tiny arcs. Had it not been rotting, had it been frozen, it would have been a beautiful thing.'

'Got yerself a strange type a beauty.'

'I knelt next to it to get a closer look. I put my hands on the ground and lowered myself down. Tiny pieces—microscopic bits—of the bird's decaying body wafted up into my nostrils. I was that close.'

The old timer's eyes narrowed. 'Find that type a thing interestin, do ya?'

'And these ants—reddish brown ones—burrowed through the bird's flesh,' the stranger said. He leaned forward as he spoke, a froth of spit gathering at the corners of his mouth. 'One of these ants climbed to the tip of the bird's rib bone—a string of osseous matter—his antennae were moving independently, a fleck of god knows what in his pinchers.'

The barrio was abandoned now. Even the barkeep was gone. The stranger stopped waxing on about the bird. The world was quiet. Before the old timer could say anything, the stranger spoke. 'I examined that ant and analyzed what he did, why he did it. I supposed the effects he had on the course of the universe. It was all the history anyone needs.'

'Learned the secrets to the whole wide world from some ants?' the old timer said. 'Sounds like injun magic to me.'

The stranger picked up his mug and drank, wiping a dribble from his lip. 'History is only half the equation,' he said. 'You have to add science.' For a second time that evening he drew an arched pathway in the air before him. 'Someday we will send men into the heavens and they will look down on us—us living like ants. They'll circle the earth at a league per second, hurtling through a cold darkness without parallel. And when those men return, they will not have lived the same life as those who stayed here. They will have actually aged slower. They will be just a little bit younger than their brethren. If I were to spend my life making these journeys—going between heaven and earth—I would live forever, knowing everything.'

The old timer's shoulders shook with stifled laughter. 'Men living in the stars that never age. Fer a second you had me nearly believin it.' He wagged his finger at the stranger.

'I can prove it to you,' the stranger said.

The old timer rolled his eyes, said he would like to hear this. He leaned forward and rested his chin on his clasped hands.

The stranger's voice brokered no guile. 'When I sat down here I added and subtracted, postulated and theorized—I did all the fool things a man of science does. Ive had time enough to think it over and I realized tonight I would meet you and tonight I would kill you.'

The old timer coughed. 'Pardon?'

The stranger looked down to where his hand rested on the table. A cleaver, speckled with rust, a wooden handle, lay next to his hand.

'That some sort a sleight of hand there?' the old timer asked.

'What?'

'That cleaver there.' The old timer nodded to it. 'Makin it appear like that.'

'It's been there, friend,' the stranger said. 'Been there since youve known that I was going to murder you.'

'You aint gonna murder me.'

The stranger snorted a stifled laugh. The old timer looked down into the earthenware well of his cup. 'You got no real cause to kill—to murder me.' He looked to the stranger. His eyes glassed over with the glaze of alcohol. 'It's the grog here,' he said. 'Worms at the head, makes the tongue loose. I—I didnt mean what I said.'

'What you said—'

'Yessir.' The old timer looked at the cleaver, the handle lightly touching the stranger's fingertips. 'Dont even recall what I said exactly.' He laughed, hiccupped. The stranger joined in the laughing. The old man wiped his eyes with the back of his wrist. He threw his head back in yawping laughter, the hard lump of his adam's apple bouncing up and down. He didnt notice when the stranger stopped laughing and sat watching him carry on. Eventually he sighed an end to the rumpus. 'Should we have another drink?' he asked.

'No.'

'Not much a drinker, is ya?'

'Prefer to be sober when I split your head open.'

Again the old timer's eyes glassed over and drifted their sights to the blade resting at the stranger's fingertips. 'Dont even reckon what I said to set this off.'

'Las palabras no son importantes. El universo se acaba aquí.'

The old timer shook his head.

'¿Usted no habla español?' the stranger asked. 'Et le français?'

'Someone send you here?' the old timer asked. He pointed his finger at the stranger. 'Send you here to murder me? You—I mean, you yourself aint got no real cause.'

'Você tem razão. Eu sou somente o efeito.'

The old timer sat in the chair, a slow sobering realization deepening the folds in the skin of his forehead.

'Ive always been here,' the stranger said. His hands remained flat on the tabletop, his gaze cutting into the old man. 'So have you.'

'No sir,' the old timer declared. He shook his head in an exaggerated fashion. 'Got the wrong man, you do. I's come from out Arkansas way.'

'Youre not listening,' the stranger chided. 'That state, Arkansas—*Akakaze* in the Sioux tongue—with its population of fifty-five thousand souls, famous for the Little Rock Nine and the National Guard—it all just got invented.'

'Dont think I rightly get what youre sayin, son.'

'Thats unfortunate,' the stranger said. 'You been dumb and afraid your entire existence then.'

'An youre gonna kill me?'

'Yes.'

'Why?'

'It was set in motion,' the stranger said. 'Someday people will park their cars—their pickup trucks—right here; they'll go into the store, buying bread made two states away and freighted in. They'll buy medicines and develop photos of their last vacation. Their cars will sit idle and leak oil and power steering fluid in the exact spot where your brains are going to spill out on the floor here.'

The old man bit at his lower lip, said it sounded like nonsense to him. The stranger said the time would come and they would see. The old timer suddenly looked sleepy. 'Jus go on and do it if you got the notion to.'

'It's not time yet,' the stranger said.

'What do you mean *it's not time yet*?'

The stranger stared at the old timer as if waiting for the right moment to come. When he blinked, the old timer flinched.

'You really dont got to do this,' the old man said.

The stranger chuckled.

'You is crazy,' the old man said. 'Shoulda figured you for a loon, dressed the way you is. Seen you cut down that injun, but I dont think you got it in you to cut down a proper folk.' The old timer stood, swayed. He looked downward at the stranger, the demure figure. The old timer took a single step, then whirled around to seize the blade.

But the stranger was already swinging the cleaver. First it sailed through the forearm of the old man on its parabolic trajectory. The down arc of the swing stopped when the blade buried into the old man's skull. The force of impact caused a fine mist of blood to spray out across the exposed breadth of the blade. Thicker, lumpier blood and matter wept from the aperture in the old timer's head after he fell to the floor. The stranger squatted over the body, watched the stillness of the man's chest. He stood once he smelled the rankness of the old man's bowels releasing.

Day came on quickly, pooling the shadows of the dunes. The man trudged on. Without the stars to guide him, he turned his sights to the sun. It blazed as a whitened orb. In his mind the man calculated where he needed to head. He kept up the pace for some time and drank the last of his canteen's contents. He picked a distant mountain peak and made it his goal. By midmorning, the sun had risen and it baked down on the sands with a mounting fury.

The man thought it best to sleep, let his legs rest. He traipsed to a low spot carved into the ridge of the dune. He plopped onto the sand and used his heels to kick out a spot to accommodate his body. He spat out the pebble so he would not choke on it in his sleep. As he reclined into the bed, he took the handkerchief, unfolded it and wrapped it over his eyes, nose and mouth.

Despite the wind and the constant barrage of sand, the man slept soundly. In his dreams he stepped out of the desert and directly to the plains. The stranger—yes, that man from the barrio—he was there, a bird perched on his shoulder.

'¿Qué hace usted aquí?' the man asked.

'Funny,' the stranger said. 'I was going to ask just that.'

The man walked past the stranger toward the hovel. As he came closer to the hovel, his face prickled with flames and the ash from the burning structure pelted his face. He squinted against the fiery tongues and saw a set of blackened bones amongst the timbers. He turned to ask the stranger if this was so, but the stranger had gone. When he turned back to examine the bones, he saw that the ribcage of the skeleton housed a much smaller and misshapen skeleton.

The man awoke abruptly. The sand whipped at his face and he sweated. Whatever dreams he had dissipated in the scorch of daylight. Pulling the handkerchief from his face, he sat up and gauged the sun. To make his way home he needed to walk against the sun, the full force of it beating down on him. In the bottom of a dust bowl he found a few sprigs of tall grass. The man pulled them up, roots and all. He gnashed the flora in his teeth and sucked the liquid from the blades and roots. He started up a dune. With each step he slid back, sags of sand collapsing behind each footfall. He reached out toward the slope and on all fours he began crawling out of the bowl toward the dune crest cut sharp against the sky. The faint countenance of the moon hung above like a half buried relic. But even the moon slipped away from the man, the earth rolling on underneath his trudging. The movement westward ho and once upon a time glimpsed our future only briefly. Our destiny always lay just beyond the horizon. And some who stood looking out over all of creation saw what the future beheld and turned to go back. But the earth is a cruel instrument and it continued on, the ground turning beneath their feet, the horizon ever changing, the future never here.

Once atop the dune the wind whipped around the man. Ghostly mists of sand blew off the peaks around him. Blisters raised by the unrelenting sun began to weep, pierced by grains of sand. In this morphing land, his path was fixed—a line cutting across the shifting sandscape toward a mountain pass. He walked, casting a backward glance. Along the ridge of a distant dune a figure rode a white horse. His existence flickered in and out with the rising waves of heat. From what the man could see the figure trooped on without regard for the canticles of the sun, a dust rising in his wake like an ether of the outer universe. For a moment the man thought to call out. But his throat was slaked dry and the stranger seemed to bid him no mind. The stranger passed as all things do, blurring into nothingness and then into oblivion. The man watched him go. Then he blinked and turned. His woman awaited him, he knew. He tried to figure out how old their child would be. He began the calculations in his mind as he began to walk. He set his gaze on the horizon and thought about the world to come.

ACKNOWLEDGEMENTS

I started this story some years ago while attending Wright State University. The Wright State community—especially Erin Flanagan and Scott Geisel—have always been supportive of their writers. They provided the best education a writer could want. While taking Erin's class, I met a fellow writer, the incredibly talented and wise Ann Weisgarber. On Ann's advice I searched for the right literary agent in the UK. It ended out being sage advice.

My agent, Anna Webber, deserves special recognition for her determination to see this story in print. She has provided me with thoughtful feedback and careful editing. Many more people involved in the publishing industry have been instrumental in turning my typewritten manuscript into a book. I would like to extend an apology for omitting their names here, but I would also like to assure them I am grateful for their efforts, kind words, and expertise.

Throughout the entire process my wife, Amber, has been a source of constant encouragement. She listens to my worries, dismisses my self-doubt, and understands me like no one else. My children too have been more than understanding. Time I spend writing often comes at the expense of many other things and my family as a whole has been unconditional in their support and love. For this I cannot thank them enough.